INCIDENT OFF RUNWAY 31L

INCIDENT OFF RUNWAY 31L

▼

Walter Carlin

Writers Club Press

San Jose New York Lincoln Shanghai

Incident Off Runway 31L

Writers Club Press
an imprint of iUniverse.com, Inc.

For information address:
iUniverse.com, Inc.
5220 S 16th, Ste. 200
Lincoln, NE 68512
www.iuniverse.com

ISBN: 0-595-15660-6

Printed in the United States of America

*To my family, for bearing the career change
with a reasonable amount of grace and good humor*

ACKNOWLEDGEMENTS

▼

A number of individuals generously donated their time to comment from their point of view on the accuracy of details portrayed in this fiction. I thank them deeply.

- Don Creswell, Russ Ray and Bill Slattery, airline management leaders, who reviewed operations, procedures and terminology;
- Irene Haskew and Dara Holbrook, whose insights into metropolitan social work were most helpful;
- Maya Napolitano, for commentary on NYPD practices;
- Ed Hogan, dean of the American travel profession, who provided both critique and encouragement.

Accuracy of details alone do not a novel make; several writers helped shape and focus an idea into final form:

- My colleagues at the San Diego Writers Studio, whose patient guidance, notes and prodding generated determination to finish this story;

- Michael Norell, who early on suggested a direction for what was then a novella;

- David Moessinger, who provided the final push toward completing this project.

Finally, thanks to my wife Ann, who spent more than a few hours undoing and fixing various computer problems I encountered while attempting to deal with that recalcitrant instrument.

"There is nothing that happens without cause"

Admonition from Buddhist ritual

(Jodo-Shinshu sect)

CHAPTER ONE

▼

END OF THE GRAVEYARD SHIFT

The six-thirty mass was just breaking up as Pat Boyle slid his formidable bulk into a pew at the rear of St. Al's and knelt. "Breaking up" was perhaps too generous a description. Twenty, maybe twenty-five people shuffled down the worn aisle and out into the damp cold of a New York morning. Mostly business people, a few older folk who were probably parishioners.

Boyle could qualify as a parishioner. While he seldom attended mass other than Christmas and Easter, and zipped in and out for a morning visit infrequently, Boyle had served as an altar boy at St. Al's back when the Third Avenue El still ran, separating the businesses of mid-town

Manhattan from the cold-water flats of the East Side.
Those cold-water flats of the 50's were now astronomically
priced apartments, condos and co-ops, but St. Al's still
remained, a faded red brick church tucked away among
skyscrapers between Lexington and Third Avenues.

They'd been married here, he and Kate, and their son,
Pat Jr., baptized. When the little boy died, he had been
buried from St. Al's. Later on, when he and Kate began
having their problems, Boyle sometimes sought the quiet
at the back of the church. No guidance had been solicited,
none given; the quiet itself sufficed.

Boyle rubbed a large hand across his broad, ex-line-
backer's face and through his thick, reddish-brown hair; he
could feel stubble on his chin already. This morning was a
typical one; up at four, on the phone with the key
European stations at four-thirty.

Frankfurt, as usual, was fogged in. ("Show me a map of
the great swamps of the world," Boyle would rant to the
delight of his staff, and I'll show you where some clown
has built an airport!"). The Germans were being German
as to when and if the airport would open, so Boyle
instructed Flight Ops to use Stuttgart as an alternate and
bus the passengers to and from.

Paris' DeGaulle was open but Pierre Blanc, the Global
operations manager, had yet to show up for work, par for
the course for "Plucky Pierre". Frequently, some newcomer to the Human Resources department would insist
that Boyle "do something" about him. Boyle would invite
the newcomer to try her hand at removing a French
national from a management position in an American
company in France. Inevitably, the newcomer would try,
only to find the severance package for a thirty-year-plus

employee was roughly the price of a chateau in the Loire valley and "Plucky Pierre" would remain on the payroll, to no-show another day.

The major station, London's Heathrow, was open and functioning. Global had a mini-hub at Heathrow and how well the airline ran intra-Europe on any given day was a function of Heathrow's performance. Penelope Warren ran Heathrow well, to the continued delight of Boyle and the disappointment of some of her antagonists at headquarters. When he appointed her to the job, the first woman at that level in Global, Boyle told her critics she "had the biggest pair of balls in the U.K. since Margaret Thatcher." Later informed of the remark, Penelope fired off an e-mail to Boyle: "Unaware you so well acquainted with our former Prime Minister."

Boyle checked his watch; time to go. By the time he walked the few blocks to the Global Air building, most of Central and South America would be in business and generate their mound of phone calls, e-mails and telexes. Then the day's operations review with the U.S. stations and his staff, followed by the late evening phone conference with Tokyo, Hong Kong and Sydney.

But he stayed in the pew and stayed kneeling. Something about the weight of skin and bone and flannel pressing down on the wooden kneeler felt right, somehow comforting.

There was more. There was some reason he was here this morning. Boyle lowered his head, shut his eyes. Years ago, years when he practiced his faith and thought he had faith, the nuns would drill him in the examination of conscience.

What have I done? Was it the right thing?

Images of Kate and little Pat, of things said and not said, of things undone. His son, dying, while he was on yet another trip, unreachable, expanding the routes of Global Air.

It's business. It's the airline business. Kate. Memories of her laughter, their loving. Gone. No, that wasn't accurate. Not gone, not even separated. She's left to take a "break" from their marriage, take some time to think. Might even be a good thing, still...

I run an airline, he thought, I run an airline.

He looked at the altar. Is that all I have ever done? "The Living Legend" was what many of his station managers called him, most to his face, in that joking and sarcastic manner men use to express affection.

One job with one company. When he started as a young man with Global Air in the early 70's, the airline dominated international air travel to and from the U.S. Today it struggled to maintain its market share in a world of new, cheaper carriers.

And for how long? He saw the confidential financial reports few others did; they detailed a grim future for Global Air.

Then there were the constant rumors—sale, merger, even liquidation—like mosquitoes in the night, they sapped your strength and will even as you fought them off.

Running an airline—is that all I have ever done?

Boyle snorted in self-derision; a little late in the game to be asking that question. Work through this—dig in, stay alert, work through this.

He remained kneeling; the church was quiet. From behind, he heard a coin drop in the poor box, shattering the silence as it clanged noisily into the empty metal container.

*   *   *

By 0630, the maintenance base of Global Air at JFK International Airport was in full swing. A small army of workers swarmed over aircraft that were scheduled to depart that day to points in the United States, Europe and Asia. Boeing 747s and 757s, McDonnell Douglas MD-80s and Airbus 300s were going through final checks in the cavernous hangar before release to the passenger terminal two miles distant.

Dom Mennotti watched the 747 nose its way from the blackness outside into the green-tinged lighting of the hangar. From the vantage point of his second-floor office it reminded him of some huge hound, head erect and stiff, pointing at a vague and distant scent.

He squinted at the aircraft's tail number, then punched that number into his desk-top computer. "C-check..damn," he thought, more resigned than angry. His shift supervisor would be in a grand funk with this latest C-check dropped into the operation.

Mennotti stood up and put on his padded winter jacket, rounding his appearance even more. The guys called him "Fireplug" and blamed his constant motion on his need to avoid nearsighted dogs. He opened the door and stepped out onto the metal catwalk which lined the hangar. Even when the hangar doors were closed, the place was chilly and damp. Perched on the southwestern edge of JFK, the hangar sucked in the winds off Jamaica Bay and the Atlantic Ocean beyond.

Mennotti clanged over the catwalk and clumped down the metal mesh stairs to the hangar floor. He walked over to the parked 747 and under its massive wing. Years of experience notwithstanding, he was still in awe that a machine the size of a football field could lift itself into the air and carry hundreds of thousands of pounds of passengers and cargo all over the world.

Rick Wenthol, the a.m. shift supervisor, was standing by the nose gear of the aircraft, clipboard in hand, a pained expression on his thin, callow face. This annoyed Mennotti, who figured Wenthol was pissed, which meant he would soon be pissed, as well.

"They sent us another C-check to do," said Wenthol, without looking up from his clipboard. "Why are they always sending us C-checks?"

"They're not always sendin' us C-checks."

Wenthol looked up. His expression reminded Mennotti of a stained glass window in his parish church, some guy being devoured by lions but looking noble and forgiving nonetheless.

"A C-check is heavy maintenance, it's overhaul! That's four, sometimes five whole days…"

Mennotti let him run on. Why the hell did I ever leave the union, he thought.

"…Global Air's overhaul base is Tucson, not JFK! We're just supposed to do line maintenance and every time I look around I've got another C-check to do!"

Wenthol wasn't totally wrong. But he whined. Mennotti hated whining.

"Look Wenthol, they designated us backup to Tucson…"

"Backup is one thing, every day is another!"

"Every day? What the hell do you mean, every day?"

Mennotti could feel the Sicilian in him rising; this was not necessarily a good thing.

"Then I need more people." Wenthol pouted.

"More people?"

Mennotti was reddening; Wenthol took a step backward.

"If we're going to be a major overhaul base, then I need more people to…"

Mennotti grabbed Wenthol by the arm of his padded jacket and pulled the taller, younger man towards him. "Hey, hey Wenthol. Let's not get excited here, okay?" He jerked him down to eye level and nodded vigorously at him. "Okay?"

Wenthol tried to pull back, but Mennotti had clamped his right hand around the jacket like a pit bull. "Okay Dom, okay. I'm not excited."

"Okay, look." Mennotti relaxed his grip and Wenthol almost sprang backwards. "Remember a couple a weeks ago, they announced third quarter results?"

"I was in Paris."

"Paris?"

"Yeah. I had some vacation time."

"Ah, Paris. Paris is a lovely city." Mennotti reached out and smoothed the wrinkles which still showed in the arm of Wenthol's jacket. "Great food, wine, the Seine, churches.."

"Yeah."

Mennotti grabbed Wenthol's jacket and jerked on it again. "While you were getting laid in Paris, this airline announced a loss for the third quarter!"

Wenthol looked blank.

"Do you know what that means?"

Wenthol tried to shrug. Mennotti released his grip.

"I guess it means we didn't make any money in the third quarter."

"Try, 'I guess it means we didn't make any money for the year!'"

Wenthol still looked vague. Mennotti sighed. "Look. If an airline can't make money in the third quarter, when everybody and their aunt's flyin' somewhere, it mean's the airline's goin' down the toilet. Okay?"

Wenthol studied Mennotti. "That why there's all these rumors about someone buying us?"

Those damned rumors. "There's always someone lookin' for a deal and right now, this airline's on the ropes." Wenthol was chewing on that—time for the clincher. "So meantime, if they throw some shit our way, we gotta do it. Okay?"

Wenthol nodded. "I just want to make sure we do things the right way."

"We're always gonna do things the right way!" Mennotti hoped that was true. "But we gotta cut costs. That's why they give us those C-checks. Saves a couple a thousand bucks in fuel to do it here 'stead a flyin' a plane the hell down to Tucson."

Wenthol considered the logic and nodded his head. "I see your point."

"Wonderful. Now let's get this bird movin'."

Wenthol turned and walked toward the two-storied service stairs pushed up to the 747's main cabin door. Mennotti watched him go. Damn! he thought, won't anybody do anything anymore without a day's fuckin' explanation?

*   *   *

The Global Air building boasted a feature unique among its midtown Manhattan neighbors—an inset balcony which wrapped around its fifty-first floor. On this floor were located the board room and executive suites for Global's senior management, providing its occupants with stunning views from their private balconies.

Pat Boyle's office was on this privileged floor. Furnished in the innocuous executive style dictated by company policy for budgetary reasons, Boyle had added two PCs, several telexes and printers, a bank of TV monitors and a phone console whose size, number of lines and web of push buttons appeared more suited for Mission Control then midtown Manhattan.

A huge world map, electronically displaying all of Global's cities and their local times, took up most of the wall facing his desk. A sitting area comprised of sofa, chairs and conference table was arranged beneath it.

Boyle was at his desk, shuffling through some of paperwork when the intercom buzzed.

"Yeah, Ginny?"

"There's a Mr. Redmond here to see you and I've got Gilberto in Brazil on the line."

"Put Gilberto on three and send Mr. Redmond in as soon as I'm finished."

"Right."

"And e-mail Kasamatsu that if the Japanese government halts another of our flights en route to Hong Kong, we're going to the State Department and raise hell."

"Gotcha."

"And ask him to call me tonight as soon as he gets into the office."

"Anytime?"

"Anytime."

Boyle punched line three.

"Bom dia, Gilberto."

"That's quite an improvement over que pasa, Patrick. You seem to be catching on."

Boyle chuckled. "Speaking of que pasa?"

"Brazilian Customs just went on strike."

"So what else is new?" Brazilian Customs went on strike about as often as the French and Italians, which was saying a lot.

"203 is due in Sao Paulo in about half an hour, Patrick."

Boyle punched in a few entries in the console. A tiny light representing an aircraft in flight started blinking in his wall map display, close to the illuminated city code "SAO" in Brazil.

Boyle tapped another button. The time display for "SAO" changed from its local time "1156" to "ETA 1234". "See it's due in at twelve thirty-four, huh?"

"Without a Customs officer to be seen anywhere, my friend."

Boyle sighed. He'd been down this path before. "Can your guy treat 203 as an aircraft-in-transit?" Most Customs authorities, even those on strike, would process passengers from an aircraft-in-transit, one whose ultimate destination was beyond that country's borders.

"Brazilian Customs does not pay very well, Patrick. My guy has a hard time making ends meet."

"You know I can't do anything about that, Gilberto." The U.S. Foreign Corrupt Practices Act, as well as Global

policy, forbade any and all bribes to officials in other
countries. This made doing business in many countries
next to impossible.

"He and his wife are fond of travel, Patrick."

"Fond of travel to where, Gilberto?"

"Munich, for Christmas shopping."

Not a real brain twister here, thought Boyle; delaying a
planeload of passengers versus a couple of roundtrips, Sao
Paulo—Munich. "Okay, do the IATA routine."

Global Air in Sao Paulo would invite the Customs official and his wife—more likely his "guest", female but
unwed to the official—to Munich for "training". As members of IATA, the International Air Transport Association,
Global Air could then legitimately offer them a seventy-
five per cent discount on their tickets. The twenty-five per
cent "fare" would then be billed to Global for "consulting
services" by the official and paid by Global's Sao Paulo
office from an impressed fund of **reals**, currency the
Brazilian government prohibited the airline from repatri-
ating to the U.S. It was all a game, but it kept people
employed.

"Patrick, you may have the stony countenance of a
Nort Americano, but I sense the true heart of a com-
padre."

"I sense bullshit, Gilberto. Ciao."

"Ciao is for Italians, perhaps Yanks in mess halls. Bao
tarde."

Boyle hung up. The intercom squawked.

"Ready for Mr. Redmond?"

"Yeah, send him in. Ah, Ginny who's this guy again
and what's he want?"

"He was referred by Mr. Allen. Mission unknown."

"Okay." Mr. Allen. That would be L. Townsend Allen III, an outside director on Global's board of directors and chairman of its compensation committee. Maybe he's going to ask if I want a raise, mused Boyle. More likely, he'll be looking for an upgrade to first from coach on an advance-purchase ticket for a "friend." Some board members felt dispensing upgrades to impress, influence or seduce was a matter of noblesse oblige, rather than the pain-in-the-ass it was to the airline employees who had to deal with the resulting demands.

The door opened and Damon Redmond strode in. He possessed the build of an athlete, the tailoring of an investment banker and the impenetrable arrogance of many who find their fortune early.

Boyle rose to greet him.

"Boyle? My name is Redmond." He looked around the office. "We'll sit here." Redmond walked to the sitting area in the corner of the office and sat down, ignoring Boyle's outstretched hand.

Boyle resisted the temptation to stay behind his desk. He walked slowly to where Redmond was sitting; Redmond watched him move.

"Larry Allen suggested I drop by."

Larry? So that's what the "L" stands for, thought Boyle. Probably spells it "Laurence". Boyle sat opposite Redmond.

"I've placed some investments for Larry. Got him together with Gerry Samuels. You know of Gerry?"

Do I know of Samuels?, thought Boyle. You asshole. "The buyout artist?"

Boyle's dart hit its target. Redmond's eyes narrowed.

"Mr. Gerald S. Samuels has made billions buying and selling shitty-assed little companies…"

Boyle awaited the, "…like Global Air." Then this guy was out of his office.

"…and I help him do that."

Boyle waited.

"The reason I'm here this morning…" Redmond shrugged, his role as a messenger obviously beneath him, "…is to tell you something you should already know— and everything I say is in confidence, you got that?"

Boyle just stared at him.

"You're losing somewhere between three-quarters and one point two, point three, million bucks a day, every day. Right?"

This guy knew the figures. Boyle said nothing.

"Right. Now you know you can't go on like this, right?"

Redmond's use of the personal pronoun was as annoying as it was trite. Boyle waited him out.

"There's been lots of speculation that maybe somebody's interested in buying this outfit, turn it around…I'm sure you've heard the rumblings."

Boyle studied his nails.

"Now this is pure speculation, right? And you didn't hear it from me. But all I'm saying is, if somebody like Mr. Samuels were to buy this outfit, then maybe that buyer would like to have his team lined up first."

Boyle looked at Redmond. Intimidation 101 for the softening up, then the close. He laughed.

"Something funny?"

"You have an interesting style, Mr. Redmond."

"I like to get to the point."

"But if you and whoever it is buy this airline, why bother telling me about it in advance?"

"Global's problems aren't operations as much as they are marketing and finance. Your department checks out." Redmond couldn't stop there. "Pretty much." He watched Boyle for a moment. "Then again, when Mr. Samuels buys a company, he likes to have his people in place."

"Not sure I follow."

"You know, somebody who's not only doing a halfway decent job himself but who can sort of point out those people who maybe need replacing, soon as the new team takes over."

"A Judas goat?"

"Excuse me?"

"You're looking for some shit-eater to point out who should be fired? And you come to me!" Boyle was on his feet. "Who the hell do you think you're talking to?"

Redmond rose slowly. "Hey, this is business."

"Let me tell you something about this business! I've worked for Global for over twenty years and it's been damn good to me." He almost added "And my family," but caught himself. "So if you want some kiss-ass, you've come to the wrong guy!"

Redmond was on his way to the door, opened it and turned to Boyle. "You know, guys like Gerry and Larry and me, all we're looking for is return on investment.

Don't let a couple of years here and my comment about you doing an okay job confuse you. You're just part of the inventory." Redmond shrugged. "Take it for what it's worth." He left the office, leaving open the door behind him.

CHAPTER TWO

▼

CHANGES

William Noren checked his appearance in the mirrored panel of the private elevator. He liked what he saw. Tall, slim, jet-black hair, a thin face which, combined with burning dark eyes, gave him the look of a Doberman, the suggestion of viciousness. It was a look he cultivated.

The breakfast meeting had been set for the Cloud Club. Noren appreciated that. With his own money, expense account and club memberships, there were very few places in Manhattan that could impress Noren. The Cloud Club was one. Perched on the 64th floor of the Trans Oil building in midtown Manhattan, it had virtually unobstructed views of the city. Depending on the table, one could see the harbor traffic at the tip of Manhattan, gaze at the vast expanse of Central Park and the surrounding million-dollar apartments, watch the planes come and go at La Guardia and Kennedy airports, or stare at the grey wastelands of Jersey stretching westward toward the distant Watchung Mountains.

Noren cared little for scenery or sights and remained untouched by what others might consider beautiful. The Cloud Club moved him because of its membership roster—primarily Chief Executive Officers, Chief Financial Officers and Chief Operating Officers, with a smattering of extremely wealthy entrepreneurs. No old-money types—not unless they were actually working, instead of clipping coupons and pestering their financial advisors. Only active doers and achievers were members of the Cloud Club, where the initiation fee was $125,000 and the waiting list two years long, unless you had some very well-placed connections. It ran a substantial annual deficit, which was a source of perverse pride to its membership. After all, the feeling went, one did not have the time to concern oneself with such trivia as an annual deficit at one's club: there was always shareholder money to cover such contingencies and that knowledge was very self-satisfying.

The Cloud Club was for heavyweights only, absolutely as members and even as guests. It was expected that a member would invite as a guest only those who might conceivably merit eventual membership themselves or who, like nobles in a feudal setting, were recognized as having some reasonably important function, while also knowing their place.

Noren included himself in the ranks of the former, both by virtue of achievement and age. Not yet forty, he had progressed through a series of positions with several companies after his graduation from NYU. Each job move had given him increased responsibility, money, power and visibility. He had come a long way from East Brooklyn, now visible to his gaze through the windows of the Cloud Club. His parents owned a stationery store there and the family lived in an apartment above the store. Both immigrants to the U.S., his parents taught him the value of hard work and the folly of honest, hard work. Results, no matter how obtained, were all that mattered. For those who understood this, the opportunities were endless.

Noren rose from the table to greet a man who understood that very well. Gerald S. Samuels was a New Yorker, and had amassed one of Wall Street's largest personal fortunes of the last ten years through a series of swift—some claimed ruthless—leveraged buyouts. He allowed himself a moment of self-satisfaction for being here, hosted by Gerald S. Samuels. Noren had been identified as a player.

"Mr. Noren." Samuels accepted the extended hand.

Noren felt the appraisal of hooded eyes in a soft, honeytanned face framed by wisps of silver hair.

"Mr. Samuels." They shook hands. Samuels' hand was dry as the desert; Noren worried his might be clammy. "A pleasure to meet you, sir." "Sir" was a word Noren did not often use. His deference was obvious and expected.

"I've heard some good things about you, Mr. Noren…may I call you William?" His voice was a baritone, statesmanlike.

"Please do."

A waiter in starched white tunic and black trousers had followed Samuels to his chair and held it for him as he sat. "May I get you gentlemen something to drink?"

"Coffee?" asked Samuels.

"Fine," said Noren. He avoided coffee, believing it carcinogenic, but would not risk introducing the faintest note of negativity into the meeting.

"William, I invited you here today to talk about something that could affect you, and which, of course, must remain confidential."

"Of course."

"You may have heard of my interest in your present employer."

"Employer" struck Noren as almost condescending; he wondered whether it was intended as such. "Sure. There's been some in-house discussion, nothing concrete."

"There will be an article in tomorrow's **Journal** speculating that my principal company, Samuels' Holdings, will be buying your employer."

"I see."

"I'm not sure you do. The story's a plant, meant only as a diversion."

Noren nodded, silently cursing himself for his amateurish presumption; he had yet to totally eradicate the spontaneity of the East Brooklyn boy. The older man stared at him. Jesus, did I blow it, worried Noren.

Samuels leaned forward. "On Monday, I'll announce a tender offer for Global Air at twenty-two dollars a share."

Noren registered mild surprise, hoping his reaction would appear neither overdrawn nor disinterested. He waited for Samuels to continue.

"The Global Air Board's outside directors are aware of this and have agreed to the price; the company directors obviously will acquiesce. The key element is surprise and then swift agreement."

"May I ask why Global Air?" Noren sought the tone of junior partner to senior partner. His throat was dry. He needed a drink of water, but did not trust his hands to hold the glass steady.

Samuels gazed off into the distance before replying. When he returned to look at him, Noren knew he had been accepted. Whatever that meant.

"As I'm sure you know, Global Air was an airline pioneer. First across the Atlantic and the Pacific, into South America, all that shit. Today their stock trades in the high teens, on a good day." The tone of the elegant senior executive vanished, replaced by that of the New York merchant. "If they had a management that didn't have its head up its ass, they could get some decent earnings, maybe nudge the stock up five, six points on earnings alone. Earnings alone!" Samuels emphasized. "That's where you come in. I need someone smart, someone with a pair of brass balls who can walk into this shithouse and turn things around." He stared intently at Noren for a few seconds. "And make himself some very big bucks doing it!"

Samuels relaxed and sipped the coffee, which the waiter had placed unobtrusively by his right hand. "When my people looked into your company, we found squat. Except for you, maybe the finance guy who's holding the whole thing together."

Noren offered a faint smile of appreciation. His thoughts exactly.

"I took a look at some of marketing stuff you did. I like it. One of my guys was particularly high on that Newrange deal."

Noren tensed. The Newrange deal was a particularly large sale for him; it also involved allegations—but no charges or indictments—of kickbacks to the purchasing officer of Newrange.

"That Newrange situation…" Noren began.

Samuels waved him off. "Yeah, yeah, I know. Lot a shit flying around that one. Point is, you got the deal done. And that's the point, the deal!"

Noren's adrenalin was pumping; his work, noticed and appreciated by Gerald S. Samuels!

"And before that, when you were at Consolidated Industries," Samuels continued.

Noren smiled. Samuels' people had done their homework. "The union never knew what hit them," Noren agreed smoothly. "One day we were negotiating a contract for the plant in Fort Wayne, the next day we open our maquiladora in Juarez and tell the union to shove it." The manuever earned notice for Noren in several business publications as a bright-young-man-on-the-move. It was one of his fondest memories.

"Initiatives like that tell me you get results," said Samuels.

"I get results," said Noren.

"So here's the deal. I want you over at Global as my right-hand guy, Senior VP Marketing. You take a little time, learn how the airline runs, get the earnings up where they should be, I make you president of the company."

"Who do I report to in the meantime?"

"Me."

"You?"

Noren was surprised and unable to conceal it. In previous takeovers and buyouts, Samuels always had someone else run the store. He stayed on the sideline and watched the finances.

"Yeah, me. Global's too big to have somebody else in there. I'm going to stay on top of this one myself." He leaned back and sipped at his coffee. "So, what do you say?"

Noren was caught off guard. He had been expecting some sort of offer, otherwise why the meeting, but had not anticipated this demand for an on-the-spot response.

"Don't worry about the details. I'll have my financial guy, Damon Redmond, contact you." Samuels pulled a business card from his jacket and gave it to Noren. "He'll get with you about salary, stock options, perks, all that shit." He leaned closer. "Think of this like an IPO. A year, two years from now, you make it work, you can look me in the eye, say, 'Fuck you,' and walk away a rich man. You don't make it work…" Samuels shrugged, sat back. "What do you say?"

Noren knew if he made no decision now Samuels would consider it a negative decision and the opportunity closed.

"I'm on board."

Samuels extended his hand as he rose from the table. "Congratulations. You've done the right thing. Sorry I don't have time for breakfast. You take your time, eat well, I'll be in touch." He turned and strode away.

"Right, see you later," Noren said to the departing figure. He was standing, feeling slightly dazed as he watched Samuels exit through the dining room, nodding to other members as he went.

Noren sat down. The waiter appeared. "Are you ready to order, sir?"

"Huh? Okay...no...er, no, on second thought, I won't be eating."

"Very well, sir," said the waiter as he placed the house check for the coffee before Noren for signature.

"Mr. Samuels didn't sign this before he left?"

"No, sir."

"I see. Would you ask the manager to step over here for a moment, please?"

"Why, certainly sir."

Jesus Christ, thought Noren. Initially elated, now quickly infuriated by this tiny, trivial detail of an unpaid check. Samuels hadn't signed, Noren obviously couldn't pay cash in the club and he didn't want to simply walk away without at least explaining the situation.

The manager walked over. "Yes sir, may I help you?"

"Yes. Sorry to bother you with something so small, but Mr. Samuels left without signing his check and..."

"But your signature is perfectly good, sir."

"Mine?"

"Yes sir. Didn't Mr. Samuels tell you?"

"Tell me what?"

The manager smiled. "Ah, Mr. Samuels does like his surprises." He extended his hand. "May I be the first to welcome you as the newest member of the Cloud Club, sir."

Noren took the manager's hand and shook it. Samuels had me read, he realized.

      *   *   *

Samuels took the private elevator to the lobby where Damon Redmond was waiting for him. As Samuels' closest financial advisor and personal stock broker, Redmond's moniker on the Street was "Remo", shorthand for "Remora," the fish that latch themselves onto the bodies of sharks and tag along for the food and the ride.

"He go for it?" Redmond asked.

"Of course he went for it," said Samuels. "People in the habit of using others never think it's being done to them." They walked through the lobby and the revolving doors. Samuels' limousine and driver awaited curbside. "I still think I should dump this guy Boyle."

"Gerry, we're going to need someone who knows what they're doing during the changeover."

Samuels looked skeptical.

"Airline's a complicated business. Anyhow, he's just a company suit—he won't give us any trouble."

Samuels snorted his acquiescence. "How soon before you think the Street's going to find out about my plans?" Samuels waited while his driver scurried around the limousine to open the door.

"Outside directors always leak, Gerry. You know that."

"If Global stock so much as ticks up an eighth..."

"I'm on it, Gerry, I'm on it."

Samuels got in his limousine, the driver closing the door behind him.

Redmond watched the limo pull away, into the traffic. Sonofabitch wouldn't even offer me a ride. Typical, he thought.

*   *   *

The helicopter picked its way through the wind gusts and landed on the roof of the Global Air building. Boyle ran up to the clattering machine, ducked under the prop wash, grabbed the handle of the door held open by the pilot and climbed aboard.

The pilot, speaking into his headset, gave Boyle a big smile and thumbs up. The chopper lifted up and eastward toward JFK Airport.

Boyle thought JFK's proximity to corporate headquarters was a mixed blessing. Global's principal hub, JFK provided a real-time source of company and competitive information, furnished a quick read on employee morale and concerns, and prevented major problems being obscured due to distance or time. However, it also encouraged some headquarter types to "play airline" with the operation, much to the frustration and chagrin of the field personnel charged with the actual field responsibility.

Boyle was especially sensitive to the latter. During the years he worked his way up the operations chain of command, few things annoyed him more than having some corporate "expert" in finance, computers or other non-public-contact function critique his operation. The criticisms, generally well-meaning, were usually wildly impractical, issued by individuals in corporate positions who demanded attention and response to stroke tender and insecure egos.

Boyle's mission today was twofold: get a feel for what the troops felt about Global's financial position and the buyout rumors; get out of the office and breathe some fresh air.

The meeting with Redmond still rankled, a nagging little cut that wouldn't heal. Not just the man's arrogance and abruptness but the realization that, should Samuels or someone like him buy Global, the airline's days were probably numbered. Boyle knew the sum of Global's assets far surpassed its current depressed stock price. Expanding rapidly in the days immediately after World War II, Global had taken advantage of a strong dollar and devastated foreign economies to build a huge international portfolio of real estate. Those investments, along with generous landing and beyond rights in countries that no longer granted such, possession of restricted gate slots at busy U.S. airports and a large inventory of owned—rather than leased—aircraft made Global an inviting target for the knowledgeable investor. The parts, sold separately, were worth more than the whole.

And the largest expense in this money-losing operation were personnel costs, the one item that was also the most expendable from an investor's point of view.

Not a great position to be in thought Boyle, as the chopper pilot began his corkscrew approach to the Global Air terminal. Not a real great position at all.

He could spot Fran Demarest at the helicopter pad, hands clamped firmly around her skirt to prevent any contingencies resulting from the prop wash. Fran was Global's JFK station manager, installed by Boyle shortly after he had placed Penelope Warren at Heathrow. "Boyle's Bimbos" they were called by the same people—primarily headquarters types—who had previously railed against Boyle's Heathrow selection.

For those who knew the airline however, and the Kennedy operation in particular, the choice was not only an obvious one, but long overdue. Just out of high school in the mid-70's, Fran Demarest hired on as secretary to the

JFK operations manager. Unable to afford either time or money for college and without stunning physical beauty, she combined an effervescent personality with an absolute determination to get things done that made her popular with her supervisors and peers. Already proficient in her secretarial and people skills, she quickly absorbed the requirements and details of her boss's job as well, to the point where she was being asked for solutions to operational problems.

Promoted to secretary to the JFK station manager, she replicated her previous accomplishment, only to languish in that position for several years as Global rotated station managers in and out on two-year stints. Her luck changed when Pat Boyle became the JFK station manager. Quickly spotting her abilities, Boyle placed her in station management, first as a shift supervisor, then shift manager and finally operations manager. Meanwhile, Global's JFK operation, considered virtually unmanageable by some due to its volume, weather, unions and the low boiling point of many of its customers, became a consistent leader in station on-time performance.

Boyle was recognized for this achievement and admitted to the officer ranks as Vice-President of the Western Division. Fran stayed at JFK and persevered through a series of mostly mediocre station managers until Pat Boyle got his big promotion.

The assumption by many in Global was that they slept together; if not now, then certainly back then. In fact, their relationship was totally limited to JFK airport. Boyle knew little of Fran's personal life, other than she was a single parent whose child, Tim, was the engine of her life.

Fran told Boyle of Tim's grades (usually honor roll), sports (baseball and hockey), hopes (veterinarian), and girlfriends ("A lovely girl, but I don't think she's the one for Tim"). But of herself, her marriage, its length, and even who her husband was and what he had done for a living, she said nothing.

So much for sleeping your way to the top, he thought somewhat wistfully, as the helicopter jounced onto the tarmac.

He held up four fingers to the pilot to designate pickup time. The pilot nodded recognition. Boyle opened the door and jumped to the ground, ran out from under the wash to where Fran was standing.

"Pat, how are you?" she shouted over the 'copter's roar, her skirt still firmly under control.

"Great." He waited as the pilot applied max power and lifted off. "You didn't have to come out here to the pad."

"I needed the exercise." Fran smiled and rolled her eyes in self-accusation.

She didn't need the exercise. Fran kept herself in excellent shape and Boyle knew he should compliment her for it as if she wasn't expecting a compliment. "Eh, yeah…" he mumbled and gestured toward the terminal. They started walking.

The afternoon bank of arrivals was in process, providing the turnaround aircraft for that evening's departures. Boyle was glad to be back in the ebb and flow of station operations.

"So what tore you away from downtown?"

"It was getting stuffy in the office." They both laughed.

"How're things going out here?" he asked.

"On-time performance is above target…"

"Yeah, I saw that."

"Overtime's a little tight…"

"Gotta watch that. We haven't put out any ban on OT yet, but…" he shrugged.

"…and Dom Mennotti says he's got to have more people if we keep throwing C-checks at him."

Boyle stopped walking. "Mennotti's lucky to keep the people he has. Tell him to stop bitching and start working." Mennotti had been installed as JFK's Manager of Maintenance before Boyle got his current position; he would not have been Boyle's choice for the job.

They resumed walking. Boyle felt somewhat embarrassed by what, for him, was an outburst. "You know, Dom's certainly a fine mechanic, but as a manager, he tends to panic. Always seems to be facing insurmountable obstacles."

"I think he feels he's under the gun." Fran consistently backed her people; it was a quality Boyle appreciated.

"Yeah, well, I wanted to talk to you about that, too." They stopped walking; she waited for him to speak. "There are a lot of rumors about us being sold."

"I know. Post Office asked me about that today in our mail meeting and it's come up in our last two Employee Encounters."

"I'm not sure myself what's going on…," he said, which meant, "There's stuff going on I can't talk about right now."

She knew his shorthand. "Uh-huh."

"...but I thought this might be a good time to walk around, talk to the troops, tell them not to get excited about these rumors."

"You want to walk the ramp?" she asked.

"Yeah." He smiled with the enthusiasm of a kid.

"Let's go."

They headed toward a group of ramp workers clustered around a tow motor on one of the gates. "Walking the ramp" was one of Boyle's signature traits. He'd wade into a group of employees, introduce himself and encourage any and all questions about Global Air, the airline business or life in general. The employees felt they had someone at the top of the airline who—at least—would listen to their complaints, suggestions and concerns. Boyle felt he was getting a straight story from the people whose attitudes— therefore their actions—toward their jobs and their customers would make or break his operation.

Fran's pager beeped. She unclipped it from her belt and read its display. "Tokyo flight's got a problem." She clipped the beeper back on her belt. "Want me to stay here?"

"Nah. You go ahead. I'll just wander around."

Fran strode briskly toward the gate at which the flight to Tokyo was parked.

Boyle went up to the group of workers, said hello and quickly had a dialogue going. Then he broke away and, slapping backs, exchanging high-fives and greeting workers by their first names, worked the ramp like an old-time ward healer working the neighborhood.

Fran climbed the jetway stairs from the ramp to the parked 747. The gate agent, standing at the control console of the jetway, tugged on the joystick and the jetway swung slowly back to the aircraft.

As the jetway eased toward the fuselage, Fran saw a group of workers gathered around Pat Boyle, enthusiastically engaged in what looked like a question-and-answer session. They love that man, she thought. She had realized long ago they were not alone in that.

CHAPTER THREE

▼

MEETING IN THE BOARDROOM

Friday nights and Sunday evenings were critical times in Global Air's operations cycle. Passenger load factors shot up substantially as bedraggled business travelers made their way home for the weekend, some to exchange dirty laundry for clean and re-join the race Sunday nights on planes bound to destinations foreign and domestic.

That pattern gave Boyle the rationale to work late Fridays and come into the office Sundays. Saturdays he busied himself with errands and paperwork while hoping he could convince Kate to join him for Saturday night dinner dates. But she insisted on Mondays, estimating correctly that any thoughts or desires either of them might have to make a night of it would be dampened by the reality of getting up early the next morning.

This Monday night he waited as usual outside the clinic for battered women where she worked. The night was cold but he preferred that to going inside the clinic. Not only might it cause Kate some awkwardness, on previous visits he felt like the enemy on alien ground.

It had been slightly more than a month since she told him she wanted a break from their eighteen-year marriage. Not a divorce or a separation, just a "break." He suggested counseling but she reminded him she had been trying unsuccessfully for years to have him do just that. It wasn't that he hadn't wanted to—it was the time. It was simply trying to find the time.

But you always have time for the airline.

He was in Hong Kong when little Pat became ill. Just a real bad cold and fever, Kate told him on the phone. He was in Jakarta when she took little Pat to the hospital with spinal meningitis. The phone service between the U.S. and Indonesia had been down. When the call finally got through to him in Medan, the priest had already administered last rites.

Boyle paced the sidewalk to keep warm. He had never been a smoker but somehow felt the need for a cigarette right now.

The clinic door opened. Kate was framed in the light behind her. He could see only the outline of her face, the gold and silver highlights in her hair.

He walked quickly toward her. "Hi."

Kate put her arms around herself to ward off the chill; she was not dressed to go out.

"Hi. Listen…"

He put his two hands around her shoulders and bent forward to kiss her; she offered her cheek.

"…Pat, I can't get out for dinner."

He backed away to look at her. "Something wrong?"

"We just got a real bad case, about an hour ago. I can't leave her."

"Want me to bring you some takeout?"

She smiled. "No, no thanks..I'm sorry."

"Well, if it's your job," he shrugged. It's my job. How often had he said that? "Eh, next week?"

"We both need more time. Let me think about it, okay?"

"Yeah, sure." He was surprised at how disappointed he felt.

She undid her arms, waved good-bye and went back inside.

*   *   *

The message light on his answering machine was blinking rapidly. Boyle methodically took off his overcoat and suit jacket and put on a comfortable old cardigan. By the looks of the number of calls, this would be a long evening.

He played the first message. "Mr. Boyle, this is Dottie Allen, Mr. Samuels' secretary." She said "secretary" as if it were a question; probably from California. "Mr. Samuels wants you to know he has called a meeting in the board-room tomorrow at eight and expects you there and your key staff people."

Boyle stared at the machine. He bought us.

"And Mr. Boyle, Mr. Samuels said for me to tell you he's had you paged on your beeper and called on your cell phone and you haven't responded and he'd like to know why." Boyle looked at the beeper and cell phone perched on the counter next to the answering machine; Kate refused to go out with him if he came equipped with what she referred to as his "corporate umbilical cords." The only time he went without them.

Boyle half-listened as the rest of the messages clicked on and off. Company employees from around the world, a few friends and friendly competitors—was it true what they heard about Global?

The phone rang. He clicked off the answering machine and picked the phone.

"Boyle."

"Are you watching the ten o'clock news?" Kate asked.

"We on it?"

"Well, Global is. They say a Gerald Samuels, investor of some sort, bought it?"

"Yeah, could be."

"Why didn't you tell me?"

"I thought you don't like me discussing business."

Kate was silent for a moment. "Well, I hope it works out for you, Pat."

"I'll call with the details, soon as I get them."

"If you want." She hung up.

He replaced the phone in its cradle and picked up the beeper next to it.

He studied the beeper, flipped it over in his hand and decided not to turn it on.

*　　　　　*　　　　　*

Boyle entered the boardroom at a quarter to eight; its immense, wood-paneled interior appeared close to capacity with attendees.

"Haven't seen this many people here this early since the last time we declared a profit," quipped one of his staffers.

"I haven't seen you here this early since I hired you," Boyle shot back and slapped him on the shoulder. "Hey, save a seat for Fran. Fog's holding her chopper at Kennedy." No quicker way than a chopper between Kennedy and Manhattan—when they flew.

"Right, Pat."

Boyle noticed Redmond standing by the head of the boardroom table, talking to an individual he didn't recognize. Whoever the guy was, he had an expensive tailor and barber, probably a personal trainer, by the looks of him. Boyle sucked in his gut and rubbed the sleeve of his off-the-rack blue suit.

Redmond saw Boyle and waved him over.

"Boyle, want you to meet William Noren. He's your new opposite number, Senior VP Marketing."

Boyle knew Global had never previously designated a senior vice-president in marketing; the title of senior VP had always been reserved for operations as a way of underlining and re-enforcing Global's priorities. "Glad to meet you, Bill." He reached for Noren's hand.

"I prefer 'William,' if you don't mind."

They shook hands. Noren's handshake was limp, his palm damp. Not as cool as he appears, noted Boyle.

"Let's all take our seats," announced Redmond to the group.

For a moment, few moved as no one was certain of the role or the rank of the person was who made the announcement. But prudence quickly asserted itself and everybody moved towards a chair, senior managers in the green leather swivel chairs which surrounded the coffin-shaped walnut table, lesser-ranked managers in the straight-back chairs lining the walls.

Boyle was distracted by a comment made behind him. When he turned to take his customary seat at the top left-hand side of the table, Noren was sitting in it. "Excuse me, that's where I sit." Boyle felt like a fool as soon as he said it.

Noren bared his teeth in his imitation of a smile. "Things change." He remained seated and turned his head away as the door to the Chairman's office opened. Boyle stood there, thoroughly nonplussed.

Gerald S. Samuels entered the boardroom and stood surveying the group. Boyle recognized the man from pictures in the paper and his attitude from years of handling self-important VIPs traipsing through airports.

There was a brief silence. Then Redmond began clapping, joined immediately by Noren, who clapped harder and more rapidly, while rising to his feet.

Redmond countered Noren's ploy by standing and walking to Samuels, right hand extended. He and Samuels shook hands, while many in the room started applauding.

Noren almost ran to join them. He also shook Samuels' hand, then turned as he and Redmond escorted Samuels to his chair at the head of the table.

The prince and his lackeys, observed Boyle.

The three were now at the head of the table. Redmond and Noren stood back from Samuels and continued to applaud, joined now by most of the group, many of whom were also standing.

Samuels raised his hands to indicate silence and wave the standees down. He looked at Boyle. "You can't find a seat?"

A lower-ranking manager at the distant end of the huge table hopped out of his chair. Mike Clancy, the vice-president of sales, seated alongside, waved Boyle over. If there was anybody in the room who failed to notice Noren sitting in Boyle's former place, they noticed it now.

"Nice start, Patty my boy," whispered Clancy as Boyle slid in the chair beside him. "I always said you had that touch."

Boyle grimaced in reply.

Samuels cleared his throat; the room became absolutely quiet. "I am Gerald S. Samuels and I'm pleased to tell you the Board of Directors of Global Air has accepted my offer to purchase this fine, world-renowned airline."

This time it was Noren who started applauding, leaping to his feet as he did so. Redmond glared at him but quickly followed suit.

"If the old man drops his pants and bends over, they each could have a cheek," whispered Clancy to Boyle.

Samuels again waved for silence. "All of you will have on your desks today a summary outlining our purchase and its details and I will not take up your time with those this morning. Rather, in this **very** brief meeting —" he paused for effect, "—brief because as of this moment **productivity** is your new key word!"

Boyle noticed several people scribbling down "productivity" as if they were hearing it for the first time.

"First, I want you to meet your new leaders."

Samuels turned to Redmond and nodded his head in that direction. "Mr. Damon Redmond, our new Chief

Financial Officer, will assist me in that critical area." There was brief and polite applause. "Since good CFOs are seldom seen and never heard, we will spare you any of his remarks. On the other hand," he turned to Noren, "I do want you to hear how our new Senior Vice-President of Marketing, Mr. William Noren, will give this company new direction."

Noren stood to greater applause. The marketing department was most heavily represented in the meeting and no one of its members wanted to appear less than enthusiastic.

"William, before you say anything, I also want to recognize—he needs no introduction—the individual we have selected, after careful review, to keep our planes flying, Mr. Pat Boyle."

"What review?" whispered Clancy to Boyle.

"Beats me." Boyle stood to tentative applause. Few in management wanted to be perceived as too close to an individual who had just lost his place at the table.

"Thank you, Gerry."

Samuels winced noticeably at the use of the familiar.

"We'll keep the planes flying safely and on time." Boyle sat down to lesser applause. He knew he had been expected to say enthusiastic and grateful things about the new management but, what the hell..there were enough politicians in the room already.

"Boyle." Samuels' curt acknowledgement communicated his chagrin. He turned toward Noren. "And now, William, tell us about your plans for the marketing department."

"Thank you, Mr. Samuels." Noren's emphasis of "Mr." was not lost on the audience. "Rather than bore you with

my marketing philosophies, practices and concerns—
those of you in the marketing department will learn those
soon enough…" The remark drew nervous laughter.
"…I'd prefer to hear from my department heads—reservations, advertising and sales—on how you run your businesses."

"Oh shit," groaned Clancy to Boyle, "and I got in at
two this morning." Boyle looked at him—bloodshot eyes,
stale breath and a thrown-together appearance told the
story. "These travel-agent dinners are killing me."

"Think of this as a job interview if you like," smiled
Noren. He shuffled through some papers on the table.
"Ms. Jepson?"

"Yes?" she replied.

"Tell us something about our reservations department."

Norma Jepson stood, shaky and totally unprepared. She
was a thirty-two year Global employee who had done little
else with her life. "Well, we maintain telephone reservations offices in Jacksonville, Gary and Albuquerque which
cover the east, central and western states respectively. In
Europe…"

"Why wouldn't anybody answer our 800 number last
night?" Noren was still smiling.

"Ah, well, what time did you call?"

"I called at eight, waited for ten minutes, no answer.
Same thing at nine and nine-thirty."

Jepson began to sway and looked as though she might
faint. "Ah…we may have had some people call in sick…"

"You don't know?"

"Well, normally I get a report every morning but this
morning…"

"Then, Ms. Jepson, I suggest you may want to rise earlier in the morning. Thank you."

"This is bullshit!" Conroy rumbled at Boyle. He used the back of his hand to obscure his mouth and remark. Boyle nodded.

"Now Mr. MacCready, I believe it is? Our advertising guru?"

Finley MacCready, another long-time employee, stood. Tweed-jacketed, tattersall-shirted and bow-tied, he looked like an ad for a literary scene long since past.

You've made your point, you son of a bitch, thought Boyle.

"Where are we at ad-wise, Mr. MacCready?"

MacCready assumed the air of a professor lecturing a student. "At Global Air, we have positioned ourselves as the carrier of choice…"

"You see the Times today?"

"Eh, no not yet, I…"

Noren pulled a copy of the Times from his briefcase and tossed it on the table in the direction of MacCready. It was open to a full-page ad for Global, showing two young people, a male and female, both white, running down a hill. "This yours?"

"Yes, yes it is."

"They look like escapees from Disneyland and about as pertinent."

"Our demographics…"

"…are changing and changing rapidly. We need to address that. Thank you Mr. MacCready."

MacCready sat down and stared straight ahead; he looked stricken.

"Nothing happens until somebody makes a sale; it is the life blood of any organization!" Noren stared directly at Clancy. "Tell us about our life blood, Mr. Clancy."

Somebody did a good job of briefing you, thought Boyle, you knew who to look at.

Clancy got to his feet shakily. Boyle could see the sweat glistening on the back of his hand.

The salesman cleared his throat noisily. "Well, sales is running slightly ahead of forecast…"

"They call you 'Boing-Boing,' Mr. Clancy?"

Clancy wiped sweat from his lip and forced a smile. "Ah, that's from an old TV commercial we did. The nickname stuck and…"

"It's been my experience that men with adolescent nicknames have never left adolescence." Noren said it lightly, almost jovially.

Clancy stood there, wavering slightly. The room was absolutely quiet.

"In any case, you were saying?"

"Yeah. I was saying we're ahead of forecast.."

"You're ahead of forecast but you're not making quota?" Noren waved a computer printout. "I don't understand?"

Clancy raised his hand to his forehead; Boyle could see a ring of sweat under the arm of his suit jacket.

"Well, the forecast number is RPMs…"

"RPMs?"

"Yeah, 'revenue passenger miles'…"

"Yes?"

"…and the quota is in dollars…"

"So?"

The sweat was pouring off Clancy—Boyle guessed the hangover was playing havoc with his thought processes.

"You can't explain this?"

A voice behind Clancy said, "It's the yield." Everyone turned to the voice, a beautiful young woman sitting behind Clancy. Noren took particular note.

"Stand up, please," asked Noren. "You are?"

"Trish Peters. I work for Mr. Clancy."

Clancy glared at her.

"Explain."

"We're beating forecast revenue passenger miles because we've lowered our prices and therefore selling more seats. But the average price of those seats is so low that we can't make the revenue quota."

"In other words, we're giving away the store to make the sales department figures look good!" Noren accused.

"Ah…" Clancy began.

"Thank you, Mr. Clancy, I've heard enough."

Clancy slumped back down in his chair.

"The next time I ask you a question Mr. Clancy, please give me a straight answer." Noren surveyed the room as if he were daring a challenge. "I think we can all agree there is much work here that needs to be done." Noren turned to Samuels. "I can assure you, Mr. Samuels, we will do it!"

A few people applauded, then stopped when they realized they would not be joined by others; even politicians have limits.

"Thank you, William, a dynamic presentation. Thank you all for coming. Now let's get back to our desks and make Global the number one airline in the world!"

The group started breaking up.

"Boyle!" Samuels shouted at him, "I'll see you in my office." Samuels turned and walked toward the door to his office, Redmond at his heels.

"A personal summons." Boyle clapped Clancy on the back. "You better get yourself some aspirins and some rest."

"Yeah, yeah." Clancy turned to Trish Peters, who was approaching.

"Mr. Clancy, I'm sorry if..."

"You ever show me up like that again and you're out on your ass!"

"I didn't mean.."

"Bullshit!"

Clancy charged off in a huff. Peters turned and followed Boyle as he made his way toward Samuels' office.

Boyle passed Noren who had already collected a few sycophants; they were hanging on his words.

"Oh, Pat," said Noren as Boyle passed him.

Boyle stopped. "I prefer 'Boyle.'"

"Whatever. I hope you didn't think there was anything personal in my remarks just now."

Boyle came closer. "I thought they all were pretty damned personal. Where the hell were you when these people built this airline?"

"Different times. This airline needs vision and action."

"Maybe I don't like your vision." Boyle turned and walked away toward Samuels' office.

Noren noticed Peters.

"Oh, Mr. Noren...", she began.

"It's 'Bill'".

"Bill, I hope you don't think I was trying to embarrass Mr. Clancy."

"Considering what we pay him, he should be able to express himself coherently. What do you do here?"

"I'm manager of Sales Analysis. I report to Mr. Clancy."

Noren studied her. "Starting tomorrow you report to me."

"Well, that's wonderful, but..."

"But what?"

"What will Mr. Clancy say?"

Noren smiled. "It doesn't matter what Mr. Clancy says."

        *   *   *

Boyle was surprised when he entered the Chairman's office: the room had been totally re-decorated. Formerly a shrine of airline memorabilia—aircraft models and pictures, historic photos of first flights and famous personalities—it now resembled the sitting room of an English club, all leather, finely detailed mahogany paneling and brass. Only the desktop computer and the sliding glass door to the balcony indicated the century.

Samuels was behind his desk, Redmond sitting in a chair in front of the desk; both stared at Boyle as he entered.

"Close the door, please," said Samuels.

Not one for small talk, thought Boyle as he closed the door.

Two things, Mr. Boyle." Samuels did not ask him to sit down. "My employees address me as **Mr.** Samuels." They stared at one other briefly; Boyle nodded. "Secondly, Mr. Redmond obviously told me of your previous conversation with him. While I can't say I agree with the attitude you expressed then, I do respect it. I am sure you will find, as we work together, that we both have the same goal, the success of this airline."

Boyle had to say something. "I'm sure we will."

"Thank you for coming." Samuels turned his attention to the cuff of his shirt, tugging at it so just the right amount would show beneath the sleeve of his suit jacket.

Boyle stood for an uncomfortable moment, turned and left the room, closing the door behind him.

Samuels looked at Redmond. "This won't work. Get rid of him."

"Gerry, we've been through his numbers. He's under budget, Global's always one of the top three airlines in on-time performance, the unions haven't called a strike since he's been running the show..."

Samuels fixed him with a cold stare, his black eyes gleaming in a reddening face. "You see the way that cocksucker looks at me?"

Redmond said nothing.

"Like he runs the airline! I run this fuckin' airline!"

"Gerry, everybody knows.."

"In that meeting just now, you watch him? He was just sitting there and looking! He shoulda been up there cheering and shouting and thanking God I bought this piece a shit and saved all their jobs!" Samuels stared at Redmond as if his financial advisor did not comprehend what he said. "I saved their jobs!" He dragged the words out.

Redmond shrugged uncomfortably. "I'm sure they know, they appreciate..."

Samuels began to calm down. "You see their faces in there? Noren had 'em by the short hairs."

"Noren turned off half the room."

Samuels considered the remark, his eyes fixed on Redmond.

"There are two ways to motivate people—self-interest and fear. Fear's cheaper." He picked up a financial report on his desk and began reading it. Redmond had been dismissed.

*   *   *

When Boyle returned to his office, Fran Demarest was waiting.

"Fran, you missed all the fun." He meant it to be ironic, humorous—it sounded angry, almost bitter.

"I heard. Sorry, fog had us down till about eight."

"Bottom line?"

"Everything delayed up to an hour and a half. No cancellations. Red-eyes from LAX and San Fran diverted to Philly, passengers being bused. Should be back to schedule by the afternoon bank." She watched as he took off his jacket and settled behind the desk. "So how'd you do?"

He grinned crookedly. "You mean my private audience?"

"Uh-huh."

"Still employed." Employed for how long? And was it worth it? He gazed at the wall map. Each city code contained part of his life, his history: LON, RIO, LAX, TYO, SYD…and JKT, there would always be Jakarta.

Fran waited while Pat was in his reverie. They had developed the type of relationship where each was comfortable with the other's silences.

He looked away from the map, back at Fran. "When's the last time we had a really good blow at Kennedy? You know, when it's dark at noon and you can just smell the storm coming and we get all the planes out and board up the glass in the terminal?"

"Oh...last fall? We caught the tail of hurricane what-ever-its-name-was."

"Yeah, well we're in for it again. Right here." He tapped on the desk with his finger. "And I don't know how it's going to play out."

CHAPTER FOUR

▼

STORM WARNINGS

Mennotti was furious. ·

It was 0602, the maintenance hangar—as usual—was full of aircraft, he had a 757 on the floor that needed to be on the line for an 0730 departure to Dallas, Ops Control was saying where the hell's the plane and Wenthol wouldn't release it!

Damn it to hell! And no one told him till just now! Jesus, did he have to do everything himself?

He hopped in the electric golf cart and weaved his way along the hangar floor, trying to stay within the painted yellow safety lines when he could, ignoring them if that was what it took. The 757 was sitting there, parked by the far hangar door, all buttoned up and no one in sight. No crew, no Wenthol, not a goddamned living thing within fifty feet of the aircraft!

0608. He looked around frantically and spotted Wenthol by the aft cargo door of an MD80. He wheeled the cart around and pushed its pedal to the floor. Christ, why don't they make these things go faster?

He pulled up to Wenthol and hopped out of the cart. "Hey! Y'know you got a plane sittin' there that's due on the line right now?"

Wenthol looked at Mennotti. "Needs a circuit breaker in the forward galley. We're waiting on it."

"Waiting on it! Why the hell don't you dispatch the plane and let them put the circuit breaker in at the line?"

"I don't dispatch planes that are not airworthy."

Mennotti sucked in his breath sharply. Take it easy, take it easy. Relax. He walked around in a little circle and came back to Wenthol. "Summarize the problem here." His voice was calm.

"Circuit breaker, forward galley."

"That a 'no-go' item?"

Wenthol shifted his feet. "Eh, no."

"Then it's an optional item?"

Wenthol paused before answering. "Yeah, but..."

"So it's not a question of being 'airworthy', is it?"

"Well, strictly speaking..."

"Just 'yes or no' speaking."

"It's an optional item," Wenthol conceded.

An optional item was one whose non-operative status on an aircraft might cause an inconvenience but not compromise the aircraft's safety.

"And since when have you refused to dispatch an air-craft with an optional item?"

"Never have. Never will."

Mennotti took another little walk by himself. Wenthol wasn't all wrong. But still…Mennotti returned to Wenthol.

"It's completely legal to dispatch this plane."

"Hey, come on, Dom, I know that. But you know that we don't release planes with optional items to the line."

We didn't used to, thought Mennotti, but that was before the buyout. Things have changed.

"Okay, Wenthol, you're right." Mennotti pulled his walkie-talkie out of his jacket. "Here, you just talk to Ops Control, tell them you've decided we don't need the bucks from this planeload of passengers to Dallas this morning and from Dallas to somewhere else this afternoon and from that somewhere to somewhere else tonight, all because of a fuckin' circuit breaker that's an optional item!"

Mennotti held the walkie-talkie straight out, Wenthol made no move to take it. Mennotti looked at his watch. "Six-twelve."

"Okay." Wenthol pulled a walkie-talkie out of his jacket and pushed the "speak" button. "Grover, this' Wenthol. Need a mechanic take…", he looked at the tail number of the 757, "…894 down to the line for an 0730 departure." A reply came squawking back. Wenthol listened, grimacing. "I know, I know. Just do it." He replaced the walkie-talkie in his jacket.

Mennotti felt drained and the day had just begun. He looked at Wenthol. What the hell, the guy was just tryin' to do his job. Besides, it was time he found out how this business really worked. "Hey kid, what can I tell ya?" He punched him playfully in the shoulder. "Ya gotta go with the flow."

         *   *   *

Boyle noted the increased frequency of Samuels' budget meetings with concern. As the new owner, Samuels initially instructed his staff to prepare for him monthly reviews, just as he did with the other companies he owned. These quickly became weekly reviews as Global's costs soared and revenues lagged, and now had become short-notice, drop-everything-for events, characterized more by political posturing than careful, methodical budget analysis. Boyle sensed a vague panic, and panic had no place in airline operations.

This meeting in the boardroom had begun promptly at seven a.m., chaired by Samuels. Redmond sat at a computer station behind Samuels, able to access immediately any financial, sales or operational data required. Noren and his staff faced Boyle and his staff across the boardroom table—it seemed to Boyle more like two warring chieftans facing off than a company seeking common solutions.

Noren was talking, as usual. "...and every time I propose another program..." Noren pleaded his case directly to Samuels, "...which is how we generate revenue for this airline..." he shot a glance at Boyle, "...so other departments can spend it, I'm told there is no budget available!"

Boyle said nothing—Noren would typically talk himself out or end up confusing everybody with a barrage of often contradictory statistics. He was more annoying than harmful.

"And then, in these meetings, where we're all looking to save money, everything in the operations budget is supposed to be a 'safety item.' If we cut it, all the planes are going to fall out of the sky!"

"That's totally misleading and irresponsible." Boyle pitched his tone and demeanor in sharp contrast to Noren's.

"The hell it is! You..."

"All right, all right!" Samuels waved Noren silent. "He may have a point, Boyle." He flipped through a computer printout. "What the hell is this, for instance: six-point-two million dollars for glycol! What the hell is glycol?"

"We spray it on aircraft during freezing weather to keep ice from forming on the wings and fuselage prior to take-off. It's a..."

"...safety item." Noren cut in.

Boyle gave Noren a contemptuous look. "This business is built on safety items, Noren. Not on bullshit."

"You don't have the..."

"All right, I said!" Samuels slammed his open hand on the table. He took a deep breath and turned to Boyle. "There are no alternatives?"

"Glycol is mandated by the FAA. If we never operated in freezing temperatures, we wouldn't need it. Otherwise..." he thought even these guys could see the obvious.

Samuels half-heartedly paged through the computer printout. "I want both of you to go back and re-work your budgets. I want you to look for every dollar, every nickel, every fucking penny we can save and I want a daily report on how you are doing!" He picked up the printout, flung it on the table and stood. "I have been in all sorts of businesses for over thirty years and I have never seen a business where the costs are so out of control!"

Boyle couldn't resist. "Welcome to the airline business, Mr. Samuels."

*   *   *

Noren turned his glance away from the computer and stared out his office window. Above all else, he considered himself a realist.

Reviewing the facts dispassionately, this morning's meeting had done him no good; it had in fact done him harm. Each confrontation with an adversary not clearly won—particularly with the Chairman present—was an opportunity lost. At a certain corporate level, your standing was nothing more or less than the opinion your superior held of you. And that opinion was subject to constant change.

Though he'd been with Global a relatively short time, Noren had been in business long enough to recognize his usual incremental budget game was not working. Like many a successful corporate marketeer, he would promise a substantial annual sales increase for an increase in budget a fraction of that amount. He would then rely on his skills to force, cajole and threaten the sales force to produce, present those results in the most favorable terms and demand an even greater slice of the budget. The plan typically worked over the two to three years Noren considered the long term.

At Global, the problem was different. His opponent for the budget dollar could and did claim costs protected by the mantra of "safety." Toss in Boyle's reputation and experience, he bulldozes the opposition. Noren had to give him begrudging credit; Boyle was using a page from Noren's game plan.

There had to be some way around that; there always was.

Noren doodled on a piece of paper. He needed some swift, visible action: remind his people that poor results produced pain; show Samuels he could shake things up.

A noise in the outer office distracted him. It was after six, his secretary long gone.

Boyle looked in the door. "Saw your lights on."

"I'll be here for a while, as usual. You making this an early night?"

"Be back here for a conference call with the Pacific stations at ten—want to join me?"

Noren laughed at the exchange. For an operations type, Boyle wasn't all that slow. "No thanks, maybe I'll get lucky tonight."

"Not married, I take it?"

"Not me. No reason to." Noren smiled insinuatingly.

Boyle looked around the office. There were no personal pictures of any kind. "No family?"

Noren ignored the question. "So what's on your mind?" He indicated his desk. "I've still got some stuff to do.."

"Oh, yeah. I was thinking about that meeting today. Thought maybe we could get more done if we didn't waste so much time on the happy horseshit."

Noren looked at Boyle. He appeared sincere. But in corporate life, you never knew. "Call off the war, huh?"

"I don't consider myself at war."

Then you don't belong here, thought Noren. "It's an interesting proposal."

The two men looked at one another.

"What do you think of our offices?" Noren asked.

Boyle looked surprised at the question. "Offices? Fine. Maybe a little fancy for my taste…"

"No, no—I mean the location." Noren stood in enthusiasm. "When I was at Central Systems, I had this corner office looking out at the parking lot. That way I could see who was coming in early or not, when they left—who was putting out."

Boyle looked at him. "You don't trust your people that much?"

"Trust didn't get me here."

"Must be very lonely where you're at."

Noren smiled. "It pays the bills and then some."

"Yeah. Well, think about what I said, if you want."

Noren watched Boyle turn and leave. A real man of the people, huh? Noren recalled the first meeting in the boardroom. He had three department heads who were with Global as long as Boyle. They probably were his friends. Certainly that appeared to be the case with Clancy.

He sat down and made a few notes to himself. Maybe it was time to have some fun. Throw a little shit into the game. He glanced at the door. Let's see how a man of the people reacts.

*   *   *

At first, Boyle thought Kate didn't want to meet at all. That had been happening a lot recently; their "regularly scheduled" Monday night meetings were being canceled because of emergency cases at the clinic, because she was too tired, because something just came up...it was inconsistent behavior which he would not tolerate in the office.

But it's not the office, he reminded himself. That's why you're here now. Marriage like a job? Orders given and rewards issued for outstanding performance? Time parceled out in selfish increments? But there's only so much time, he defended himself, each day is a constant choice of things to do. Then maybe your choices were poor.

Through the plate glass window he saw Kate approaching. Boyle slid out of the wooden booth to greet her.

They were meeting in Schlicter's, an old Austrian restaurant hidden away on a side street in Yorkville, a part of the upper East Side that once had been known as Germantown. The restaurant was seldom crowded; its food was good, the portions large and not expensive, the place well-lit and its patrons usually spoke to each other quietly—in short, it was not a fashionable establishment.

Entering the restaurant, Kate swirled off her raincoat, tossed back her silver-gold hair and walked to where he stood. He could not remember the last time they made love.

"Hi."

"Hi there." He reached for her raincoat to hang it up but she flipped it into the booth and slid in behind it.

He sat down. "How you doing?"

"Oh, okay. Fine." She rubbed her hands together. Boyle noticed she was not wearing her engagement ring and wedding band; he had not noticed that before.

"Would you like some wine?" He was drinking the house white.

"No, no. I don't think so." She looked at him. She took a deep breath and smiled. He hadn't seen her smile in a while. She reached out and touched his hand holding the wine glass. "Pat…"

She's coming back, he hoped.

She sighed and withdrew her hand. She looked at him and blinked her eyes. "I talked to the lawyer…"

He nodded his head. She's gone, he knew.

"…he'll be filing for divorce."

He had prepared for this moment but had nothing to say. "If there's…"

She started to cry. "I better go now." She smiled at him again; he felt as if his insides were no longer there. She picked up her raincoat and slid out of the booth.

He stood. "Let me see you back to the clinic…"

"That's okay" she answered too quickly, "I've got a ride."

"Oh."

She turned and walked away. He watched her go. So that's how eighteen years end, he thought, just like that.

*   *   *

Noren had a busy day planned.

Norma Jepson entered his office at ten a.m., precisely on time. He stood behind his desk and, all smiles, indicated the chair she was to sit in. His secretary had told her the unexpected meeting was called by Mr. Noren to discuss a new development for her telephone reservations department. No, the secretary told her, you don't need to bring anything with you.

"Thank you for coming, Ms. Jepson." He could see the wariness in her eyes, the slight trembling of her hands.

"Of course, Mr. Noren," she said as she sat down.

"How are we doing meeting standard?" Global's telephone response standard was 80/5, eighty per cent of customer calls answered within five rings, and was tracked continuously by a computer. Noren had the tracking report on his desk.

"Well, we have been struggling a bit…"

Noren stopped smiling.

"…if we could use some overtime, perhaps.."

"No overtime in the marketing department, Ms. Jepson." He sighed theatrically. "Unfortunately, the operations department eats up all the overtime dollars." He stared at her; she made an effort to smile. "I think I've found the problem."

"Yes?"

"And I'm guilty of this too," he confided. Jepson was leaning forward in the chair. "We spend too much time at headquarters. You have to get out and see your people in the field. Motivate them to do more—show them you are there and you care!"

She nodded her head dully.

Noren had read her file carefully. Jepson seldom traveled anywhere, either on business or pleasure. Someone in Human Resources had offered the explanation she took care of her elderly mother. Or was it an invalid brother?

Whatever. "When was the last time you visited the Res Centers?"

"I haven't traveled a great deal, Mr. Noren…I know that sounds strange for an airline employee, but…" her voice trailed off.

"Well, we've got to change that, Ms. Jepson. What you should do is plan to spend a week each month at each of your res centers—Jacksonville, Gary, Albuquerque. See what their problems are first-hand." He was smiling again.

She was silent for a moment. "I don't know that I can do that."

"Ms. Jepson, that's not acceptable. We all have our jobs to do and sometimes we may just have to adjust our personal lives accordingly." He let the thought sink in, then reached for a large envelope on his desk. "You know, Global Air is very appreciative of your past services." He toyed with a corner of the envelope. "I don't know if you've had the opportunity to check your benefits recently…," he handed her the envelope "…but you have accumulated a very attractive retirement package."

"Retirement?" She said it as if the word had been "cancer."

"Look at the package, talk to Human Resources, take your time. If you decide not to do it, then let me know your travel plans for the rest of the month by close of business today." He stood and offered his hand. "Thanks for coming by."

Jepson looked at him, then dropped her eyes, stood and walked out of the room without shaking his hand.

She carried it off well, he thought. It's always interesting to see how they react once they realize the game is over.

*   *   *

Clancy was a toucher, a hugger, a backslapper. He was a poker, a chortler, a joke-teller. He was a drinker, the life of any party, a womanizer of the Presidential level, and knew everybody there was to know on the sales side of the airline business. He was Vice President of Sales for Global Airlines and he was increasingly unhappy. His new boss, presented as some sort of marketing genius, had as much personal warmth as an enema. Clancy was puzzled. Sales type, marketing type: they were all cut from the same cloth. They got you laughing, they got you drunk, they got you laid, they got the deal. This new guy Noren was a stiff. No matter what Clancy would tell him, this guy wanted documentation. Documentation and plans. Fifty fucking reports every time you turned around.

It wasn't the way Clancy worked. He knew people; he knew everybody who could put asses in seats. We need more bodies to Europe? No problem. Get a dozen, maybe twenty U.S. travel agents. Put 'em on a plane. Send 'em to Amsterdam. All expenses paid. Get 'em laid. Get 'em a blow job. They came back. All of a sudden you're carrying more passengers to Europe. No mystery.

Running light to Tokyo? Go out to L.A. Go to J-Town. Meet with six travel agents who control eighty percent of the business. Give them an extra fifty, seventy-five bucks a head per passenger plus their regular commission. All of a sudden, you're not running light to Tokyo anymore.

Who needs reports for this? Give people what they want: some money, some laughs, some nookie. For this you don't need an MBA; you certainly don't need reports.

Clancy was returning from a total waste of time; lunch with some Japanese tour operators who hardly spoke English. Why Noren insisted he go, rather than someone on his staff, Clancy couldn't understand. That was one strange guy.

He entered the Global Air building and took an elevator to his office on the thirty-fifth floor. Stepping off the elevator, he saw one of his staff.

"Hi, Fred."

Fred looked at him as if he'd never seen him before.

"Oh, hello Mr. Clancy."

Mister Clancy? No one on his staff called him "Mister Clancy". He was going to make a comment but an elevator came and Fred hurried on to it, not looking back. Strange sonofabitch, thought Clancy. He walked down the corridor to his office.

His secretary was not at her desk when he entered his outer office. That was annoying: he hated to leave his phone unanswered when he was out. He walked into his office. There was a security guard sitting behind his desk.

"Who the fuck're you?" demanded Clancy.

"Mr. Clancy?"

"Yes?"

"I've been directed to escort you to Mr. Kreiger's office."

Arnold Kreiger was Global's Vice President of Human Resources.

"What the hell for?"

"That I don't know, sir. I was only instructed to escort you there."

The security officer rose from Clancy's chair. He wasn't the typical, seven-bucks-an-hour rental cop, pot-bellied, pock-marked and non-English speaking; this one was young, powerfully built, and looked serious. Clancy did not feel like challenging him.

"Well, if Kreiger wants to see me, I'm perfectly capable of going to his office on my own."

The security officer moved toward Clancy. "I'm sure you are, sir. But my instructions were to escort you there as soon as you arrived back from lunch."

"Well, I'll call him now and tell him I'll see him later. I've got some phone calls to make." Clancy headed toward the phone on his desk.

The security officer walked in front of the desk. "I'm sorry, sir. My orders were very clear. You're to come with me now."

Clancy and the security officer locked eyes; Clancy could feel himself sweating. He shrugged. "Okay. Let's get this over with, whatever it is."

"Yes sir," said the security officer, reaching for Clancy's arm.

"Don't touch me! I know the way!"

"Yes sir," said the security officer. "We'll walk there together."

They walked down the hall. Empty. No one in the hall, no one hanging around bullshitting. Totally empty. What the hell was up?

They entered Kreiger's office. Arnold Kreiger, Vice President of Human Resources, sat stiffly behind his desk. He and Clancy had begun their careers as passenger agents at the 42nd Street ticket counter some twenty years ago. Kreiger had always been Clancy's friend. But he didn't rise to greet him.

"Arnie, what the fuck is going on here?"

Kreiger ignored the question. He spoke to the security guard.

"Thank you, Sergeant."

"Yessir. I'll be outside." He left, closing the door behind him.

"Arnie, what is this bullshit? What's the deal?"

"Mike, I hate like hell to be the one to have to do this."

"Do what? Somebody complain about me or something?"

"You're...let go."

Clancy stopped, stunned. He knew what he heard, but hoped maybe he heard wrong.

"What do you mean, let go?" He had a hard time breathing.

"I'm sorry, Mike. You're fired."

He groped for a chair.

"What do you mean, fired...why?"

"Mr. Noren. He called this morning. Ordered you off the payroll immediately."

"But why, Arnie. For Chrissake, why?"

Kreiger shrugged. "He just called and said you were out."

"Just like that?"

"I'm afraid so, Mike."

"Can you do that?" he asked, hating the naivete and tremor in his voice.

"You don't have a contract, you're not in a union, you're an employee-at-will. Yes, we can do that."

"That's bullshit, Arnie. I've been here twenty-two years. You know that. Christ, we started together."

"I know, I know," said Kreiger. "I know."

"Just out? No settlement? No nothing? Twenty-two years and he can shit on me like this?"

They looked at one another briefly; Kreiger looked away.

"Christ, Arnie, I've still got two kids in college. What am I doing to do?" Then he felt it happening. Oh Jesus, oh no, he thought. His hands and jaw had been trembling. But now he felt a rush of warmth up the side of his nose, spreading out and lodging itself beneath his eyes. He sucked in his cheeks hard. Oh Jesus, no. He could feel the tears swelling up, now beginning to trickle down his face. Oh Jesus, no, don't let me cry. He tried to clear his throat. He looked around. He started to cry. "Oh, God, I'm sorry Arnie. Jesus, I'm sorry."

Kreiger stood. "Ah, Mike, why don't I leave you alone for a few minutes, okay?"

Clancy waved Kreiger back in his chair and shook his head no. He sucked in a few deep breaths and became quiet.

"Mike, it's time to go."

"Time to go," Clancy repeated. Twenty-two years. Gone.

"The Sergeant outside will escort you downstairs and out of the building."

"And then throw me into the street?"

"I'm sorry, Mike. We all got jobs to do."

Clancy stared at him for a few seconds, then stood. "Tell me one thing?"

Kreiger said nothing; arched his brows in anticipation of the question.

"Why?"

"I don't know, Mike," he answered truthfully, "I don't know. He didn't say."

*   *   *

The Global Air building was pulsing with rumors.

"He gave her five minutes to decide—move to Gary or it's out."

"The guard took him to the freight dock, wouldn't even let him leave through the lobby."

"They say Boyle is next."

"She's talking to a lawyer now."

"Your resume up to date?"

Noren sensed the immediate change—the deference, the hesitancy to speak to him first, the sidelong glances, not only from his staff but others—in meetings, walking the hallways, even standing in the elevator. Now they know who's going to run this outfit. He sat in his office and stared at the phone. Time for the next step. He picked up the phone and punched in a number as an amusing thought occured to him—don't have to worry about people going home before six anymore.

A few blocks away, a telephone rang in a partner's office at the Scott, Foster & Dean advertising agency. The telephone, a lavender and gold reproduction of a French antique, stood on the desk in elegant contrast to the commonplace, multi-buttoned telephone console alongside. As soon as it rang, the two individuals seated at a conference-table extension of the desk got up and left the room, closing the door behind them. The woman behind the desk, tall, blond, tailored in expensive casualness, picked up the phone on the fourth ring.

"Leslie Foster."

"In the **Ad Daily** tomorrow there's going to be a story, based on unattributed sources, that says Global Air is dumping its in-house advertising department and bidding the account."

"How much?"

"Twenty-two mil."

"That's all?"

"And it's got to be back-loaded."

She sighed. "How long do you need to look like a hero for?"

"Three to four months."

She was silent.

"After a year, it'll double."

"When do you bid the account?"

"Monday."

"When do you make your decision?"

"What are you doing tonight?"

She laughed. "You don't give a girl a whole lot of time to get ready."

"How much time do you need to close an account?" he insinuated.

"Depends what it takes to close the account."

"You know how to close this account."

She made her decision. "My place at eight?"

"Till then."

"Oh!" she added quickly, "What about your people there now? We're not going to have any complications, are we?"

"If the story in **Ad Daily** doesn't give them the message, I've got a guy in Human Resources to spell it out for them."

"The Noren style," she said ironically.

Noren didn't seem to notice the irony. "See you at eight." He hung up.

She replaced the phone in its lavender and gold base and pushed the intercom button on her telephone console twice. Her two subordinates entered the room and looked at her expectantly.

"Something just came up," she said. "We'll finish this discussion in the morning."

They went to the conference table to clear away their story boards and sketches.

"Oh, by the way," she said, "I'll need a full-blown presentation ready by next Monday for Global Air."

They looked at her in surprise.

"Global Air? I thought they did all their ad stuff in-house," said the young man with the sketches.

She smiled. "There's some new thinking at Global Air."

*   *   *

The senior executives who occupied the suites on the fifty-first floor seldom ventured outside their exclusive domain to visit offices on lesser-regarded floors; occupants of those offices were summoned to fifty-one.

Except for Pat Boyle.

Just as he loved "walking the ramp", Boyle would wander the corridors of the Global Air building, poking his bulky frame and always-inquisitive, good-natured manner into the wide variety of endeavors undertaken by members of a huge worldwide organization. He wanted to know from the advertising department if they had the overnight ratings for the drama Global had underwritten for Public Broadcasting (he'd watched it and thought it very good); if the sister of the kid—Luis Mendoza—who ran the mailroom was okay after her appendectomy (she was; Boyle had a bouquet sent to her house); even what the cook in the employee cafeteria put in her pea soup—the lunch special on Wednesdays—that made it so irresistible (basil; basil and my own sweet disposition, the cook giggled).

So Arnie Kreiger, Vice-President of Human Resources, wasn't too surprised when Pat Boyle came into his relatively cramped office and squeezed into the visitor's chair on the other side of the desk.

"What's going on, Arnie?" Boyle watched Arnie simultaneously wiggle, smile and sweat. Arnie reminded him of one of his uncles who sold life insurance; the uncle had never been successful selling life insurance.

"Well...how do you mean?"

Boyle didn't answer the question, just stared at Arnie.

"You mean, the changes Mr. Noren has made?"

Mr. Noren? "Uh-huh."

Arnie shrugged as if the question had never occurred to him. "Well, I guess...he thought it was time..." he was alternately patting down what little hair he had and fiddling with a pair of reading glasses on his desk, "...make some changes."

Boyle continued to stare. "How many years total you think those three people gave this company?"

Arnie shook his head as if he had no idea.

"Close to eighty, maybe more?" Boyle pressed.

"They were all senior, Pat." Arnie conceded.

"Damn shame."

"Jesus, Pat! We offered Norma a job, you know." Arnie struggled back. "She didn't have to quit."

"Running the res center in Gary?"

"Gary's not the greatest place in the world, but..."

"You know about her brother."

Arnie conceded. "I was just following orders, Pat." He returned Boyle's stare. "I have to make a living too."

*   *   *

Boyle left Kreiger's office, not entirely sure why he had gone there in the first place. The terminations were not in his department and beyond recall. By going to Kreiger's office instead of summoning that man to his, Boyle knowingly gave weight to those who rumored he was losing his clout, another overpaid exec on the way out.

But what the hell! Straight ahead—what you see is what you get. That was the way Boyle operated and would continue to operate until they axed him. He was not without artifice—no individual succeeds in any large organization without a touch of the actor, a bit of the gambler, perhaps even a dab of the charlatan. But there were standards, if not of conduct, at least of style.

He was in the hallway and waiting for the elevator. When it arrived and he got on, its few passengers made an aisle for him, some murmuring "Mr. Boyle," in awkward greeting. As the doors slid shut, he remembered Redmond's warning: "You're just part of the inventory."

*   *   *

Arnie Kreiger flipped through the stack of memos in front of him, but couldn't concentrate. Who the hell did Boyle think he was? Senior VP and all that, Kreiger didn't report to him; what right did Boyle have, coming into his office and hassling him for doing his job?

He picked up a memo from the top of the pile and skimmed it. Personnel grievance—"I said, he said, she said, blah-blah-blah." His life's work: little people with little problems which they brought to him for his solemn consideration. And now he was expected to step in between two senior VPs and arbitrate their pissing contest? The thought made him laugh.

Besides, it was obvious what was happening—this wasn't going to be much of a contest. If they'd found anybody half decent to replace him, Boyle would be gone by now. What was so special about running operations? You had to know something about planes and equipment and FAA regs and that stuff, but basically it was managing people.

Everyone knew Arnold Kreiger's strength was managing people—had to be, why else would they put him in charge of Human Resources?

Arnie studied his phone; he felt himself courageous, a battlefield commander at the moment of momentous decision. He picked up the phone and tapped out a number.

"Mr. Noren's office," a voice answered.

CHAPTER FIVE

▼

THE PLANNING PROCESS

Late afternoon was down time at Kennedy Airport. The morning block of departures were long gone, most of the afternoon arrivals were at their gates and the airport quietly hummed as workers and crews prepared for the thunderous bank of evening departures.

Fran occasionally looked up from her paperwork to check on Boyle; he sat in a chair by the window, looking out at JFK's southern runways, the water and setting sun beyond. During all the years she had worked for him, she rarely saw him sit in one place for more than five minutes. He was in that chair now for ten, maybe fifteen minutes.

"Sure you don't want coffee or something?"

He looked around, focused on Fran. "Nah." He swiveled the chair around to face her. "Sorry to go in a trance like that…"

"Don't worry about it."

"..but sometimes you just got to wonder."

She knew that "Noren's Nightmare," as it was now known by people at Global and in the industry, affected him deeply. Friends of his were let go and Noren had effectively challenged Boyle's leadership. "Let's see what Boyle does about this…if anything," was a widespread reaction. Just like little boys. If you wanted to know how big companies worked, just watch little boys at play.

"Have you talked to any of them?" It was a sensitive question but she felt he wanted to talk about it.

"Yeah. Spoke to Mike Clancy yesterday. He thinks he's going to be okay, work as a travel agent on the Island. Worried about keeping his kids in college, though." He brightened considerably. "Got a big kick out of old MacCready. Said he'd had it with the ad business anyhow and was going to go in and piss all over Noren's desk, but was afraid that if he did, Noren wouldn't understand what he was trying to tell him."

They both laughed heartily. Good, got you laughing, she thought.

"Norma's the one I'm worried about." The light tone evaporated. "She's got that brother, paraplegic, injured in a car accident—what, twelve years ago—she's been taking care of him ever since. I called some of my contacts at the other carriers…I'll find her something."

"Did Samuels say anything?"

"Oh yeah, next day's staff meeting. Said he wished he had more people like Noren, looking for ways to cut costs." He laughed. "There was a bit of poetic justice though. Samuels said Noren had done such a 'surgical' job he could cut out another five million bucks from his budget."

"You come out okay?"

"From that meeting, yeah, but they challenge everything."

Word had already leaked out that Arnie Kreiger had aligned himself with Noren and was after Boyle's job. Like many people who spent their entire careers in field assignments, Fran felt an understandable resentment toward those who passed all their time in the perceived comfort of staff positions, totally insulated from the often raging beasts known as passengers. But Arnie Kreiger? Fran wouldn't trust that weasel Kreiger with changing paper towels in the men's john.

"Fran, while I'm over in London for the European station meetings next couple of days, watch my back, will you? I don't like being out of New York that long...under present circumstances."

As if he had read her mind. "Sure."

"Helluva way to run an airline." Boyle turned in his chair and looked out the window.

Many of the Global veterans she talked to on a daily basis were thinking of getting out; they could see the handwriting on the wall. "Pat, have you and Kate ever thought about just chucking the whole thing..."

Boyle abruptly spun back to face her. Said the wrong thing there she realized, but didn't know why.

He looked at his watch. "I think I better go check in."

"On the deuce?"

"Yeah."

"That's almost three hours from now." Boyle was booked on Global's flight 2, the first of their three evening flights to London. "Think I'll go over the flight plan," he smiled, his tone lightened up, "make sure the captain's putting on enough fuel to get us there."

Whatever nerve was touched, Fran knew he wouldn't resent her innocent question. But that was some reaction; what else was going on?

*   *   *

Showered and wrapped in thick, terry cloth robes, Noren and Leslie Foster sat down to the light supper her cook had left for them: pate, cold grilled salmon with endive salad, washed down by some Louis Roderer Cristal champagne. Seen from her twelfth-floor apartment on Sutton Place, the East River glistened like strands of Christmas-tree icicles set among slabs of polished black stone.

"How're things going with the new job?"

"You mean the ad budget?" he kidded.

"Since you brought it up…" she grinned.

"Actually, I had help bringing it up." He nodded toward the unmade bed, visible through the bedroom door.

She clinked her champagne glass against his. "You needed help bringing it up, darling."

He laughed lasciviously. "I was only checking your level of enthusiasm for your new account."

"Speaking of which…" she reminded him.

"Ah yes, my ad budget. I bet you know as much about it as I do."

She took up the challenge. "I know most airlines spend one to two percent of total revenues on advertising."

"Uh-huh."

"Last year Global did what…three billion in revenue?"

"Yeah, say maybe three point two."

"So at three bill you should have done, say forty, forty-five million?"

"That's ballpark."

"And you did what, twenty-two?"

"Twenty-one, twenty-two."

"Round numbers, you're twenty mil below where you should be."

"Lots of room to grow." He took her hand and pulled it slowly along his naked thigh.

"I like to see budgets grow." She leaned toward him, following the path of her hand. "Nice things happen to little boys with big budgets."

He took her hand and wrapped it around his throbbing penis. "I'll guarantee you a big budget."

*   *   *

Noren knew where he made his mistake. Should've let Samuels know he had a plan—with limits—before he shook up his department. Now Samuels stuck him with a "Great job! Do it again!" scenario and expected him to come up with an additional five million bucks in cost reductions. Shit.

"Okay, run it by me again," said Noren, swiveling about in his chair. "Oh, and Trish? You might tug down your skirt a bit…I could get a look at something I shouldn't see."

Trish Peters ignored the remark, as she typically did with all the sexual innuendoes that came the way of an attractive and ambitious young woman in the business world. "We're talking a hiring freeze, ending the sales incentive program, closing three sales offices."

"Bottom line?"

"Two point seven, round to three mil a year, depending how quickly you get started."

"That's not going to do it."

"Cut any more and you're going to jeopardize the whole sales program." She looked at him. "You can't get operations to kick in any savings?"

He made a face. "Ah, we go through that at every budget meeting. Boyle'll come in and announce they're switching from almonds to peanuts for the coach class passengers and save a lousy ten thousand bucks a month. And all the rest is untouchable. All the rest are fucking safety items!"

"Why deal only with Boyle?"

Why deal only with Boyle? As if he had a choice. Kreiger had already made his pitch for Boyle's job. Noren often hired quislings—they made good subordinates—but there had to be some level of competence for a job like Boyle's. "You got an alternative?"

"The VP Maintenance is a guy named Spears, Hank Spears. Friend of Boyle's."

"So?"

"He's been out for months, terminal cancer. Boyle keeps him on the payroll as a favor."

Noren was disappointed. "Trish, we're not gonna come up with shit by pulling some VP off the payroll."

"The guy who runs Kennedy maintenance is a guy named Mennotti, Dom Mennotti. He's very frustrated with the way things are going, thinks Global could do things quicker and cheaper. He also thinks he ought to be the VP Maintenance."

"How do you know all this?"

"Met him at a managers' conference last summer. I guess he thought we hit it off and he told me his life story. Seemed to be knowledgeable, ambitious and frustrated. I also got the impression he and Boyle don't get along all that well." She shrugged in summary. "Might be able to give you some insights into the operations budget."

"Sounds like you've been studying your Machiavelli."

"Business is business."

She was ballsey; he liked that. She was also very attractive. Could be two opportunities here; get some inside information to use against Boyle, get to know Trish Peters better, a lot better. Had to be careful these days, he reminded himself, hop in the sack with them day one and day two they're back with a lawyer in tow. But there were ways.

"Trish," he sat upright in his swivel chair and leaned across his desk towards her, "…let me share something with you."

She instinctively crossed her legs and leaned back in her chair. He seemed not to notice.

"It's been very frustrating, in many aspects, my time here at Global Air. So many people have been here so long and they only know one way to get the job done—their way, the old way."

"I know."

He stood, walked around his desk and sat in the chair opposite her, no longer boss-and-subordinate, now colleague-to colleague; body language 101. "I'd like you to sound out this Mennotti. Think he can be trusted?"

"Trusted?"

"Trusted to keep this between just you and me." The promise of secrets shared between boss and subordinate can be very seductive.

"I think so."

"Then—and you tell Mennotti this, you'll be speaking for me—when we get what we need, big cost savings from Boyle's operation, that job as VP Maintenance will be his when the old guy, what's his name?"

"Spears, Hank Spears."

"When Spears kicks off…no better yet…" he reached out and placed his right hand on the top of her crossed leg. She flinched. "Tell him if this thing works, we'll get Spears off the payroll—dead or alive—and put him in instead." He kept his hand on her knee.

She slipped her pencil under his hand and lifted it off, much as one might carry a bird on a stick. "I'd better be going and get this project in motion." She stood from her chair to leave. He rose to intercept her.

"You know Trish, more than one person has found it very helpful to their careers to become acquainted with their bosses on a more personal level."

"Oh, I know," she replied, as breezily as she could, "but at Wharton they told us never to mix personal with business."

He watched her walk toward the door. "I'm starting interviews soon to find a replacement for Clancy."

She turned and looked at him.

"It's a VP slot…you might think about that."

Trish stood still for another moment, then turned and left the room.

Noren felt good. This had been a productive meeting.

*   *   *

Trish met Mennotti in one of the scabby diners which surround Kennedy airport.

"How is this supposed to work again?" she asked, sipping corrosive coffee from a thick white porcelain mug which looked as though it had not been washed after its use by the previous customer.

Mennotti sighed inwardly. Marketing types were all the same, he thought. Great on the "big picture," seemingly incapable of grasping details. Maybe they all came from California. He would try again.

"Each plane has two wings," he said. She grimaced at his patronizing attempt at humor, but said nothing. "Some planes—like our 747s—have two engines on each wing. Some planes—like our A300s—have one engine on each wing."

She rolled her eyes; apparently she was still following him.

"Each engine is held onto the wing by a pylon. It sort of looks like a finger." He extended his left index finger to illustrate. "When we remove an engine for maintenance, or to inspect the wing, first we take the engine off, then the pylon. To replace them, we do just the reverse—pylon first, then engine." He demonstrated the procedure by using a salt shaker as the engine and moved it to and from his outstretched finger.

"And you say you can take them on and off together?"

"Exactly!"

"What's that worth in savings?"

"Figure a four-man crew, average two point something engines per aircraft..." he pulled a ballpoint from his pocket and scratched some numbers on the napkin, "...say eighty, eighty-five hours at forty-some bucks an hour, close to thirty thousand bucks a plane. Say four hundred planes in the fleet...you're talkin' twelve million bucks a year."

"Twelve million dollars?"

Bingo! Her eyes just lit up! "And that's only savings! That doesn't count the extra revenue from additional flying hours per aircraft!" She understands that.

"That's great! So we're creating cost savings as well as incremental sales!"

He mugged false modesty. "Marketing types call it a win-win situation." Damn! Finally someone from headquarters was listening to Dom Mennotti!

"But why hasn't Global done that before?"

Here we go again. "The one-step procedure? Global's too conservative." Then he saw another opportunity. "And, let's face it," now sotto voce, sharing confidences with a trusted friend, "Boyle likes to do things the old way, the way things are always done." She nodded, she knows; Boyle's job is soon gonna be open.

"So all this extra expense is simply...habit?"

Mennotti struggled with himself. "Well," the words came reluctantly, "I guess to be fair about it, there's a feeling that handling the engine and pylon together can put more stress on the wing which, under very unlikely conditions of max takeoff weight..." Her expression said he'd lost her. Keep it simple. "Put it this way; other carriers do it all the time. It's basically a question of knowing what you're doing."

She looked unconvinced.

"Look, it's like packing eggs. There are few things more fragile than eggs, right?"

"Yeah."

"So suppose all the egg farms never switched to machines to load their cartons and still packed by hand? Would that be cost-effective?"

"Don't those machines ever break any eggs?"

"What kinda question is that?" he asked.

*   *   *

Her years as a secretary convinced Fran Demarest that most managers equate a meeting's length with its worth. She was determinded to keep her own staff meetings short and to the point. Her direct subordinates—the JFK managers of passenger services, cargo services, catering and maintenance—were expected to report accordingly. Three of the four typically did. The exception was Dom Mennotti, who always seemed to bring to these meetings insurmountable problems with his budget, overtime, equipment, weather and other variables.

Until recently. For the last few days, Mennotti was downright placid; either he has finally come to terms with his job, given up on it entirely or was on Prozac. She glanced at him as the Passenger Services Manager was finishing up his report.

"...so we run out of the Pouilly Fuisse and serve this perfectly fine California chardonnay. Well, there's a lawyer in first…" the attendees groaned, "…and now he's gonna sue for pain and suffering." The manager threw up his hands in mock appeal.

"He's looking for a free ticket," said Fran, "send him a one-class upgrade coupon and we'll never hear from him again." She paused. "Until next time." The group laughed appreciatively. "If that's the biggest problem we have today, sounds like we're in pretty good shape. Anybody with anything else?" She looked around the table. "Dom? Everything okay in your shop?"

Mennotti looked surprised to be called on. "Yeah. No problems."

"Owww!" the Cargo Services Manager hollered; everyone looked at him. "Oh sorry, but when Dom said he had no problems, I had to pinch myself to see if I was dreaming." Everybody laughed, including Mennotti, who reached over to the man, grabbed him by the neck and shook him playfully.

"Okay, that's it," Fran announced. "Same time, same place tomorrow. Keep those planes on time!" The four people stood and left her office.

She watched Mennotti, who was leaving with his arm around the shoulder of the cargo manager. Something's going on with Mennotti. She'd mention it to Boyle.

Mention what? That the man's not complaining? But it was so unlike him. Besides, Fran was in an awkward managerial position. Mennotti reported to her administratively because he was based at JFK. But he reported functionally to the vice-president of maintenance who'd been on sick leave for months, which meant that he reported to Boyle, for all intents and purposes. Pat Boyle didn't have the time

to be concerned with yet another manager and his problems. Or lack of them.

Fran sighed. This would have to wait. Boyle just got
back from his European stations meeting, he'd be in the
office a few days and then off to Honolulu for the Pacific
stations meeting. This would just have to wait.

*   *   *

Now's the time, Mennotti told himself as he drove the
Global station wagon the two miles between the passenger
terminal and the maintenance base. I'm handing these
cocksuckers ten, twenty million bucks on a plate and this
guy Noren doesn't want to talk to me. Bullshit. They think
Dom Mennotti doesn't know what's going on? Noren's
gonna be a hero; Peters is gonna be a hero; Boyle's gonna
get dumped and I'm gonna sit at Kennedy playing with
my dick? No way!

Mennotti pulled into his parking space and turned off
the engine. Too many years doin' all the work, watchin'
everybody take all the credit. Including Boyle and his girl-
friend, the station manager. If this guy Noren wants a
favor, he's gonna deal with me direct.

*   *   *

Noren was pacing. "Jesus, Trish, there is no way I'm
going to meet this guy!"

Trish sat in a chair by his desk and waited for him to
calm down.

"I mean, why can't he take your word? You work for
me—everybody knows that—when he becomes a VP he
can talk to me all he wants."

"He says there's a problem he can only talk to you about."

"A problem? Great! Why the hell is it all of a sudden there's a problem?" He swiveled back and forth in his chair. How stupid was she? She wasn't that stupid. Why meet Mennotti? From what she told him, he was just another scuzzball like the types he grew up with and left behind in East Brooklyn. But deniability! Did he have to spell out the importance of deniability for an executive? There's stuff you don't want to know about, can't know about. Christ, everybody knows that!

But tomorrow was Samuels' meeting. Shit. He stopped swiveling. "Tell him okay. Tonight."

"Tonight? Where?" She had her pencil poised, pad ready.

Where? Needed someplace there was no chance he would be recognized—that left out all the decent spots—and no place anywhere near Kennedy.

"The bar in the Staten Island Ferry terminal."

*   *   *

Mennotti couldn't believe it when she told him. This guy is sitting there in the Global Air building midtown, surrounded by probably the biggest number of bars and restaurants in the world and I gotta drive in from the airport to the fuckin' ferry? He wants to be discreet. Discreet my ass.

The drive through the rush-hour traffic took the full hour and a half that Mennotti forecast plus another ten minutes trying to find a place to park at the ass end of Manhattan Island. He entered the bar and looked around;

most of the commuters were gone, only a few serious drinkers remained. He spotted a guy in a booth who looked just the way Noren had been described, a wolf with a hard on. He walked over. The guy looked at him.

"Mr. Noren?"

"Mennotti?"

Already Mennotti didn't like him.

"Sit down."

Mennotti slid into the booth. He noticed Noren was drinking club soda; musta run outta fuckin' Perrier.

"Trish Peters said you wanted to see me."

"Yeah, well I figured if we were gonna work together I oughtta talk to you direct."

"So I understand." Noren smiled.

Here comes the hand job, thought Mennotti.

Noren concentrated on the soggy cocktail napkin he was toying with. "It's just that you and I have to be...you know..."

"Discreet?"

"Exactly."

"I know that's important. But I wanna make sure that you understand I'm expectin' certain things to happen for me when you show up Boyle and become a corporate hero."

"I'm sure Trish has told you..."

"I wanna hear it from you."

Noren cleared his throat and looked around. "When I am in a position to do so, I will fill the vice president of maintenance position and you are my candidate." He gulped some club soda.

"Good."

Noren wiped his fingertips with the cocktail napkin. "Trish said there was a problem?"

"We got a C-check comin' in this week." Noren looked blank. "C-check. Heavy maintenance. Engines and pylons...

"Oh right, okay."

"...and this would be a good time for the one-step procedure, but..."

"Yeah?"

"...when you change procedures you gotta change the procedures manual."

"So?"

"So authorization for that would normally come from Hank Spears..."

"The VP who's out sick."

"...or his boss."

"Christ!" Noren pounded his fist on the table. "Don't you understand? Boyle can't be involved in this!"

Mennotti raised his hand to signal time out and withdrew a piece of paper from his jacket pocket. "He's already authorized it."

"What?"

He handed the piece of paper to Norton. "Read it."

Noren read the Service Bulletin, used to announce a change in an operations procedure.

"Effective immediately, aircraft engines and pylons will be handled as a unit during C-check. They will no longer be handled separately.

"Exact procedures are found in manufacturer's specifications manual, 6.20 through 7.00.

Authorized by: Patrick J. Boyle, Senior VP. Operations."

Noren looked at Mennotti, awaiting an explanation.

"Ya gotta understand. We change procedures all the time."

"Understood."

"Now, normally I'd call up Spears, he's been out, so I'd call Boyle, tell 'im what I wanna do. If he's got no problem, he says okay, I print this out...," Mennotti tapped the piece of paper, "...with Boyle's authorization—ya gotta have authorization—give it to my guys, they do the work." He leaned toward Noren. "It's in my PC now. Before I print it and hand it out tomorrow, I want your assurance that any shit hits the fan, I got your back-up."

Noren sat back. "I see." He wiped his fingertips again with what was left of the cocktail napkin. "Boyle knows nothing about this?"

"You gotta be kiddin'."

"Just want to make sure." Noren balled up the napkin, looked at it, then nodded his head. "The timing on this is good, real good." He sat up straight. "Look, let me be as frank as I can. Boyle blocks every attempt that Mr. Samuels and I make to save money. Every one. You've come up with a way to do just that. You go ahead and put this out." He looked around as if someone might be listening and leaned toward Mennotti. "I have Mr. Samuels' backing on this. You got my word."

"Okay. I'll take your word."

Noren looked at his watch. "Have to run. Lots of things to do tonight." He grinned at Mennotti, slid out of the booth, stood up and tossed a dollar bill on the table. "This should cover the club soda."

Won't cover the fuckin' tip, Mennotti thought, but said nothing.

"Keep in touch with Trish." Noren turned and walked away.

Mennotti watched him leave. Where do they get these guys, he wondered. A blowsy, frizzy-haired waitress meandered by and stopped at his table. "Thought maybe everybody had gone home," he said.

"It's been busy, hon. Ya wanna drink?"

"Nah. I'll just have a glass a red wine."

She wandered away. Mennotti reached into his jacket and pulled out a small tape recorder. Let's see if the pickup's as good as the guy said. He pushed the rewind button and waited as the recorder whined. It stopped. He pushed the play button and listened. Background noise. Noise coming into the bar. More noise. "Mr. Noren?" the tape began. Mennotti smiled and clicked it off.

Not that I don't trust this guy...

   *   *   *

Boyle slammed his fist on the boardroom table. "We've been over this before! Reserve fuel onboard an aircraft is not a negotiable item! There are specific FAA regulations which dictate precisely how much fuel must be carried."

He knew his face was flushed, his voice choked and tight. Hold on, don't lose it now, he cautioned himself. Samuels looked at him impassively. Noren wore his grimace smile.

"Pat," said Noren, spreading his hands as if in supplication, "we all know about the regulations. I'm only asking about the additional fuel captains take on at their own discretion."

Bastard managed to sound sincere.

"No reason to be defensive," Noren added.

"Let me try one more time." Boyle tried for biting sarcasm, but damned if he didn't sound defensive.

Samuels drummed his fingers on the table; Noren continued to grin inanely. Boyle felt the room was unusually warm and cleared his throat again. "Each flight has an individual flight plan tailored to the specific route, aircraft, passenger and cargo load, and weather the aircraft will be flying through."

"I understand that," smiled Noren.

"If you do, then why the hell are we wasting all this time?" Boyle shot back.

"Just give him an answer and get on with it," Samuels ordered.

"When the captain of an aircraft is given a flight plan, he not only has the right, he has the **responsibility** to check that plan against his knowledge and experience and change it, if necessary, including the addition of more fuel."

Noren yawned broadly.

"Suppose our pilots are overly cautious and always take on more fuel, isn't that a waste of money?" asked Samuels.

"We've got a computer program which measures reserve fuel requests by pilots. If an individual pilot continually exceeds programmed averages, the Chief Pilot brings him in and finds out what's going on."

"And you're sure this program works?"

Boyle detected a note of contempt in Samuels' voice. He rubbed his sweating palms down his suited thighs, a linebacker awaiting the snap of the ball. "The program works." His throat was dry. "If we err, we err on the side of safety."

"Yeah well, let's not 'err' ourselves out of business," Samuels shot back. "I cannot tell you how sick and tired I am of dealing with costs that you seemingly can't—or won't—control!" Samuels snorted in frustration and cocked his head over his shoulder toward Redmond, seated at the computer work station. "Where are we at, costwise?"

Boyle watched Noren smirk.

Redmond typed several entries and read the computer screen. "According to Aviation Daily our cost per available seat-mile is third highest in the industry, year-to-date."

Samuels threw up his hands; case closed. He paused, templed his fingers, looked over them at Boyle. "And you're off to Honolulu today?" Scorn, mixed with theatrical disbelief.

Boyle nodded deliberately. He had spent most of his adult life in this company and now was being treated like a kid in school. "Pacific operations meeting. Be back Thursday." Then the thought occurred: Why? Why come back at all?

"Goddamnit! It was London last week, now it's Honolulu, where the hell are you going when you get back?"

The question and Samuels' mock outrage struck Boyle as funny. He smiled and failed to suppress a slight laugh— might as well pour it on. "Chicago."

"Chicago?!" Samuels' face was purpling.

Boyle pointed at Noren. "It's his party."

Samuels almost leaped at Noren. "Party?!"

Noren looked like he'd just been discovered playing with himself. "Ah...it's not a party, Mr. Samuels, it's a major sales and service promotion!" Noren was speaking too rapidly, a little boy being blamed for something he didn't do. "We're starting service from O'Hare to Athens and we've got TV, radio, print media, the mayor…"

Boyle was smirking.

"Alright, alright." Samuels waved him quiet and turned back to Boyle. "Doesn't sound like a party to me."

Boyle winked at Noren and beamed at Samuels. "I must have been misinformed," he said in all innocence.

The room was absolutely quiet, all eyes on Samuels as he glared at Boyle. Samuels broke off eye contact and toyed with the notepad on the table before him. "When you eventually find the opportunity and motive to return to your office, you and I will discuss your costs in detail, item by item."

Boyle knew he could get away with a challenge like that only once—once might be enough.

"Okay." Samuels looked around the room. "Anybody with anything else?"

"Mr. Samuels, I need a few minutes of your time." Noren's tone was appropriately subservient.

Samuels looked at Redmond, who shrugged. "Okay Noren, but Redmond and I have a lot of financial shit to go through, so it's got to be brief." Samuels stood and headed for his office.

Boyle watched Noren scurry after the departing Samuels. Wonder if Noren's going to complain about his hurt feelings, he mused.

*   *   *

"Sit down", Samuels indicated a chair to Noren. "What do you got?"

Noren's scenario was planned and rehearsed: review of his accomplishments; summary of the problem; statement of its solution and request for approval. "When you and I first discussed my joining Global, the stock was depressed, earnings were flat..."

"Yeah, yeah I know. Stock's up to twenty-six and what, three-eighths yesterday, first quarter sales up nine-point-seven per cent—that could be better—your costs are improving but I gotta tell you, if you're here to blow smoke up my ass about what you're been doing, I don't need it. I know what you've been doing. And my schedule is real full today."

Noren swallowed hard. "I think I've got a fix on maintenance expenses."

"Oh?"

"The guy who's running Kennedy maintenance now is filling in for his boss who's out with cancer..."

Samuels raised a hand. "Don't have time for a soap opera."

"The point is—I think I can control maintenance costs. But that's Boyle's department and I may need your backing." Samuels waited for him to continue.

"There's what they call a C-check, a major overhaul..."

"How much money you talking?"

"Ten million a year to start." Staring boldly at Samuels, Noren tilted his head slightly, lowered his voice. "And that's conservative."

Samuels looked at him with interest. "This works, you got backing. Fuck up, I never heard of you."

"I'll deliver the results," promised Noren.

"Good. Now please have Redmond come in here when you go out."

Noren jumped to his feet. "Right."

"Noren," Samuels stopped him at the door, "I haven't forgotten our conversation. The presidency of this airline remains open for someone who can do the job."

"I appreciate that, Mr. Samuels."

Noren bounded out of the room. Redmond entered immediately.

"What's with Noren?" Redmond asked. "He almost flew out of here."

"I told him he could still be president of Global. He believed me. So where are we at?"

Redmond spread out some papers on Samuels' desk. "The Singapore group estimates they'll have the financing lined up in a month, six weeks outside."

"We talking dollars or yen?"

"They're talking yen."

"I want dollars and I want the dollars locked in when we sign, not when we close."

Redmond made a face. "Don't know if they'll go for that one, Gerry."

"You see where the yen is going against the dollar?"

"They look at the same figures."

"Get it."

Redmond sighed acquiescence. "Okay. The deal for the European and South American routes looks a lot firmer. Dresden Bank's the lead bank but they have to get a U.S. bank to front the deal because it'll exceed the twenty-five percent foreign control law."

"What's the time frame?"

"Spoke to Dietrich this morning, he's talking weeks."

"How about the planes?"

Redmond threw up his hands. "You know who we're dealing with on that one, Gerry. I mean, one day he's going to write a personal check for the whole fleet, the next day we're haggling over the price of a twenty-year old 747. I can't tell you."

"That's his style. Stay with him."

"With the phone bills I'm running up to Vegas, I might as well move there."

The plan was beginning to fall in place. Samuels stood up and walked to the balcony door; a lovely spring day. He slid the door open and stepped out on the balcony. His view was to the south, towards the tip of Manhattan Island and the lower Eastside where he'd been born, grew up, where his father owned a dry goods store. Samuels still owned and operated the store, although it typically ran in the red, the only possession in Samuels' empire in which an annual loss was tolerated. Redmond joined him on the balcony.

"So what you're saying..." Samuels began.

"What I'm saying is, if all goes well—the Singapore group, the Europeans and our billionaire friend in Vegas—within two months you will have pulled off the largest sale of assets in U.S. airline history!" Redmond was about to lean on the balcony.

Samuels grabbed his arm. "Watch out for that damned railing, it's loose." Samuels shook the railing to demonstrate. "I called building maintenance about it, someone's on strike..."

Redmond started laughing.

"What's funny?"

"Gerry, come on! We're talking about the biggest airline deal ever and you're complaining about some stupid railing!" Redmond continued laughing.

Samuels did not have a sense of humor. But Redmond had a point. For once in a very long while, Samuels had to smile.

*   *   *

Fran Demarest stood at the podium in the boarding area for Global flight 85, the daily noon nonstop from JFK to Honolulu. All passengers were on board, save one. The gate agent waited at the jetway door for Fran's okay to pull the jetway. Fran looked anxiously at her watch; airport managers were measured by a plethora of indices—none was more important than on-time departures. "It's okay, Melissa," she assured the gate agent, "I'm watching the time."

Fran was looking toward the passenger concourse when she spotted Boyle jogging toward the gate.

"We don't hold flights for full-revenue passengers, let alone non-revs," she shouted at him. She meant it with good humor but both were very aware an aircraft off the gate more than three minutes past scheduled departure required a written and detailed explanation.

"I know, sorry," he wheezed as he approached the gate, "got hung up on a call."

She took a step back when she saw his face—it was drained, ashen: was it the running or was he having a heart attack? "Are you okay?"

"Just got off the phone with Penelope in London." He looked at his watch and the gate agent. "Better have her standby to button up."

"Go, Melissa. We'll be right down." The gate agent flung back the door and ran into the jetway.

Boyle cupped Fran's elbow in his hand and guided her toward the jetway. "Strictly confidential and unconfirmed." Boyle whispered the words but his voice was strong. "Penelope was contacted by a friend of hers— heads up the foreign currency department at Manchester Union Bank—said he'd been told by a source at Dresden Bank they were putting together a deal to buy our Atlantic routes."

Fran stopped, Boyle dropped his hand; they were at the jetway door. "What would that mean?"

"We could survive, but…"

Three-quarters of Fran's arrivals and departures were trans-Atlantic flights. "Global Air without Atlantic flights?"

Boyle shook his head in disbelief. "I'll be seeing Arthur Liu in Honolulu, maybe he can check it out."

They moved quickly through the door and into the jetway—whatever else might be happening, an on-time departure remained paramount.

Fran pulled an index card from her jacket pocket as they walked down the ramp. She maintained a summary list of items in priority order to brief Boyle about when he transited JFK, but doubted there were any worth bothering him with in these circumstances. She looked at the list: late freight dispatch from cargo, causing delays—that could wait; Mennotti's changed and untypically placid behavior—another time; a flight attendant's suggestion concerning meal service on the Bermuda trip…an item at the bottom of the card caught her eye. "Pat?" She reached out and tugged the sleeve of his jacket as they neared the aircraft door. "Johnnie Vernon, used to work in load control'?"

He stopped and looked at her questiongly. "Yeah?"

"I didn't even know whether this was worth mentioning…"

"Go ahead."

"He's down in Phoenix now, working as a travel agent."

"Uh-huh'?"

"He heard from a big charter operator in Las Vegas that they're talking about buying our fleet! I mean, I thought this was just another wild rumor…"

"Sonofabitch," Boyle said quietly. He thought for a moment, much as a physician might before telling a patient her cancer had been confirmed. "The sad truth is, Fran, this company is worth more dismembered than whole." He held her arm.

"We better get you on board!" Fran said.

They walked swiftly to the aircraft. Boyle strode on board, past the waiting gate agent. No sooner had he disappeared than he popped back out, frowning and pointing his finger sternly at the gate agent.

"I expect you to keep this airline on time, Melissa!"

Melissa appeared stunned.

Then Boyle broke into a big grin and winked at her.

"Oh sure, Mr. Boyle!" she blushed and pulled the jetway back from the plane.

"See you, Fran." Boyle waved, as the aircraft door slid into place.

"Take care, Pat." Fran looked at Melissa—the gate agent was beaming. Fran knew how she felt.

CHAPTER SIX

▼

NOTHING WITHOUT CAUSE

Mennotti was fanatical in tracking the progress of all machines sent to his shop for maintenance, whether a 747 in for a C-check or a forklift for a re-alignment of its blades. Much like a conscientious military officer, he tried to personally monitor the care of his charges as much as he could, while their status was constantly updated in his computer.

Aircraft N412GA was right on schedule. A three-engine wide-body, it would be back in service tomorrow, completing its C-check a full sixteen hours ahead of what would be a normal cycle. Sixteen hours of labor costs saved, sixteen hours of additional revenue flying; aircraft

N412GA would make Dom Mennotti a vice president of Global Air. He re-played his fantasy in the boardroom: Noren, maybe even Samuels, escorts him into the meeting with all the suits around the table—including that phony, Boyle—and introduces Mr. Dominic S. Mennotti, Jr., Vice President of Maintenance for Global Air!

He broke off his reverie and checked his clipboard. Only a few people were aware of the new procedure. The analysts in Aircraft Scheduling seemed to be impressed, though they'd never admit it. Trish Peters said Noren was "anxious for results," which meant he couldn't wait to run to Samuels and claim credit for Mennotti's work. And then there was Wenthol; he was the only guy who wasn't enthused, at least he didn't act enthused. But that was typical; he didn't like change. The hell with him.

Mennotti flipped through the worksheets on the clipboard till he found his supervisors' schedules. There's fun: the plane would be buttoned up early tomorrow morning on the graveyard shift. Wenthol was the supervisor on duty. If he thinks he's gonna get any glory for this, he's shit outta luck. The people who count know this is Dom Mennotti's project: idea, implementation and result.

He punched up the flight schedule display in his computer. Sonofabitch. Airline Scheduling had his feet to the fire. They designated aircraft N412GA as a First Flight tomorrow! Company performance standard was eighty-five percent of departures within five minutes of schedule. Flights designated "First Flights" were judged critical for the system to achieve its on-time goal, due to the tight scheduling of their transit and/or turnaround times; they were expected to achieve one hundred percent of exact schedule. If a First Flight failed to operate precisely on time, people fell all over themselves looking for someone to blame. Maintenance was a candidate for the collar if they didn't get the aircraft to the line in time for fueling and loading. Sonofabitch! Betcha that's that little cocksucker Harry Langer who runs Scheduling; a chance to show me up if I can't push the plane out in time.

He checked the aircraft's itinerary. N412GA was set up as flight 119, an 0700 departure to Chicago, transit on to San Francisco. No chance that sucker's gonna be late. This plane's goin' to Chicago tomorrow if I have to push it to the gate myself.

*   *   *

Boyle sat at a table in the lounge on the top floor of the Ilikai Hotel, anchored at the western sweep of Waikiki Beach. He watched the setting sun tinge Diamond Head rosy-pink. Maybe there are too many tourists, too much concrete and traffic, he thought, but this is still one of the world's great sights.

Once he and Kate and little Pat had lived in Honolulu for two years while he ran the airport operation for Global. That seemed so long ago now, it was as if it never happened; perhaps that was because they were so happy then, so carefree, so different from the present. He took a swig from the glass of beer he was holding absentmindedly. That's going to change. He wasn't sure exactly when he had made the decision, maybe on the flight over, maybe during one of the meetings, maybe now; this was his last meeting, he would go back and resign. They could have the title and the money and all the bullshit; he would go back and try to make it work again with Kate. If not that,

what was there? Another twenty-some years on the job—
or some job—and then what? Retirement? With whom?
He and Kate cared for one another once, no doubt about
that. Maybe it can work again...he would try. He sensed
somebody standing behind him.

"Looks like you're carrying the weight of the world."

Boyle turned to Arthur Liu. "Hey Arthur, sit down,
join me."

Arthur Liu was one of Boyle's best friends and Global's
first local hire in Singapore some forty years before. The
only apparent concessions he had made to age were silver
temples in a head of otherwise thick, jet-black hair. Now
Global's Vice-President for Southeast Asia, he maintained
active and agressive business interests in Singapore's
Chinese community, owning controlling interest in a large
tour operator, two fine restaurants, and a fleet of taxicabs.
Though Boyle and other Global peers would kiddingly
accuse him of hanging on to his airline job for the free
transportation, they knew that the airline business was
part of the warp and woof of this man's life. Like many of
them; like Boyle himself.

"So how do you think the meetings went?" Boyle asked
as Liu slid a chair over, sat down and signalled a nearby
waitress for a beer.

"Good. They were good."

Boyle waited for the rest. The older man was a mentor
to Boyle, not only on Asian business but larger issues as
well.

"You seemed..." Liu was searching for an appropriate
word, "...distracted?"

"It showed, huh?"

"We have become accustomed to your manner; straight-forward, charge ahead, take no prisoners!"

Boyle managed a smile. "So just because I ask you to take a few prisoners, you think I'm getting soft?"

Liu smiled politely. The waitress appeared at the table with a bottle of beer, poured it into a chilled glass and scurried away.

"My brother called me just now," said Liu. He sipped his beer.

Boyle nodded his head in recognition; Liu's brother was Managing Director of a very successful stock brokerage in Singapore.

"He confirmed your story. A consortium of European banks are negotiating to buy our Atlantic routes..."

Boyle felt as though Liu had told him of the death of a friend who had been seriously ill—it wasn't a total surprise, but it left him with an unexpectedly powerful sense of loss. Global Air without its flights to London, to Paris, to Frankfurt, to virtually every city on the European continent?

Liu was studying him, gauging his reaction. Boyle sensed there was more.

"In the course of my brother's queries, he learned of an investment group—not many details, the information vague—apparently Australian, proposing to acquire the Pacific routes."

They can't do that, he thought, immediately correcting himself and the pitiful naivete the thought represented. He corrected himself—of course they can do that. He corrected himself again: of course Samuels would do it.

Boyle started to say something; he was surprised that he had to clear his throat. "And the Las Vegas deal?"

Liu frowned "no." "My brother found no evidence of that at all, not even a good rumor. If Samuels is attempting to sell the fleet, it must be a one-on-one negotiation." Liu paused. "But it would make sense."

Good sense. Boyle had to agree—it made real good sense. He looked at Diamond Head, now shrouded in dusk, a necklace of lights surrounding its base. Maybe Kate would want to return here? He thought of little Pat, learning how to swim in the bathtub-warm waters of Hanauma Bay. No, probably not.

Liu toyed with the gold band of his watch. "Of course, these are negotiations. Not all negotiations result in a deal."

"Umm."

Liu looked down at his beer and back at Boyle. He had something else on his mind.

"Some of us were hoping Kate might have been able to join you on this trip…"

Boyle moved his glass of beer in a circle; it left a ring of moisture on the shiny black table top.

"Yeah, I was kind of hoping that too."

Liu pondered a moment; he became solemn. "You have had a very honorable career, Patrick." He focused intently on his boss and friend. "But there is always change." He lifted his glass in a toast to Boyle. "We must be open to change."

Boyle lifted his glass and clinked it against Liu's. "To change."

They both took a swallow and replaced their glasses on the table. Liu became chipper and businesslike. "So. Our closing dinner tonight and you're back to New York tomorrow?"

Boyle looked at him. "You son of a bitch," he said with great affection, "At least you're not calling it my farewell dinner." Both men knew it would have been an accurate description.

*   *   *

The clock radio went off at four p.m. but Tug Wallace had been awake for quite some time. He felt the cold coming on two days ago, realized it was more than a cold while in the hangar yesterday and knew now he had a full-blown case of the flu. The chills and fever, sweats and coughing had kept him up since he went to bed. Going back tonight to that cold and drafty hangar would only make things worse. Still, he hated to call in sick. For a grown man to say, "I can't come in today," was like saying, "My mother won't let me out to play." Besides, he was Tug Wallace; they had others there who could drive the tug and run the fork but they weren't Tug Wallace.

Tug Wallace's first name was Frank but nobody at Global knew or remembered that. For the twenty-seven years he'd been there he was known as "Tug," the best damned tow motor and forklift operator there ever was. On his tow motor, he could hook up to a 747 at max take-off gross weight of three-quarters of a million pounds and maneuver that sucker backwards and forwards, in and out of gate positions, past other aircraft wing-tip to wing-tip with the precision and smoothness of a surgeon. On his forklift, he could do a William Tell and push an apple off a post with one of the blades, damaging neither apple nor post.

His passion was fishing. This weekend the blues were running in Long Island Sound and he had promised his son they would catch some. Tug appreciated the serenity and intellectual gamesmanship of fly fishing in some remote and rocky stream, reveled in the one-on-one struggle of man, fish and line on the open ocean but enjoyed nothing as much as putting about the Sound in his little runabout, surrounded by the flashing and gnashing of bluefish in a feeding frenzy.

He had to make a decision soon. If he was going to go to work, there were numerous things he had to do beforehand; pick up his wife from her job, they would pick up their son from his job, go shopping, shave and shower while she cooked dinner—his breakfast—and off to work.

On the other hand, one phone call and he could stay where he was.

What the hell. He didn't do it that often. Tug Wallace picked up the bedside phone and punched in Wenthol's number.

*   *   *

Noren thought the request simple enough; he wanted to set up an appointment with Mr. Samuels and Mr. Redmond before the weekly budget review next week. But Dottie Allen, who had been Mr. Samuels' personal administrative assistant before the Ice Age ended, was in her control mode. Since she managed to "misunderstand" several requests from Noren's secretary—why would anyone expect Mr. Samuels' administrative assistant to deal with a mere secretary?—Noren was forced to make the pilgrimage to her office and explain his request in person.

"I don't understand why you need a meeting with Mr. Samuels and Mr. Redmond before you're going to meet with them anyway."

That's not all you don't understand, you stupid cow, he thought. Noren was smiling sincerely. "There's a...sensitive issue we need to discuss."

Dottie Allen never liked subordinates of Mr. Samuels discussing sensitive issues with him without her being clued in beforehand. "Perhaps if you were to tell me what the issue is, I can discuss it with Mr. Samuels and allow him to decide if it deserves a separate meeting." She paused. "He is a very busy man, you know." She smiled a sour little smile at him.

Noren didn't have time for this. She was hanging her huge, ancient ass out there for an embrace. He lowered his voice and cocked his head slightly. "Dottie, I need your help on this one." He could taste the bile in his mouth.

She brightened immediately. "Oh! Well why didn't you say so?" She hit a few keys on her computer. "I've got you scheduled for fifteen minutes. Is that enough time?"

That'll be enough time to hang Boyle. "It is, Dottie." He stood and smiled with all the gratitude he could muster without throwing up. "I want to thank you."

She took a plastic bottle of hand lotion from her credenza, squirted some on her hands and rubbed them together. "Anytime I can help."

Noren strode rapidly back to his office. Trish Peters was waiting for him.

"Okay Trish, all set. I've got fifteen minutes with Samuels and Redmond before the budget meeting next week. Now what I need from you and...whatsisname?..."

"Mennotti."

"...is a complete breakout of operating costs saved and revenue gained for this particular plane; those costs and revenues applied to the fleet—per plane and total—and then projected on an annual basis."

Peters was taking notes. "Can do."

"I present those to Samuels and Redmond, they take a look at 'em. Samuels calls in Boyle, says why didn't **you** do this and it's goodbye Boyle." He wondered if Samuels would announce him as president of Global at the same time as he announced Boyle was out.

"If you're going to be in Chicago tomorrow, when do you need this data?"

"Saturday." Peters grimaced; another Saturday shot.

"I'm going to have the agency spike it up and put in CD-ROM format for the meeting."

"Humph." Peters was impressed.

Noren knew she would be. "Seen this?" He slipped a CD-ROM into the laptop lying open on his desk. The laptop in turn was hooked up to a rear-screen projection unit behind the desk. "Watch this!" On screen came the latest Global thirty-second commercial.

"That's great!"

Noren ejected the disk. "I'm bringing this with me to Chicago tomorrow. This'll be the most exciting thing they've seen since the town burnt down." He looked at her. "Trish, you gotta remember, in marketing never let the numbers do the job for you. You've got to sell! You blow them away with your presentation, you can use any numbers you want and the other guy's left holdin' his dick."

"Or whatever."

He leered. "Yeah, right." He stared at her; she returned the stare. Good. No more blushing virgin act. Soon it'll be sack time. But not right now. "You find out what Boyle's schedule is?"

"Spoke to his secretary. He's on the nonstop from Honolulu, coming into the office tonight to pick up some stuff for Chicago and'll meet you at the flight at Kennedy tomorrow."

"We're booked on the same flight?"

"One-nineteen at seven a.m."

"No way. I really don't want to spend a lot of time one-on-one with Boyle before the meeting next week. At least in Chicago we're gonna be involved with a whole lot of other people...book me for something later. Long as I'm there by eleven-thirty, I'm okay."

"Will do."

His eyes followed her as she stood and left his office. He saw no panty line beneath her tight skirt. Wonder if she didn't wear panties? He'd find out soon. Real soon.

        *   *   *

Boyle typically used his flights as uninterrupted office time. Between the contents of the pilot's map case he carried—letters and memos for signature, various studies and industry publications—and the seemingly infinite work which resided in his laptop—flying time was a welcome respite from the phones and everyday crises of the office.

Not today. On a flight of almost nine hours duration through five time zones, he reviewed and re-played his decision. Regardless of repetition, the conclusion was the same: it was time to move on, time to restore that which he and Kate once shared. He'd had a good run at Global, did the best he could, achieved much but had placed much in jeopardy—the words, the lesson, *"What profits a man..."* weaved their way in and out of his thoughts as ceaselessly as the whoosh of air outside the plane's cabin.

With assist from a strong jetstream, the Global nonstop from Honolulu arrived at Kennedy fifteen minutes before its scheduled eight fifty-six p.m. arrival. Boyle was downtown and in the Global Air building by nine-thirty.

Ginny, his secretary, had sorted his mail and stacked it in three piles, each topped with a note. The "urgent" pile was mercifully the smallest. The "next week" pile told him held have no lack of evening reading material, while the "whenever" pile, the largest, was aptly named. He slung down his suit bag and placed his laptop on the desk. Funny thing about this bold new computer age; he took the laptop with him to Honolulu and faithfully responded to the eighty or more E-mails he received daily and read the hundreds of messages he was copied on. Yet the mail and paperwork which these machines were supposed to eliminate seemed to have increased in volume. Covering your ass had a lot to do with it, he suspected.

He sat down and picked up the "urgent" pile. At the top of the heap were the itinerary and schedule of events for tomorrow's O'Hare/Athens inaugural flight. The Mayor of Chicago will be joined by the leader of Chicago's Greek community...an archbishop of the Greek Orthodox Church...high school band...TV and radio interviews...the usual inaugural stuff. He noted he was booked on 119 at 0700. He could go through the "urgent" pile now, go home and try to get some sleep, be back here for an hour or so in the morning and catch the 0612 chopper to JFK. That's a plan.

He caught himself. Would that be the plan if Kate were still there?—Hi hon, I'm home. For a few hours, gone again. Can't help it, it's the job I've got, what do you expect?— Yeah, it would be the same. That's why she's not there. And maybe won't be coming back. Next week he would tell Samuels he was resigning. He would stay on for a month or longer or leave immediately, that was Samuels' call. But suppose she won't come back? Change. *We must be open to change.*

He looked at the phone. He called her from Honolulu daily but she wouldn't accept his calls at the clinic and she had the recorder on at the apartment she was renting. She'll still be up; he picked up the phone and touched a fast-dial button.

The phone rang four times, then the recorder kicked in. He listened to the message and waited for the beep. "Hi. If you're there, could you pick up?" He waited. "Well listen, I know it's kind of late but if you're there I'll still be in the office for a while. I just got back from Honolulu and I'll be in Chicago tomorrow...," he heard what he just said "...ah, well anyhow, we need to talk and I'll call you later." He started to replace the phone, then stopped. "I need to talk to you about change, Kate." The recorder disconnected. He was not sure if his last comment had been saved.

*   *   *

Wenthol had a message from Mennotti on his recorder at home, on his E-mail in the office and on a little yellow stickum affixed to his office phone. They all said the same thing: **Aircraft N412GA has to be on the gate at 0600! They set it up as a First Flight! I'll be in at 0500 to see how things are goinq!**

Things were not going that well. Tug Wallace called in sick. The hangar was backlogged with aircraft awaiting maintenance, there was a ban on overtime and the only guy he could spare to run the heavy fork was Ben Machado, which meant negotiating. Wenthol called Machado off the hangar floor and into his office cubicle, as if its three flimsy partitions offered either privacy or protection from the cacophony of machines screaming, whining and banging.

"Come on Ben, it's not that big a deal."

"Hey, I'm supposed to work on baggage container repair tonight."

"I need you on the heavy fork."

"You need me on the fork but if there ain't enough bag cans on the line, Mennotti's gonna be all over my ass."

"I'll handle Mennotti."

"Like you usually do?"

They both laughed. Machado wasn't a bad guy.

"Come on, gimme some OT."

"I would if I could but, y'know, there's no OT."

"Then you're gonna owe me big."

"How big?"

"A day. My call."

"Half-day. Subject to workload."

Machado thought about it. "Okay. But I may need to leave early some day next week."

"I'll cover you for two hours."

"Where you want me take the fork?" Machado sprang to his feet.

"Stookie on the C-check. It's a First Flight tomorrow and they gotta finish the engine-pylon assembly tonight."

"Pleasure doin' business with you." Machado left the cubicle.

Yeah, a real pleasure, thought Wenthol. Not enough people, no OT, some asshole in scheduling makes a First Flight outta a C-check; it's a real pleasure...Well, I'm not gonna be around a whole lot longer to worry about it. He took an envelope from his desk, slipped it under the chromed clip on his clipboard and walked out on the hangar floor.

*   *   *

Ben Machado's normal assignment was container repair, where he inspected and repaired the various lower-deck containers for baggage, freight and mail which air-lines carry in the bellies of their widebody passenger aircraft. Machado was very pleased with tonight's assignment; not only was he getting some comp time, he'd have the chance to show some of these old farts around the hangar there was more than one guy who was a swingin' dick on the forklift. "Tug" they called him cause they thought he was so hot. Ha! Just watch Ben Machado whip that heavy fork around tonight, he'd show them!

Machado walked to the forklift storage area and climbed aboard the giant of Global's forklift fleet: a Komatsu EX Series model, certified to lift 36,800 pounds. It was to your ordinary, run-of-the-mill forklift as a Testarossa is to a Taurus. Capable not only of straight up-and-down lifting, its tines could be both tilted and yawed left-to-right, its controls as responsive and sensitive as those in an aircraft cockpit.

He backed out of the area and maneuvered the forklift slowly and carefully across the hangar floor crowded with aircraft to the C-check area. He was surprised when he saw aircraft 412. "Hey Stookie," he called to the lead mechanic, "what's with the engine? How come the pylon's attached?"

Stookie squinted at Machado on the forklift. "Where's Tug?"

"He called in sick."

"Aw, shit. I gotta explain this all over again?"

"Explain what?"

"New procedure. We handle the engine and pylon together, not separately. Think you can do that?"

Machado felt insulted. "Whaddya mean, can I do it? How'd you get the other one on?"

"Tug handled it."

"He did it, I can do it. Let's go."

The engine and pylon unit rested in an engine cradle, a rubber-lined metal stand shaped to hold and support an aircraft engine. It rested on a support base with slots wide enough to accommodate the forklift tines in the side of its base. The entire unit was positioned beneath the gaping hole in the port wing of aircraft 412.

Machado moved the forklift in from the side of the aircraft and under its wing, slid the tines into the base of the unit and lifted its 12,000 pounds slowly and gingerly to the wing. Stookie and his three mechanics began the task of re-attaching the pylon and engine to the wing. He watched them work, responding quickly and precisely to their shouts for a change up or down, left or right. He knew these bastards were impressed with his work but there wasn't a chance in hell they'd let on; not when he was replacing Tug Wallace, even for a shift.

The work went smoothly. From Machado's viewpoint, it looked as though they were just about finished. Then he felt it.

A slight twinge in the controls of the forklift, nothing dramatic, almost imperceptible. Just a twitch, as if some weight had shifted slightly in the unit.

"Hey Stookie! You guys feel anything?"

Stookie, sweating profusely as he labored over the inboard side of the pylon, looked up. "What?" he shouted back.

"I said, 'You guys feel anything?'"

The din of machines working, the sounds of metal being pounded and shaped, the whoosh of the air blowers as they roared overhead in an attempt to warm the vast expanse of the hangar made hearing difficult.

Stookie cupped his ear.

He doesn't want to hear, thought Machado. It's getting close to shift change. Ah, fuck it. If something had moved, they'da felt it. Had to; they were right on top of the wing and pylon. He waved his hand. "Forget it," he mouthed.

*   *   *

Mennotti came bounding into the hangar at 0448 and almost ran to the C-check area. Wenthol was right where he should be—clipboard in hand, standing by the plane. The plane itself was buttoned up; everything looked in order. He charged over to Wenthol. "Looks good, looks good! Everything okay?"

Wenthol took his time to answer Mennotti. "Under the circumstances, yeah, I guess everything is okay."

"What the hell do you mean you, 'guess'?" This guy is just pullin' my chain, Mennotti counseled himself.

"All the systems check out, so..." Wenthol didn't finish the thought.

"So?"

Wenthol leaned toward Mennotti. "So how comfortable would you be if your family flew on this plane?"

Mennotti exploded. "You sonofabitch! Don't you ever mention my family! Who the fuck do you think you're talkin' to?!"

Wenthol took a step backwards.

"You got somethin' to say, you say it now!" Mennotti bellowed.

"Yeah, I got something to say." Wenthol waved at the aircraft behind him. "I don't like what we're doing here. We always handle the engine and pylon separately and one day you waltz in and say we're gonna do it different and save money and I say that's bullshit, all we're doing is cutting corners!" Wenthol's anger dissipated. He let out a large breath in exasperation, looked around the hangar and back at Mennotti. "Ah, what the hell's the use." He removed the envelope from his clipboard and handed it to him.

"What's this?"

"Read it."

Mennotti opened the envelope and read the one-sentence letter of resignation. "So you're quittin'?"

"Two weeks and I'm gone."

Shit. He wouldn't miss the constant hassle with this guy but could he be replaced? A hiring freeze was on. "Let's talk about this."

"Nothing to talk about. I don't like the way things are going, I got another job, I'm history."

"Just because of this new procedure...?"

"Ah, that's only part of it. I mean, look around Dom. We can't hire new people, there's no OT, we've got deferred maintenance up the ying-yang...it's not right." Both men had calmed down. "Nothing personal."

"Yeah, yeah...I understand." Mennotti looked up at aircraft 412. "The bird's ready?"

"She's checked out."

"Gotta be on the gate by 0600."

"We're gonna taxi it down at 0520. Plenty a time."

Mennotti nodded. Wenthol turned and walked away.

The prick's got some good points, Mennotti thought. Gonna be some changes around here when I'm VP of maintenance.

CHAPTER SEVEN

▼

DAY OF DEPARTURE

Hy Ascher was up and he was furious. He was furious first because his boss—the boy wonder who ran Mainstream Merchandising—calls him at nine at night and tells him he's got to go to Chicago right away tomorrow and find out what the hell was going on with our sales! Our sales are shit and you gotta find out what's the problem! What's the problem? He'd spent the last month telling him there was a problem in Chicago and now, in the middle of the night, this asshole calls and tells him we got a problem in Chicago!

That dumb fuck. The only smart thing he did was call Hy Ascher. Hy Ascher was not in retail, Hy Ascher was retail. He could walk into a store here, there, anywhere—you name it—-talk to the people, watch how they treat their customers, look at how they display their merchandise, take a good look at their books, and tell you exactly what your problem was and how to fix it.

But it wasn't enough he had to be called in the middle of the night to go to Chicago. No. He had to call the airlines and make his own reservations. His travel agent was long gone, probably out at some party drinking somebody else's booze, while he, Hy Ascher, had to call and make his own reservations! And the assholes he spoke to at Global Air! "I'm sorry, Mr. Ascher, but we're sold out in first class on Flight 119. I can confirm you in coach on this flight."

Coach!

Hy Ascher was a member of Global Air's Million-Mile Club, an honorary member of their Commodore Club (they gave him the membership others pay for—he didn't pay a cent), he knew members on their Board of Directors…Hy Ascher did not fly coach. Hy Ascher flew first class only! The dumb broad on the phone didn't seem to understand that…maybe they put all the dumb ones on at night. He spoke to her manager. The manager said we can put you on the waitlist for first class or confirm you in first on the next flight. Hy Ascher would not be put on anybody's waitlist! No hotel, no restaurant, no airline, no Global Air was going to "waitlist" Hy Ascher!

It was now five-ten in the morning. He paced the floor of his Manhattan apartment; the limo was due downstairs at five-twenty. He was packed and dressed, pacing and fulminating, working up a good head of steam for his arrival at the airport. Then he'd tell those cocksuckers that Hy Ascher was going to be on that flight in first class, period, no matter who they had to bump or what they had to do. At this moment, to Hy Ascher, it was a matter as significant as life or death.

      *   *   *

Often friends or passengers would ask Lois Lipscomb what was the hardest part of her job as a flight attendant; all that time away from home, the hotel hassles, the weird hours and time-zone changes, the passengers themselves?

No, Lois would say, it's leaving my kids, not being able to see them off to school every day, welcoming them home in the afternoon, that's what I miss.

Lois Lipscomb—"Lil' Mommy" Lipscomb to her friends and co-workers, a play on the "Big Daddy" moniker hung on her husband due his resemblance to the hall-of-fame football player—had worked as a flight attendant for Global Air for twelve years. She had gained enough seniority to become a senior flight attendant and chief, responsible for the overall inflight service as well as the other flight attendants on those flights she worked.

In gaining her seniority, she also earned a tremendous amount of respect from her fellow cabin attendants and flight crews, and had a veritable following among many of Global's frequent fliers. When she first started flying professionally, she sensed the occasional surprise, withdrawal, aloofness of a few passengers, unaccustomed to seeing a black face in a position of some authority. But times seemed to have changed somewhat, though perhaps it was she who had changed, maybe it was a little of both; most people appeared to be more accepting of others for what they were, not what some pre-conceived notion insisted they be.

Lois Lipscomb was proud of her job, proud to be with Global Air. She knew every feature of every aircraft she worked on and spent a good deal of time absorbing technical aspects of flying so she could reassure passengers when they appeared anxious or concerned about what was to many of them either a new or frightening experience, or both. Though she was now a veteran flyer grown accustomed to stepping into an aluminum tube and placing her life in the hands and judgement of others, she empathized with those who considered flying an unnatural and dangerous act. More than anything else, she exuded a warm, pixyish quality which others found captivating. As many an irate passenger found out, Lois was hard to resist when she set out to calm them down from some grievance—real or imagined—which they felt they had suffered at the hands of Global Air.

She finished packing for what was a three-day pattern: to Chicago and San Francisco this morning, overnight SFO; to Miami the following day, overnight MIA and back to New York on the third day. She walked into the kitchen to double-check the contents of the refrigerator. Her husband, a sergeant in the New York City Police Department, had a desk job—thank God!—in the precinct house close to where they lived in Kew Gardens, a stone's throw from Kennedy. He was a good provider, but had a very poor memory when it came to buying sufficient quantities of food to supply himself and the children while she was gone on one of her trips.

Her inspection of the refrigerator was reassuring; enough milk, juice and vegetables—if they'd eat the vegetables—

and meat and fish for three dinners. The kids would eat lunch at school, her husband at work, so all appeared in order.

She checked her appearance in the hall mirror; uniform clean and pressed, pocket handkerchief just so, makeup— what little she wore—okay.

She went into the children's room and kissed them both goodbye. Sabrina, seven, squirmed as she was kissed. Mark, nine, registered no reaction and continued sleeping soundly.

As she left the room, about to close the door behind her, something made her pause and look back. Two little heads framed by fluffy white pillows. How precious they were. How lucky she was.

*   *   *

Aircraft N412GA, now designated Global flight 119, was taxied the two miles from the maintenance hangar to the passenger terminal and tugged into position at Gate 17. It was now 0543. Passenger boarding would begin in approximately forty-five minutes.

Once the aircraft was on the gate, groups of workers attacked it, each group going about their specialized tasks. At the two service doors, fore and aft on the starboard side of the aircraft, commissary workers stowed the meals and refreshments that would be served to the passengers on both the JFK/Chicago leg, as well as the Chicago/San Francisco flight. Extra meals and their aluminum carts added more weight to the total gross weight of the aircraft, but transit time at Chicago's O'Hare was too brief to reprovision and still maintain the flight's schedule,

Outside the aircraft, fuelers had hooked up their lines to the fuel tanks. They were pumping 114,000 pounds of jet fuel, an unusually heavy load. Far in excess of the fuel required for the JFK/O'Hare leg, it was calculated to permit the fuelers at O'Hare to top off the tanks and save precious transit time.

While the fuelers and commissary workers went about their tasks, two large load-lifters moved into position against the open fore and aft cargo bellies of the aircraft. These hydraulically driven platforms would be loaded with baggage containers for the forward compartment and cargo containers—mail and freight—for the rear compartment. The containers would then be lifted to the hold of the open compartment door and pushed off the roller-bed floor of the platform onto the roller-bed floor of the aircraft, where they would be moved into position and locked down.

Flight 119 carried an unusual freight load this morning, Carrara marble from the Serra quarry outside Milan, Italy. It had been hewn to the precise specifications of the architect who designed the newest hotel of the Quentin chain in San Francisco, and was being flown, rather than shipped by ocean and rail, as time was drawing near for the hotel's completion. The marble was loaded on two freight pallets and weighed 9,000 pounds per pallet, close to maximum allowable weight. All these weights: provisions, fuel, cargo, estimated weight of passengers and their luggage, empty weight of the aircraft itself, were entered into a computer which produced a flight plan for Global 119.

In the flight ops office, Captain Harry Walker, a twenty-two year veteran of Global Air and a transport pilot with the U.S. Air Force for five years before that, was reviewing the flight plan. "Hey, Chief," he said to the chief dispatcher on duty, "looks like this one's loaded to the gills."

"Right you are, Captain. You got a helluva load of cargo."

"And that thru-fueling and provisioning adds a pretty hefty chunk..." observed Captain Walker. "What's the weather like?"

The dispatcher handed the captain a weather chart for the U.S., updated every hour by the U.S. Weather Service.

"There's a cold front moving down from Canada," said the dispatcher. "Gonna hit the Chicago area just about the same time you do."

A cold front usually meant flying through turbulence. It could also mean snow, even this late in the season. Snow at O'Hare could mean holding aloft and possible diversion to an alternate airport. Under Federal Aviation Agency regulations, every flight was filled with enough fuel to enable it to fly to destination, hold for forty-five minutes and proceed to a pre-designated alternate airport. Even so, cautious command pilots often took on more fuel, thus more weight.

"Let me take a look at the weight and balance." For an aircraft to achieve takeoff at rotation speed, its weight had to be precisely distributed so that it was balanced fore and aft. The weight and balance sheet told Captain Walker how the aircraft was loaded by compartment to obtain a viable CG—center of gravity—for takeoff. It also showed him he had 6,259 pounds ACL—allowable cabin load— of available weight remaining on flight 119. "Think I'd better take another five thousand pounds of fuel, Chief," said Captain Walker.

"It's gonna put you close to max takeoff gross weight, Captain."

"I know. But if I have to hold over O'Hare, I'd feel better with a little more gas in the tank."

"You got it." The dispatcher hit the button on the mobile phone console.

"Dispatch to fueler 119. Dispatch to fueler 119."

A few seconds passed. The speaker hissed. "Fueler 119 here."

"Give me five thousand pounds more fuel on 119. Repeat. That is five-zero-zero-zero fuel on 119."

"Repeating. Five-zero-zero-zero fuel 119. Gotcha. Fueler out."

Captain Walker continued his study of the flight plan. "See this bird just got out of C-check, huh?"

"Yessir."

"Fred," his co-pilot was studying the route maps and radio coordinates for the flight, "we got a C-check bird this morning. Take a real close look on your walk-around, will you? Those grease monkeys have been known to leave strange things in strange places."

Both men smiled at the remark, though both knew it had a very real basis in fact. More than one screwdriver, monkey wrench or power tool was found in an engine nacelle or wheel well on an aircraft coming out of maintenance. The results could be embarrassing or disastrous.

"I know what you mean, Cap" nodded the co-pilot, "I'll give it a close look."

The chief dispatcher tore a document off the computer printer and handed it to Captain Walker. "Final weight and balance, Captain."

Walker studied it for a moment. "With all this weight we're carrying Fred, you and I better pass up the dessert cart this morning."

"Glad I didn't have that second donut for breakfast," the co-pilot said, winking at the chief dispatcher.

*   *   *

Fran Demarest arrived at 0551. Shift changes were always critical to a smooth airport operation, particularly the one at 0600 which set the tone for the day. Since it was also a time when only a few managers were on duty, the temptation for employees to shove problems onto the next shift was great. Fran had spent too many years backstage at the airport listening to tales of the graveyard shift not to know the value of an unanticipated early-morning visit from the boss. Besides, she received an E-mail from Boyle that he was going out on 119 and she wanted to see him off.

That is, if 119 took off this morning. Conditions were marginal, early-morning fog was rolling in and out. The red-eye from LAX was in and on the ground but the one from San Francisco was holding over Jersey. Fran did a quick walkaround of the terminal; other than the lingering fog, the operation looked in good order. She entered the passenger service office where Lead Agent Nels Martin was reviewing the morning's passenger pre-flight manifests in the computer. "Looks like the transcons are pretty heavy today," he said, turning the computer screen toward her.

Fran took a look, made some computer entries. "Yeah, but the Caribbean's wide open and Miami and Rio are bowling alleys...Uh-oh."

"What's the problem?"

"119 to Chicago."

"Yeah?"

"It's over in first by three."

"Let me see." He looked at the flight manifest display as if it were a mail bomb ready to explode. As a lead agent, he would have to explain to irate passengers why they were being bumped out of first class. While first class obviously offered more creature comforts, its most attractive feature for many flyers was the rigid separation of the good and the worthy from the coarse and the vulgar. To these passengers, being placed in the back of the aircraft with "them" was a shocking loss of status, a challenge to their self-esteem. They would no more willingly sit in coach than they would ride the New York City subway system.

"Guess who's number three on the waitlist?" he asked.

She looked at him apprehensively. "It wouldn't be, would it?"

Some frequent fliers were well-known to the airport staff; Martin nodded his head gravely. "Hy the Hump."

"Uh-oh. One of those days."

Fran's walkie-talkie squawked to life. "Mrs. Demarest?"

"Yes?"

"This is Marcia on gate 17. I've got a call for you from Mr. Boyle."

Fran looked at the number on the phone console. "Transfer him to 3834." She looked at her watch. 0621. Must be calling from his car.

"And Mrs. Demarest, I have Mr. Ascher here. When I went to check him in for 119 just now, the computer gave me a coach seat and he says he's booked in first. He wants to see a manager immediately."

Fran rolled her eyes at Martin. "Tell him I'll be there as soon as I talk to Mr. Boyle."

Some static crackled on the walkie-talkie. "Mrs. Demarest? Mr. Ascher says he wants to see you now."

Martin waved at her as he stood and headed for the door. "Tell Marcia I'm on my way."

"Thanks, Nels," she hollered to the departing Martin. "Marcia, inform Mr. Ascher Mr. Martin is coming to the gate now and I'll be there shortly."

"Transferring Mr. Boyle."

Fran turned off her walkie-talkie. The telephone rang and she picked it up. "Hello, Pat? Where are you?"

"Hi. Still in the office. Don't think I'm going to be on the 0612 chopper this morning."

She spun the computer screen towards her and displayed the helicopter schedule. "That helicopter is still here at Kennedy—fog."

"I know. Listen, here's the plan. I'll hang around here till 0630. If the chopper's still grounded I'll take a cab and shoot for the 0800 to Chicago. Who knows, maybe 119 won't have left yet."

She accessed the local aircraft operations display. "I don't know about that. We're still showing all departures operating on time and the San Fran red-eye just landed. You know how conservative the tower is with clearing helicopters."

"That I do. See you at some point."

*   *   *

"Don't you know who I am?"

"Mr. Ascher, we've been through that. I do know who you are and I'm trying everything possible to get you an this flight."

"I thought you said there were seats on this flight."

"Yessir, there are. What I meant to say is that we're trying everything possible to get you in first class."

"I don't think you know what the hell you're doing! I want to see the manager!" For about the fourth time, Ascher slammed his fist on the counter.

"Mrs. Demarest will be here as soon as she can, sir." Martin was hoping that was soon; somewhere he had a limit and he felt he was getting close to it.

"I want to show you something," said Ascher.

Here comes the card trick, thought Martin.

"Let me show you these cards." He pulled out a large, richly patinated leather card holder from his suit jacket pocket. "Here's the Admiral's Club," he slapped the plastic card on the counter,"...here's Delta"...slap..."I've got United"...slap..."the Ambassador's Club"...slap..."and here," he was holding the piece of plastic in Martin's face, "is Global Air! Anyone of these airlines," he waved his arm over the assembled cards, "would jump through their assholes to get me a seat in first class, but not Global Air! They're too fucked up!"

Some of the other passengers were beginning to stare. Those behind Ascher on the check-in line were shifting about. Martin knew he had to move him on. He wondered if his union would back him up if he took a swing at the little prick.

"Why, Mr. Ascher! Are you playing cards so early in the morning?"

Martin could not believe what he just heard. He turned. Lois Lipscomb was checking in for the flight.

"Oh hello, Mrs. Lipscomb," said Ascher in a suddenly subdued tone of voice.

"You giving Mr. Ascher a hard time, Nels?" she asked with a wink.

"Trying not to, Lois. But we are oversold in first and Mr. Ascher wants to ride in first."

"Why, Mr. Ascher, you won't ride with me unless it's in first class?" Her tone was mock accusatory.

"Well, ah, Mrs. Lipscomb, I didn't know it was one of your flights." Martin tried to keep from staring; Ascher was obviously uncomfortable and actually appeared to be blushing.

"Good morning, Mr. Ascher." Fran arrived with a boarding pass. "We've got you all taken care of." She handed him a boarding pass. He grabbed it and scooped up his card display. Lois put a hand on his arm and lightly but firmly guided him away from the counter.

Well done, Lois, thought Martin. "How'd you do that?", he said out of the side of his mouth to Fran.

"Headed off a frequent flyer at the ticket counter. Gave her five thousand flyer miles and a seat on the eight o'clock," whispered Fran. They looked at Lois and Ascher.

"Now you're all set, Mr. Ascher!" Lois beamed.

"Yes, but..."

She looked at his carry-ons, anticipating the next problem. "My! That is a big ol' suitbag and...is that your attache case?"

"It's my laptop," he said proudly.

"Oh, a laptop!" she squealed, as if he had really accomplished something. "Tell you what." She lowered her voice conspiratorially. "I'm going an board now and I bet you'd like to come on board with me and store that big ol' suitbag in the closet so it's out of the way!"

"Yes Lois, but I've got a bit of a problem…"

"Oh!" she cooed with concern, "What is it?"

He proffered his boarding pass like a little boy pulling out his pecker for his first short-arm inspection. "I'm in 1-C, on the aisle, and I need to be in a window seat…"

"…so you can use your laptop!"

"Yes!"

Lois took the boarding pass, pulled off the boarding stub and handed the remainder to Fran. "Well you just come on board with me now and sit where you want and when the person who has that seat comes on we'll just see about exchanging it!" She slipped her arm through his and patted it. "I bet we're not going to have a problem!"

Ascher looked directly at Fran in triumph. "I'm sure we won't!" He hefted his suit bag and lap top while Lois opened the jetway door and held it for him. Ascher entered the jetway without looking back. Lois let him pass her, then turned to Fran.

"Thanks Lois," Fran sighed, "you're an angel in the nick of time."

"No problem." She rolled her eyes in the direction of the jetway, contradicting what she said. "Say, when I get back, maybe we can talk about my schedule…"

"Your schedule?"

"You know, that weekend trade I requested?"

Fran got the point and laughed. "'No problem.'"

"Toodles!" Lois waved and entered the jetway. The jetway door closed behind her and hissed into its locked
position.

      *   *   *

From his seat in the helicopter, Boyle could see an aircraft being pushed back from gate 17. He looked once
again at a copy of today's schedule in Chicago. This morning was mainly internal Global meetings; the public func-
tions didn't really get underway till noon. As long as he
was on the 0800 departure held be okay. Noren would
probably stir up some shit with Samuels about his missing
the flight but that would be next week and by next week
that would no longer matter.

He could see Fran waiting at the copter pad. He wanted
to tell her and other members of his staff about his decision to resign—that was only fair, he wanted them to hear
it from him and try to explain why he had made this decision. But that would have to wait until he had a chance to
discuss it with Kate—if she would ever return one of his
calls. The chopper landed with a jolt. He hopped out,
ducked under its prop wash and trotted to where Fran was
standing.

"If someone doubles my salary real quick, I'll never be
the one to tell the world the senior VP of operations
noshowed his flight."

Boyle laughed; airline people were always in a snit
about "noshows", passengers who failed to show up for
their flight and didn't cancel their reservation. "Let's make
that our secret." He motioned toward the plane now taxiing toward the runway. "That 119?"

"That's the one. I've got you re-booked on the o-eight hundred departure."

"Thanks. How about coffee and the phone in your office meantime?"

"All yours."

As they walked towards the terminal they saw a parade of different aircraft in varied and colorful livery taxiing toward the runways; the morning rush hour was underway.

Boyle sniffed the air; a light onshore breeze was blowing, carrying with it the tang of the ocean beyond. The sun was burning off what was left of the morning fog. "A great day for flying, after all," he said.

*   *   *

"Global one-one-nine heavy, hold for departure," crackled the voice of Departure Control over the pilots' headsets.

"Global one-one-nine. Holding for departure," responded Captain Walker. He nodded to his copilot. "Okay Fred, give 'em the spiel."

"Right, Captain." The copilot picked up the passenger cabin phone and began the standard welcome and pre-flight announcement. He was good at it, one of a number of commercial airline pilots who fulfilled the PR part of their job with style.

Captain Walker was not one of them. In the cockpit, he was taciturn to the point of abruptness. When he was sitting in the left-hand seat, only items pertinent to that flight were discussed: heading, altitude, fuel burn, engine temperature, radio coordinates; all the minute details involved in piloting a machine through skies populated by many other aircraft. Flying was too serious a business to have anything else on your mind.

"Global one-one-nine heavy, position yourself on runway thirty-one left for departure."

"Global one-one-nine, moving on runway thirty-one left," repeated Captain Walker.

Runway 31 Left, nicknamed the "Bay Runway", is the longest of Kennedy's five runways. Flight 119 was positioned on it, the nose of the aircraft pointed toward New York City in the distance, the waters of Jamaica Bay and the Atlantic off its port wing. Captain Walker was pleased his flight had been assigned 31 Left. The aircraft was loaded close to its maximum takeoff gross weight of 412,000 pounds and he estimated he would use about three-quarters of the 15,000 foot runway on his takeoff roll. It took a lot of runway to allow a plane this heavy to reach takeoff speed.

"Global one-one-nine heavy, cleared for takeoff."

"Global one-one-nine starting takeoff roll."

          *   *   *

Ascher was forced back gently into his wide leather seat as Flight 119 lifted off and climbed skyward. He was in the seat he wanted—3A, window, left-hand side—and Lois Lipscomb proved correct; no problem. In fact, she even turned the situation into a positive by suggesting to the man who was originally assigned the seat—a lanky fellow—that he'd be more comfortable in the aisle seat at the bulkhead where he could stretch his legs out.

Matter of fact, her behavior was just what Ascher tried to teach employees in his customer-awareness sessions at Mainstream Merchandising; there's always a way to meet customer objections, you just gotta use your smarts. He made a mental note to use this experience as an example in his next session. And that Martin kid wasn't half-bad either. Maybe I was a bit of a prick; I'll drop him off a bottle next time I'm through.

He turned and looked out the window. It was a peaceful sight, the land growing smaller, the glare of the sun ricochetting off the silver-blue Atlantic beneath him. Peaceful and calming.

A movement at the edge of his peripheral vision caught his attention. He glanced left, at the wing. He froze. The engine appeared to be twisting on the wing. Something's wrong. He felt a severe jolt.

The man seated next to him looked around, concerned. More jolts. Something fell in the aisle. No one spoke, as if everyone in the cabin was suddenly holding his breath. The only sounds were the rush of air, the clanging of metal in the galley as the plane bucked and jounced, like a fish hooked, fighting for its life.

The engine, twisting more now. Twisting. Ascher stared out the window at something which could not be happening.

Without a sound, as if it were a silent movie, the engine tore away from the wing and fell toward the water, far below.

Ascher heard himself scream.

*   *   *

First he sensed it, then he felt it, then the instruments confirmed it; total loss of power, left engine.

Captain Walker heard his copilot shout, "Left engine, zero power!" even as he applied full power to the remaining two engines and lowered the nose of the aircraft, the precise textbook reaction to the failure of an engine in flight.

If the aerodynamics of the aircraft were unchanged.

"Stall! Stall!" shouted the copilot.

His actions put the plane in a stall! How could that be? The shaker stick—which would indicate a stall—never moved.

Pilots are trained to fly on their instruments. Captain Walker concentrated totally on the instrument panel before him.

What was wrong?

He tore his focus away from the panel and turned to his left. Because of the aircraft's design, he could see only the tip of the port wing. And it was normal—nothing wrong there.

He looked back at the instruments. Holy God, we're in a power dive!

"Nose up! Nose up!" he cried as he desperately pulled on the yoke, one man trying to right a plunging 400,000 pound missile seconds after something went wrong.

   *   *   *

Lois Lipscomb was strapped into the flight attendant's jumpseat at the cabin door. At the first jolt, she thought they had hit a pocket of severe turbulence. As she felt the plane nose over, she knew the captain was struggling for control.

But now they were twisting down, out of control.

Loose items in the cabin were crashing around as storage bins burst their locks.

There was a scream. Silence again. Then it seemed as if everyone were screaming.

Oxygen masks deployed from their compartments and added to the nightmare, writhing against the overhead bins like yellow-headed snakes.

Her training told her to remain calm and help the passengers but tremendous G-forces pinned her to the seat.

The screams began to sound distant, remote, as if she were entering some long, dark tunnel. She began to hum; sweet Jesus, she thought, I'm coming home, I'm coming home.

She saw two little heads framed by fluffy, white pillows. Please let them be okay, God, let them be okay.

The screaming faded away.

CHAPTER EIGHT

▼

AFTERMATH

They were in Fran's office when Boyle's pager beeped just as her walkie-talkie crackled to life. He knew what his message would be when he heard the static-skewed voice on the walkie-talkie, "Mrs. Demarest, we have a serious incident."

She looked at Boyle and pressed the transmit button. "Yes?" She released the button.

"Flight one-one-nine ma'am, it..." the voice faltered, "it's..."

Instinctively, they turned to look out towards Jamaica Bay and the Atlantic, as if they might see Flight 119 climbing skyward.

"...it's off the screen and we lost contact...he called mayday."

"When, where, details?" she asked.

"Wheels up plus two-twenty. Climbing to altitude, over the Atlantic. No independent sighting of crash reported...yet."

"Load?"

"One hundred, eighty-six passengers, seven crew."

"I'll be right down." She stared at the walkie-talkie.

Boyle's pager was beeping with the frequency of a pin-ball machine in an arcade; its pitch and volume seemed to increase in intensity and loudness. All of the buttons on Fran's phone console were lit and blinking.

He held out his hand. "You okay?"

She placed her hand in his. "Yeah, I'm okay." She allowed her hand to linger momentarily, then withdrew it.

Boyle had been through this before; all incidents, minor or tragic, were his job. "You go down to Ops Control, see what you can do. Have them forward all calls to my office downtown. I'll set that up as communications control and get the crash committee up and running. Make sure everybody understands they make no comment. All calls must be forwarded to my office, absolutely no exceptions."

"Right." She stood, steadied herself, picked up the walkie-talkie and headed toward the door.

"Got another one of those?" He indicated the walkie-talkie.

"Sure." She pulled one from its re-charging unit next to her desk and gave it to him. "See you." She went to the door.

"Fran?"

She stopped.

"Next couple of days are going to be tough. You're going to do okay."

"Thanks." She left the room.

He wanted to go with her but that would be irresponsible. Whatever had happened, he had to keep the airline flying. Whether the accident had occurred half a world away or half a mile away, the hard fact was the airline could not stop for it. Yet as he reached for the phone, a bitter thought intruded: What if...? Scenes of countless meetings, endless debates—had safety finally proved too expensive? What if...? No. No one could have—no one would have. He picked up the phone, touched the speed dial for his office. Ginny picked up on the first ring.

"Mr. Boyle's office."

"Ginny..."

"Hi Pat, you out at Kennedy now?"

They haven't heard the news downtown yet. "Yeah listen, looks like we've had a pretty bad incident with one-nineteen to Chicago." He heard her draw her breath in sharply. "I need to alert the crash committee. You got the list'?"

"Yes, but I thought Mr. Samuels..." Her voice was shaky.

"I know and I'll talk to him next. Just have everyone stand by. Okay?"

"Okay."

"Get ahold of PR. Alert them and relay all media and customer contact calls to them. I'll handle all government calls. Have the duty officer in Ops Control notify all corporate officers. I'm in Fran's office. I'll call you back as soon as I speak to Samuels."

"Pat?"

"Yeah?"

"Wasn't that the flight you…"

It hadn't occurred to him. Wasn't that strange. "Yeah."

"Oh, thank God you're okay!"

Boyle was silent for a moment. "Yeah."

Ginny did not respond.

"Gotta go, Ginny. Bye now."

As with all airlines, Global had a planned response team to handle major accidents. Typically described by a euphemism, it was invariably known within the airline as the "Crash Committee." Comprised of all major department heads, it was the single entity that coordinated and communicated within the airline as well as between the airline and all other parties—the general public, government agencies and news media—who had any stake in an accident.

Pat Boyle had headed up Global's "Emergency Coordination Group" until Samuels' arrival. At that point the new owner and chairman—for reasons presumably of ego, obviously not of expertise—designated himself head of this committee. Boyle knew an amateur would be quickly overwhelmed by the sheer amount and volume of confusion, anger and frustration generated by a crash. Although his pager was full with messages and no longer beeped, he could not respond to any of them until he had contacted Samuels and set up the crash committee.

Kate.

He left a message on her recorder last night saying he would be on the first flight to Chicago this morning. If she hears about this…better call her. But suppose she never got the message, maybe she was somewhere else? Can't take the chance; he picked up the phone and punched in her number. As it rang, he watched the flashing lights on Fran's console; his stomach was writhing.

"Morningstar Clinic. May I help you?"

"Kate Boyle, please."

"Who may I say is calling?"

"It's her husband."

"Ah, let me check and see if she's come in yet, Mr. Boyle." The operator used to call him "Pat". He clicked through the messages on his pager; mostly Global, one FAA, two TV stations, nothing from Samuels. He started to sweat; this call was wasting time.

"Mr. Boyle?"

"Yes."

"She hasn't come in yet." She sounded embarrassed. "Is there a message?"

"Yeah. Just tell her I'm okay." He knew it sounded stupid, and her pause confirmed it.

"You're okay?"

"Yeah."

"Oh. Okay. Goodbye, Mr. Boyle."

Best he could do. He punched in Samuels' number.

"Mr. Samuels' office." Dottie Allen sounded shaky.

"Dottie, it's Pat Boyle. Is he there?"

"Oh Pat, what's happening?! I just got a phone call for Mr. Samuels about a crash!"

"Yeah listen, I've got to talk to Samuels."

"He and Mr. Redmond are on a conference call with Europe and he said he can't be disturbed until they're finished."

"Dottie, this is urgent."

"I don't know, Pat..."

"Look, just go in there and tell him I need to speak to him now!"

"If he gets upset, you'll tell him you insisted I do it?"

"Yes Dottie, for God's sake!" The phone was getting slippery in his hand. He heard her place the phone down, a chair squeaking.

"Pat?" The walkie-talkie was on. He picked it up. "I'm in dispatch." Even through the static, the despair in Fran's voice was evident. "I heard the tape. He called mayday. Said they were in a left-wing stall, power dive...He said, 'one-one-nine, out. God help us all.'..."

Her voice was breaking; she shouldn't be there. "Fran, are you okay?"

"Transferring your call," Dottie Allen said over the phone, "he's really pissed." she added.

"I'm okay," Fran said. He heard the steel in her voice. She was going to be all right.

"Boyle?! Boyle?! What the hell is this?!" Samuels'was on the line.

"I got Samuels on the phone," he said into the walkie-talkie, "I'll call you back."

"Boyle?!"

"Yes Mr. Samuels, I..."

"What the hell do you mean, interrupting my conference call?! I know Mrs. Allen informed you I was not to be disturbed!"

"We apparently have had a crash."

"What do you mean 'apparently'?"

"It was over the ocean when it went down so right now there is no debris to confirm it. We do have the tape."

"What happened?"

"At this point, we don't know."

"How could something like this happen? Isn't that your department?"

"Yes it is and right now I don't know, but..."

"Well find the hell out and don't interrupt me again unless you have all your facts straight!"

Boyle was standing up, choking the phone with his hand. "Mr. Samuels!" His voice was neither excited nor high, it was more of a growl and deadly calm. Samuels was silent. "There has been a crash. You are chairman of our emergency response committee. I have given instructions to activate that committee so we can deal with this situation in an organized manner."

"Without clearing it with me first?"

"I'm clearing it with you now."

"That could be construed as insubordination."

"That's your call."

Samuels paused, as if he were actually considering the charge. "Alright. I'll meet with the committee in the board room at four o'clock this afternoon."

"But we need immediate…"

"I expect you to take charge of events, not the other way around!"

Boyle looked at the phone. He had planned to resign. Why not leave now, he thought, just walk out and let Samuels handle all the shit that was about to happen?

"Boyle?"

It was tempting. But he had a job to do. And it wouldn't be fair to the people at Global; he couldn't walk out on them. Boyle was sure that to Samuels the crash was nothing more than another cost of doing business.

"Understood."

"Fine. I'll see you at four."

*   *   *

Word spread rapidly at the maintenance base. Workers put aside their tools, drivers got off their forklifts, secretaries emerged from their offices and wandered out of the hangar onto the ramp, toward the bay in the distance. Whether they felt they could do something about what had happened or whether they hoped the news was wrong and they would see the plane returning to Kennedy was unclear.

This tide of people parted to make way for Dom Mennotti, who shuffled into the hangar. He continued further back, deeper inside the hangar. Stunned, he felt nothing, only that his feet were moving him along. He could see a tall figure approaching; it was Wenthol. Mennotti stopped. He could see Wenthol looking down at him, leaning toward him.

"You sorry son of a bitch," Wenthol said.

He thought to fling out his left arm at Wenthol to distract his attention, follow up with a hard right to his gut. But he did nothing, he just stood there and saw the contempt in the younger man's face. Then Wenthol walked past him and was gone to the ramp with the others. Mennotti stood for another moment and felt it coming. He looked around. There was an empty parts tub by the wall. He made it just in time, vomiting in spasms into the tub.

When it was over he knew he should wipe his mouth but he was too tired. He had to go home, get some rest. Then he could think. No one would say he meant to do this. They would understand. A mistake. It happens, it happens. But first go home and get some rest.

*   *   *

The meeting had started promptly at seven a.m. in Noren's office. He demanded the ad agency be on hand at one more run-through of his presentation for later in the day, before he caught the 10:30 flight to Chicago.

Leslie Foster brought her chief copywriter, her VP for Creative Projects and her VP for Consumer Research. When the announcement had been made that Scott, Foster & Dean won the Global Air account, she had let it be known she planned to handle the account personally. Knowledgeable Madison Avenue gossips speculated on just how "personal" her handling would be.

The group was sitting around the conference table in Noren's office. He was annoyed when he heard the phone ring, as he had left explicit instructions with his secretary he was not to be disturbed. He grabbed the phone. "Yeah?"

"Mr. Noren, sorry to bother you," his secretary said, "but I have the Director of Operations on the other line. He says it's urgent."

"Isn't he one of Boyle's people?"

"I believe he is, sir; should I ask him?"

"Nah, put him on. I only hope to hell this is important."

He put his hand over the phone's mouthpiece. "Major operations problem," he said to the ad people, "we got a rock group and their groupies going out to Paris and they've just run out of condoms on board!"

The advertising group responded with a fusillade of laughter. That's what I like about advertising types, thought Noren, they've got some wit about them.

"Mr. Noren?"

"Yeah."

"This is Jack Ransdall."

"Yeah?"

"I'm Director of Operations."

"Congratulations. Whaddya got?"

"I'm notifying all corporate officers, sir, that if you haven't heard already, we just had an aircraft incident at Kennedy airport."

"What kind of incident?"

"A crash, sir."

"A crash?"

The group looked at each other.

"Are you gonna tell me what happened? Big plane, small plane, any survivors, no survivors? Any details?" Jesus, these operations people are slow.

"I'm sorry, Mr. Noren. It's been pretty busy here this morning. It was flight one-one-nine, JFK to Chicago. Hundred eighty-six passengers on board, seven crew. Crashed on takeoff into the Atlantic off Jamaica Bay. Cause unknown at this time. No reported survivors. Police, fire, FAA and FBI on scene. NTSB notified and investigation team en route. Aircraft manufacturer rep alerted…"

"Okay, okay, I get the picture. No survivors?"

"None reported, sir."

"No one knows what happened?"

"No sir, not yet. There is an unconfirmed report of a lady who claims she saw an engine fall off."

"An engine fall off?"

"Yes sir."

"Oh shit; that'll look great on the six o'clock news!" Ransdall did not respond. "Okay, anything else?"

"Mr. Boyle asked me to tell you…"

Boyle? "Ah, wasn't Mr. Boyle supposed to be on that flight?"

"Not that I'm aware of, Mr. Noren." The voice was suddenly stiff and formal. "I spoke to him only a few minutes ago."

Noren said nothing.

"Mr. Boyle asked me to tell you he has postponed plans for the inaugural activities today in Chicago."

"What?!" Noren shot to his feet. The advertising people looked startled. "Without consulting me?!"

"Under the circumstances, it wouldn't be appropriate, Mr. Noren." The voice was flat and ice cold.

"Godamnit, I'll decide what's appropriate! Get Boyle on this phone right now!"

"Sorry, Mr. Noren, I have important things to do." The line clicked dead.

Noren slammed the phone into the receiver. "Shit! Who the hell does Boyle think he is!"

No one spoke; the ad people watched Noren. A few seconds passed while he flipped through the story boards in front of him. "Well, looks like our plans for the inaugural are postponed."

The ad people groaned collectively. "And after all your hard work," commiserated the VP for Creative Projects, wringing his hands to underscore his sympathy.

"Yeah…Well, you can believe I'm going to be discussing this with Mr. Samuels." Noren looked at the group. "So, I guess this meeting is adjourned."

*   *   *

The 112th precinct is considered one of the choice assignments in the New York City Police Department. The neighbors are the pro-police, middle-class apartment dwellers and small shop owners of Forest Hills, Kew Gardens and Rego Park. The station house, located close to the Tudor-style homes and apartments of Forest Hills, was a relative oasis of quiet compared to some of the zoos in the NYPD. Still, it was a precinct house, not a library; the usual ebb and flow of human traffic created a workaday din similar in decibel level to that of a high school gym during a basketball game.

Sergeant Dan Lipscomb, thirteen years a cop and four of those a sergeant, noticed a sudden, perceptible drop in the noise level as he went about his duties as Desk Sergeant. He looked up from his paperwork. The same people seemed to be there, only talking and shouting less, perhaps more quietly or with some restraint. He shrugged and went back to the paperwork in front of him.

"Dan?" the ancient intercom squawked, its dark grey plastic ribs permanently caked in dust.

"Yeah?"

"Could ya come here a minute, please?"

"Yeah."

Lipscomb stood up. Two teenagers, sitting sullenly on the bench opposite his desk, stared at him. He returned their stares with a level gaze. They dropped their heads to stare at the tops of their hundred-dollar foot gear. This was not a cop you would want to cross.

He walked back to the Precinct Commander's office and knocked on the door.

"Enter."

Lieutenant Wiley was standing behind his desk. That was unusual; typically he was always seated, surrounded by stacks of paperwork. He would look up just long enough to say what he had to say, listen to a response—if any—and return his attention to the paperwork.

"Why don't ya close the door and siddown, Dan."

Lipscomb closed the door behind him. Something was up. It was rare the lieutenant would ask anybody to sit down. Maybe this was about the overtime budget. Must be. Overtime had become a real problem. The lieutenant took a step toward him, then stopped. He appeared to be in pain. "Dan, I've got some bad news." Lipscomb tensed; this was not about overtime.

"There's been an accident." Lipscomb stopped breathing. He made no guesses, came to no conclusions. He concentrated totally on the man standing before him and what he was about to say.

"A Global Air plane has crashed off Kennedy..."

Lois!

"...we've been told by the airline your wife was on board."

The two men stared at one another.

"I'm sorry, Dan...I..."

"Survivors?..." he half-asked, half-suggested.

"It went into the ocean, Dan..." The lieutenant shook his head no as he approached Lipscomb and put his hand on the seated man's shoulders. "I'm sorry."

Lipscomb was only slightly aware of the hand on his shoulder...Lois...It couldn't be...maybe she substituted at the last minute...she'd be calling any time now...maybe she got sick just before getting on board and couldn't fly...he allowed himself to think of all the possibilities that

would make everything alright while, at the same time, he
felt the growing, icy emptiness…he would never see her
again.

"…thought you'd wanna pick up the kids at school…"

The lieutenant was talking to him, something about
the kids…Yes, of course…he must pick them up and hold
them and tell them…He heard himself agreeing with the
lieutenant, almost as if it were another person speaking…Another person had taken over his speech and his
body and now was planning how he'd take the children to
Lois' mother's house…Now some other cops were in the
room with him…yeah, his friends were there now…there
was Wally and Brent…and Charlie from the PBA…He
was standing now. Someone had brought him his police-
man's cap so he could go to the school and get his children. He felt himself moving now, surrounded by other
men in blue. They were walking out of the lieutenant's
office and through the station and outside. He would go
with them to pick up his children, they said. Everything
would be okay.

*   *   *

Boyle was on the phone when Fran re-joined him in her
office. He motioned urgently to her to pick up another
phone whose light was blinking. "Someone from the
Times," he said, covering the mouthpiece on the phone he
was holding, "tell her to call PR downtown." He listened
to the voice on the other end of his line. The voice
belonged to some minor official at the FAA, delivering a
lecture on the importance of full public disclosure in incidents such as this. "Uh-huh," Boyle said to the voice.

"Pat?" Fran held the phone away from her, hand over its mouthpiece. "She says she doesn't want some PR bullshit, she wants to talk to you."

"Jesus!" Boyle throttled the phone in his hand. "Tell her..." He caught himself, took a deep breath—Fran looked at him like the messenger being blamed for the message. "Tell her I can't talk to anyone from the media right now." The voice on his phone droned on. "I understand," he said to the voice.

Fran delivered the message and replaced the phone. "She says she's got other sources. Says she'll report you refused comment."

"Swell." The voice on the other end of his line had just posed a rhetorical question and now was about to continue. Boyle jumped on the pause. "Look, I understand all that! What you've got to understand is we don't know what happened yet and as soon as we do, I'll share it with the world! You got that?!" Silence. Boyle took another deep breath—winning friends and influencing people at the FAA, he thought. The voice resumed, a tone of haughtiness now added to its previous officiousness. Boyle nodded. "One-thirty. I'll be there." He was about to say goodbye, but the voice had already hung up. He sighed and looked around Fran's desk, opened the top drawer. "Got any gum or anything?"

"Ah, no..." She looked surprised; they had worked together on and off for years and he never chewed gum before. "I may have some mints in my purse..."

"What's the story on the engine?"

"Right now there are two confirmed eyewitness reports that an engine fell off the aircraft. One guy was out fishing and called it in on his marine radio, the other was a woman bird-watching by Howard Beach."

"Where the hell is Mennotti?"

"Doesn't answer his phone or beeper, no one's seen him since just after the crash was reported."

"How about his house?"

"Called several times, no answer."

"We've got to nail down this engine thing." He looked at his watch. "I should go over to maintenance myself but they've called this press conference at the IAB for one-thirty and then it's downtown for Samuels' meeting at four."

"Want me to send one of my people?"

"Yeah. Get ahold of the writeup on the plane. Dispatcher says Captain Walker made some comment about it's being a C-check."

Fran rose slowly.

"Sorry about the, eh..." he motioned toward the phone.

She smiled. "Pretty mild under the circumstances."

Boyle appreciated the remark and the sentiment behind it. He knew there wouldn't be much of that in the days ahead.

*   *   *

Redmond watched Samuels pace. "Those bastards! Did you hear their change in attitude?!" Samuels' fury was stoked by his sense of self-righteousness. "Those bastards!"

Redmond spread his hands. "Gerry...what can you do?"

"What can you do?! How the hell can you just sit there and say, 'What can you do?' when it's my money that's going down the toilet?!" Samuels continued to pace. "Those goddamned Germans!"

"They're just the lead bank."

"What's the stock at now?"

Redmond picked up the phone from the table next to him, pecked in a speed dial code and waited. "…It's me. What's it at now?" Samuels was glaring at him. "Got me on hold." Samuels snorted in disgust. Hell, if he wanted a quote fast, all he had to do was look at the computer on his desk. "Yeah?" He placed his hand over the mouthpiece. "Down three and an eighth."

"That's two points in the last hour!"

"So what does it look like?" Redmond projected an aura of calm. Then again, it wasn't his money. "Okay." Samuels was staring out at the balcony. "He thinks it may be bottoming out."

"Bottoming out? I'm a point and a half from where I bought it!"

"What's the Dow doing?…Up five and three-quarters," he informed Samuels.

"Damn!"

"Later." Redmond replaced the phone.

"What about Vegas?"

"I've called the guy four times already. All I get is his voicemail."

"Did you leave messages?"

"Of course I left messages."

"If you were doing your job he'd of called you back by now." Samuels stalked back toward Redmond. "I don't even have to ask about Singapore, right? They're all in bed over there!"

"Not only that, Gerry, my guy is dealing with people in three other countries in Asia, plus the fund in Australia. Gonna have to wait a few hours on that one."

"So I'm supposed to just sit here with my finger up my ass, waiting for somebody to call?" Samuels returned to staring out at the balcony.

"If you want my advice…"

"Your advice! It was your advice that got me into this fucking mess! I never shoulda put any money into this sinkhole, let alone run it!"

Redmond had to suppress a smile. Gerald Samuels had built his huge fortune through tireless, individual endeavor, with particular emphasis on "individual." If something went wrong however, it was always his advisors who misled him. Redmond wasn't going to challenge that perception—no use—while the size of his brokerage commissions made the burden more than bearable. "Gerry, look…" Samuels was glaring at him again but at least he was listening. "This is the airline business—crashes happen."

"Yeah, but…"

"Hold on, hear me out."

Samuels snorted in exasperation but didn't interrupt.

"Crashes drive down the price of the stock every time, right? I mean, who'd expect it to go up? But we're talking a few points and short term."

"A few points?" Samuels' objections were becoming less vehement.

"Gerry, I know, it's not my money. But let me finish." Samuels crossed to his desk and sat down behind it. "Now

we heard the Germans this morning, and if the guy from
Vegas ever calls and if the guy from Singapore was in this
room right now, they'd all say the same thing. I still want
to buy but I want to pay less cause you're selling damaged
goods. Right?"

"That's obvious."

If it's so obvious, why the hell were you screaming
about the fucking Germans five minutes ago? No matter.
"So number one, selling off may take a little more time
then you'd like. At your price of course, or close to it."
Samuels just stared at Redmond, no comment. Though
Redmond handled many of Samuels' investments, advised
him on a wide spectrum of financial matters and served as
his CFO at Global, he had no accurate picture of the
man's net worth. Only Samuels knew that. Postponing the
sale of Global's assets might be no more than an annoyance to Samuels, put some mega-project in jeopardy or
threaten his financial existence—it was all a poker game.
"The next thing is, they've got to understand you're not
selling damaged goods so they can't leverage the price. I
mean yeah, there was an accident, it was a one-time thing,
it'll never happen again, blah-blah-blah."

"Makes sense."

"Now there'll be an investigation of the crash and natu-
rally everybody and his brother's going to want a part of
the action, so this thing could go on for months."

"Which doesn't help me." Samuels stood and began
pacing again.

"Exactly." Just watch my lips move, Gerry. "So what
we've got to do is—right up front—say, we had a problem,
we looked at it, here's what we did about it." He took a

sheet of paper from his leather portfolio and handed it to Samuels.

"What's this?"

"Read it."

The letter was from Samuels to Boyle: "Your employment with Global Air is terminated, effective immediately."

"What does this get me?"

"No matter what really happened, there's got to be a problem in operations. That's Boyle's department. You're a strong executive, the Street expects you to do something, you can him." Redmond nailed the conclusion. "It's good PR in a situation where you need some."

"Suppose he sues?"

"What's he gonna sue about? Hurt feelings? He's got no contract. Besides, civil court cases in New York City are backed up almost two years; you're long gone from Global Air if it ever comes to that." Samuels was mulling it over—time for the close. "We can handle this in a way he's just gonna want to leave town."

Samuels waited.

Redmond took the pause as encouragement. "Remember that stunt Noren pulled when he was at Consolidated? The Indian grain sale?"

"Yeah, vaguely."

"They sold a bunch of tainted wheat or something to India, all sorts of people got sick, a few even died. Noren's fingerprints were all over the deal but somehow, once the media got hold of it, the bad guy turned out to be Consolidated's production head, who didn't even know about the deal. I mean, it was a PR masterpiece."

Samuels jingled the change in his pants pocket.

"Gerry, you got a horse collar. What you need is a horse to put it on."

Samuels walked over to his desk and pushed the intercom. "Mrs. Allen, please tell Mr. Noren I want to see him immediately."

          *   *   *

The garage was at the rear of the lot, separate from the house. It was accessed by a cement roadway which ran alongside the house. The house itself was a row house in the borough of Queens, one of hundreds built in the 1920s as vacant fields were developed as a middle-class community for workers from Manhattan. Built by his immigrant grandfather, the house was now home to the third and fourth generations of the Mennottis.

It wasn't difficult opening the garage. It had an old-fashioned latch bolt secured by the strongest steel-tempered lock Mennotti could find. Though there wasn't much to steal inside—Mennotti had an ancient workbench where he liked to do leather crafting—he was determined no one in this changing neighborhood was going to walk in uninvited. He drove the car in and left the motor running. It had taken him a long time driving back from Kennedy airport, maybe an hour or more. Probably more. That was strange because the house was only fifteen, twenty minutes—with traffic — from Kennedy. He wasn't quite sure why it had taken him so long but it had.

He was very tired and needed to sleep. He knew he had thrown up, he could still smell some of it on his work shirt. Maybe when he was throwing up it affected his mind because his mind seemed empty, like he'd had too much to drink and couldn't assemble a whole lot of thoughts.

He closed the door and heard the latch fall in place on the outside. There was a handle inside the door so it could be opened, but it had broken some time ago and he couldn't find replacement parts. It was an old lock. He started to cough and his eyes were burning. The neighbors kidded him when he insulated the garage—why would anybody do that?—but he could come out here even on cold winter days and do his leather craft without needing any heat.

He got in the car, left the door open and sat down. He shouldn't be doing this, he knew that…They'll be sorry…He heard people screaming like they were falling, must be that roller coaster they went to at Six Flags…But that's not here, that's somewhere far away…He saw a tall kid looking at him, staring, sneering—is that Wenthol? Wise-ass…He saw a light somewhere up ahead. He was coughing a lot now.

CHAPTER NINE

▼

PLACING BLAME

Noren's hands were sweaty and shaking as he skimmed through his Rolodex, then punched a number in his phone.

The phone rang several times on the other end. "Olin."

"Bill Noren."

"Hey, Bill…Samuels must be shitting bricks with that plane in the water."

"That's why I'm calling. Anonymous source."

"Strictly anonymous. Lemme get something to write with…Shoot."

"Senior management at Global Air is very unhappy with the performance of Pat Boyle, Senior VP of Operations."

"This have something to do with the crash?"

"He runs operations, they fly the planes, what do you think?"

"I think you don't like this guy."

"Ah, he's one a these self-righteous types but you know I never let my personal opinion sway my professional judgment."

They both laughed.

"I'm on tonight at six forty-eight."

"I'll be watching."

"And millions like you."

"Appreciate it."

"Say, Bill…"

"Yeah?"

"My friend and I were thinking of going to Greece this summer."

"Greece is nice."

"But airfares are pretty high."

"So let me know when you got the date you're going."

"First class."

"First class is nice too." Noren laughed at the banter. "We take care of our friends."

"Six forty-eight." The line went dead.

Noren hung up. Yes! That was the nail in Boyle's coffin. This hits the news tonight, he's finished at Global, finished in the airline business. Finished in any business, for that matter; who wants a guy with that kind a cloud over his reputation? Better yet, Samuels gave this little assignment to Noren. "Just between you and me, Bill…" Yeah, that was a good sign; it's the type of delicate, confidential task you give to the president of your company. Maybe Samuels would announce him as president when Boyle got canned. Timing would be good. Then he could do something with Mennotti and Trish Peters. Mennotti wouldn't be a problem; he gets his VP slot, he's happy. But Trish Peters—that was the problem with women in business, the emotion. She went off like a geyser when she heard about the crash; what the hell for?

*   *   *

Boyle stood in the second rank of representatives, backed up against the wall of the VIP lounge, roasting in the heat of the TV lights. The VIP lounge in JFK's International Arrivals Building was designed as a convenient place for transiting celebrities or politicians to hold forth with a dozen media reps at most. It now was packed solid with sweating, shoving bodies.

Representatives from the New York/New Jersey Port Authority, FBI, NTSB, FAA, Coast Guard, NYPD, Nassau County Sheriff's Department, as well as Global Air, jostled for elbow room with reporters from all the major TV and radio networks, local radio and TV stations, and all their cameras, lights, microphones, and tape recorders.

The print media were represented by New York's four daily newspapers, the **Wall Street Journal** and **Aviation Daily**, **Time**, **Newsweek**, and **U.S. News**, several foreign newspapers and magazines.

The pre-press conference meeting had been mostly a jurisdictional pissing contest from which the representative of the NTSB largely emerged the winner, in that she would act as coordinator of questions for the rest of the group and thus have her face and agency appear on the six o'clock news. But she was not to act as spokesperson; her peers made that quite definite. She would have to refer all specific questions to the agency or individual charged with that responsibility in the investigation just beginning. A question about sea search, for example, would be directed to the Coast Guard, while a question about land search—if any—would be treated as a jump ball between the New York City and Nassau County Police Departments.

Surprisingly, Boyle had to field only one question so far: What was Global doing about bringing victims' relatives to the crash scene? The reservations department was arranging free transport and hotel rooms. The representative of the FAA jumped on several other questions he could have answered—she seemed determined to prevent the NTSB delegate from hogging the spotlight—while the Port Authority rep kept interjecting reminders that the airport was still open and functioning, with no delays planned or anticipated.

"What about these eyewitness reports that an engine fell off the aircraft?" Someone shouted the question from the back of the room. The NTSB woman looked at Boyle. "Mr. Boyle, would you care to comment on that?"

Boyle squeezed his way to the microphones. "We are aware of those reports but have been unable to confirm them." He had given copies of Captain Walker's tape to the FBI, NTSB and FAA and was told not to discuss its existence until they had a chance to analyze it.

"So you're denying those reports now?"

"What I'm saying is we are aware of them but cannot confirm or deny them at this time."

"In other words, one of your planes simply fell out of the sky on a nice clear day and you don't know what happened yet?"

The room quieted; Boyle could sense them sniffing blood. "To tell you the truth," Boyle looked straight at his inquisitor, "we don't know what happened yet but we will find out." There was a brief pause; apparently both the reporter and his colleagues took Boyle at his word, for the next question was directed to the Port Authority regarding airport security measures. He edged back to his place by the wall; he realized his shirt was soaking wet.

"Nice job," said the Coast Guard officer standing next to him. "This is a tough crowd."

"Thanks," said Boyle. This crowd doesn't know what tough is, he thought, it's the poor unfortunates at the bottom of the ocean and their families and friends left behind; that's the tough crowd.

Recognition was growing between those before and those behind the cameras that the room and working conditions were becoming too uncomfortable to continue. Besides, questions were becoming repetitive and media deadlines had to be met. After a brief exchange between the representatives from the NTSB and FAA over who would conduct press briefings and when—they agreed to hold separate briefings and announce the schedule the night before—the news conference broke up.

Boyle was hanging back to let the crowd clear out, engaged in a discussion with the FAA rep and the Coast Guard officer when he saw her. It was only mid-afternoon, but he felt wrung out from the day's events. He blinked to make sure fatigue was not playing tricks on him. Kate. She was edging her way through the departing crowd. Kate. He walked towards her as quickly as he could, fending off microphones and questions as he went, merging with the rest of the crowd as they all shuffled towards the one, narrow door. He was standing before her. "Kate."

The crowd bumped and jostled its way around them. She looked at him, shrugged her shoulders and smiled. He felt as if they had never really been apart, just visiting elsewhere, separately.

"The Bridge of Sighs?" he said. His voice cracked like that of a teenager.

*   *   *

Kennedy Airport, then known as Idlewild, was laid out and built in an era before the sterile architecture demanded by cautious and unimaginative bureaucrats became the norm in airport design. Rather than one large, faceless terminal, Idlewild consisted of seven separate and individual terminals, most with unique architectural features. The Pan Am terminal was elliptical in shape and entered through an air curtain; the American terminal incorporated one of the world's largest stained-glass windows; the Eastern terminal made lavish use of travertine marble in its check-in lobby while the gem of the airport, the Saarinen-designed TWA building, appeared ready to take flight. The nexus of the layout, the International Arrivals Building (IAB), was attached to the control tower by a footbridge raised over the vehicular traffic. Beyond the control tower was a pond and chapel buildings of the three major American faiths. It was this footbridge which

Pat and Kate called their "Bridge of Sighs," for here they would meet at shift's end when both had worked summer jobs at the airport, to plan their future together.

With Kate behind him, Boyle pushed through the crowded VIP lounge, walked through the IAB and onto the footbridge which no longer led pedestrians to the pond and chapels, but rather to a gap-toothed, multi-tiered parking lot. Beneath them cars darted like water bugs back and forth between traffic lanes.

"Long time since we've been out here," he said.

"I know."

He studied her face—it seemed taut, strained. But her eyes gave her away. Her liquid, hazel eyes were not looking at him coldly, angrily, as they seemed to have done for so long. They were the eyes of the Kate he remembered and had longed for.

"You know, when they told me you were on the phone at the clinic this morning, ah…" she turned away to clear her throat, "…I didn't listen to the radio so I hadn't heard about the crash…my God, it's so terrible…" she reached out and stroked his arm, "…and then they gave me your message and I said, 'What does he mean, he's okay?' Then someone told me about the crash, I thought, what are we doing?" She turned and looked at him. "What am I doing?…And I don't know…But I do know, I knew this morning, that if you had been on that plane I couldn't bear it." She bit her lip and looked away.

He put his arm around her. She made no attempt to move, then leaned into him. "Can we start again?" he said.

"I don't know…I don't think it's starting again so much as it is just going on, maybe trying harder." She shrugged.

"Oh Christ, I don't know Pat. All I know is I was scared to death this morning and I'm so glad you're here!"

He leaned towards her and, like tourists, they kissed on the Bridge of Sighs.

*   *   *

The crash committee met in the boardroom at four p.m. Samuels chaired the meeting, flanked by Boyle to his left, with two of his staff and Fran Demarest; Noren on his right, accompanied by his usual phalanx of analysts, assistants and gofers. Redmond assumed his accustomed position at the computer terminal diagonally behind the chairman. The heads of Reservations, Public Relations and the Legal department were there, as well as representatives from Global's three unions: pilots, ground-service employees and flight attendants.

Trish Peters caught Boyle's attention; though it was understandable given the circumstances, she looked terrible. Her hair appeared uncombed, her makeup was streaked and she wrapped her arms around herself as if she were freezing. He had attempted to greet her when she entered the room but she scurried away as if he carried some fatal and communicable disease. Even now across the table, she would not look at him, keeping her head bowed and staring straight down; for some reason she seemed to be taking the accident very personally.

Samuels looked up. "Let's begin. I'm sure everybody knows what happened this morning so I'm not going to waste a whole lot of time rehashing it. The important thing is to get it behind us and go on with our jobs!" He took a moment to compose his thoughts, then began with real feeling. "I don't know how many of you are in the market, that's not important, but let me tell you this: today Global Air closed down five and one-half points in a market that was up eighteen and three-quarters!" He looked around the table, challenging the faces in the room to hold his stare. Few did. "Now I'm here to tell you that when your stock closes down in an up market, it's...it's unacceptable!"

First things first, noted Boyle.

"Alright, let's go around to each department. Make it brief, just tell me what's happening." He turned to a slim, intense-looking woman, her grey-streaked hair pulled back into a tight bun. "PR?"

Toni Moore, director of public relations, was a news-woman before joining Global; it showed in her straight-forward approach. "The crash was a bulletin on all major networks and will be their lead story on six o'clock national news tonight. We can expect the same on local news at eleven here and in most major markets. The Times, LA Times, Washington Post—those are the ones I've checked with so far—are all running it as the headline story in their editions tomorrow morning. Turns out there were quite a few foreign nationals on the flight and we've got requests for interviews with at least a dozen foreign media. No surprise to anyone, this is a PR disaster."

"How long do you expect it to go on?"

She shrugged. "The crash story'll be off the front pages and out of the national and major market TV markets in two, three days. But the background story—interviews with family, speculations on cause, profiles of the victims..."

"Excuse me," Wayne Alton, the head of the Legal Department cut in, "we should refer to them as 'passengers'".

"...profiles of the passengers," Moore didn't miss a beat, "those will probably hang around until the cause is determined."

"And how long will that be, Boyle?" Samuels' question seemed to reverberate about the room.

Boyle knew the question was coming, just a question of how it would be phrased. "We have the Captain's comment on tape..."

"Yes, and two eyewitnesses say they saw an engine fall off, I know that. When are you going to find out exactly what happened?"

A fair question. But Mennotti was nowhere to be found, neither his wife nor his son—both at their jobs—had heard from him; Wenthol was off duty and had not returned several phone messages, and the crew that did the C-check would only comment with their attorney present, on advice from their union. And every time he turned around, someone from some other government agency wanted to talk to him, had to talk to him. Then there was the airline to run. "Crash investigations typically take months to complete. We're dealing with investigators from the FAA, NTSB..."

Samuels slammed his fist on the table. "Godammit, that's not good enough!"

The two men stared at one another, the room totally silent. Someone muffled a cough.

Samuels nodded, as if he had made a decision. He looked at Noren. "Reservations?"

Noren leaped to his feet, obviously eager to display managerial competence following Boyle's stumbling performance. "Our team is prepared, Mr. Samuels!" He smiled at the newest member of his team. "Sandor, bring us up to speed, please."

After Noren had fired Jepson, Clancy and MacReady, he re-wrote their job descriptions, re-aligned their reporting relationships and hired five MBAs to replace them. The res position went to Sandor Labash, a tanned and pin-striped-suited young man who was now standing, looking at Samuels with what appeared to be confidence. "Our telephone call volumes are up considerably in New York, Chicago and…"

"How much are they up?" Samuels spoke at a normal volume, but it seemed as if he shouted the question.

Labash looked blankly at Samuels—the interruption appeared to surprise him.

"Ten, fifteen, three hundred percent?" Samuels demanded.

Labash moved some papers on the table. "My staff hasn't furnished me with that information yet."

Boyle found this amusing; Noren obviously taught his people the staff shuffle quickly and well.

Samuels snorted with annoyance. "As soon as this meeting is over, you find out and get back to me! That's all cost, you know."

"Yes sir."

"What else?"

Labash pulled at his collar and forced a smile. "Our bereavement teams are all in place…"

"Bereavement teams? What the hell are bereavement teams?"

"Well sir, as I understand it, we have some volunteers who are specially trained for situations like this who stay with the families of the victims, I mean passengers…"

"They on overtime?"

"Ah, if need be…"

"Dammit to hell! Look, people, I don't know how plain I can make myself. I run an airline, not a social services agency!" He looked over his shoulder to Redmond for support.

Redmond shrugged. "It's something we got to do, Gerry, I checked around."

Samuels stared at Redmond in frustration, then fixed Labash with a glare that seemed to hold him personally responsible for the crash. "Sit down."

The young man, his tan now replaced by pallor, looked pleadingly at Noren as he sat. Noren was completely absorbed with a paper clip.

Samuels turned to Wayne Alton, Global's Senior Legal Counsel. "Legal?"

Alton was a relaxed and casual individual, secure his knowledge of the law shielded him from common concerns. "Hull Insurance will cover the aircraft, that's the good news. The ultimate bill for liability will largely be determined by the cause of the accident, whether or not there was any negligence involved, and whether we had more illegal aliens on board than lawyers." If it was a joke, no one laughed. "But I will tell you this; some of my brethren in the legal profession will have full calendars and bursting cash registers for years to come."

Samuels looked totally disgusted. "Marketing?"

Noren had another opportunity. "We've done a call-around to all our major sales offices. No one reports any major cancellations in group bookings, a few cancellations of individual bookings. We've already met with our ad agency to sketch out a new ad campaign..."

"A new ad campaign?" Samuels cut in.

"I should have been more specific," Noren smiled. "We are re-engineering our previously-budgeted campaign to subtly enhance the integrity of Global operations...," he looked at Boyle, "...a step we feel is required at this time."

My few minutes are coming, Boyle counseled himself, relax.

Noren appeared disappointed at the lack of a rebuttal. "We feel confident, Mr. Samuels, this adjustment in our advertising will restore public confidence in Global's operations." Noren paused. "Hopefully we won't be lying to our customers."

Easy does it, Boyle cautioned himself, Noren just smells the blood in the water. "Noren, our commitment to safety is, has always been, our number-one priority." He tried to say it coolly, matter-of-factly, but he could feel his face flushing, his throat tightening.

"Horseshit," Noren grinned, awaiting a response.

Boyle took a deep breath; don't rise to the bait.

Noren swiveled casually in his chair. "I mean, since I've been here you've been bellyaching about nothing but safety and now there's a planeload of passengers at the bottom of the Atlantic..." Noren stopped swiveling and looked directly at Boyle. "I'd say you've presided over one of the biggest fuckups in aviation history."

Boyle moved with the speed and agility of the linebacker he once was. Before Samuels could move, Boyle was past him and lunging at Noren who was rising from his chair. Boyle grabbed him by the lapels of his jacket.

The momentum of his charge carried them back a few feet, smashing Noren into the paneled wall of the board-room. Boyle wrapped his left hand around Noren's throat and pinned him to the wall. "You lying bastard!"

Several people were trying to separate the two. Redmond grabbed one of Boyle's arms. Fran was at his side. "Pat..Pat, it's okay, let him go!"

Samuels was behind her. "That's enough, that's enough!"

Boyle held Noren a second longer, then relaxed his grip and backed away.

"This is outrageous!" Samuels screamed at Boyle, "You stay here! Alton," he shouted at the lawyer, "you and Noren come into my office!...Miss Moore, you too!" Samuels stormed off to his office, accompanied by Redmond and followed by Alton and Moore. Noren, who was massaging his throat and looking warily at Boyle, fell in behind.

"You okay?" Fran asked Boyle.

He smiled grimly. "I haven't felt this good in a long time."

Samuels stormed into his office, marched through it to the door leading to his outer office and shouted for Dottie Allen, "...and bring that statement I dictated!" He turned on Noren as he entered the office. "What the hell do you think you're doing?"

"I didn't know he'd react like that."

"You thought he was going to sit there and smile?"

"I thought he might argue..." Noren let his defense trail off.

"Gerry," Redmond suggested, "this timing might not be so bad."

"Ah…!" Samuels exhaled in disgust. He strode to his desk, grabbed a sheet of paper off the top and thrust it at a baffled Alton. "Read this." Samuels waved his hand in Moore's direction. "Read it aloud for her."

"The letter is from Mr. Samuels to Mr. Boyle, dated today. 'Effective immediately, your employment with Global Air is terminated.' Signed by Mr. Samuels." Alton handed the paper back to Samuels.

"I was going to let him go today anyway," Samuels said, "but this forces my hand." He looked at Noren, who was grinning smugly. "You see any legal problems?" he asked Alton.

"None. Boyle has no contract, your letter contains no recriminations. Actually, I tend to agree with Mr. Redmond—since you planned to terminate him anyhow, this is good timing." Noren was rubbing his throat and beaming.

Samuels turned to Moore. "How does this play PR-wise?"

"You mean his firing?"

"His firing same day as there's a crash."

"Obviously it's going to appear as if he had something to do with the crash."

"And equally obviously, Global management is stepping up to a bad situation?" Redmond asked her.

"Yes…yes, I think it'll be read like that."

"Fine." Samuels appeared to relax somewhat.

"Just a caution, Mr. Samuels?" Alton interjected. Samuels waited. "You don't want to be the one to explicitly tie his termination into the crash. If that later proved false, it would leave you open to possible liability—slander, wrongful termination…"

"Read that statement I dictated earlier," Samuels ordered Dottie Allen. "This is for employees only," he said to Moore, "but I want you to think how it would play if someone leaked it to the press."

Dottie Allen cleared her throat and began reading from her steno pad. "To all members of the Global Air family. From Gerald S. Samuels, Chairman and Chief Executive Officer. Today was a black day in the proud history of Global Air. We are cooperating fully with all government agencies in seeking the cause of the crash…"

"Incident." Alton cut in.

Dottie made the correction. "…cause of the incident. In the meantime, the employment of Mr. Patrick Boyle has been terminated. This action should not necessarily be seen as having anything to do with…" she made another correction, "…the incident."

"Well done," Alton told Samuels. "Gives them a conclusion without making an accusation."

"In the difficult days ahead…"

"Yeah, okay," Samuels waved her off. "The rest is PR bullshit—no offense, Miss Moore…"

"None taken, Mr. Samuels."

"…about working together, pride in the airline, that type of shit. Anything else?" He looked at Alton.

"Liability. You may want to put in something about no matter who you talk to, including family and friends, nothing should be said which could be construed as liability on our part."

"You work with Miss Moore, polish it up, let me see the final copy before it goes out." Samuels looked at Moore. "Can we get this on the six o'clock news?"

She looked at her watch. "Going to be very tight. Certainly on the eleven."

Samuels glared at her. "I wasn't asking a question, Miss Moore."

Noren stopped massaging his throat. "Mr. Samuels, I should call the individual we discussed earlier."

"Do that. You want to drop something off on the way?"

"Excuse me?"

Samuels handed him Boyle's termination letter. "I thought you might enjoy this."

"Thank you, Mr. Samuels, I will." Noren took the letter; he was lusting with anticipation.

Redmond turned to Dottie Allen. "Get Security in the boardroom immediately. Tell them they're to escort Mr. Boyle out of the building. Absolutely no stops at his office. Have them change the locks on his office door right now."

When he returned to the boardroom it had emptied out except for Boyle, Demarest and one of Boyle's people sitting next to Demarest. Noren didn't know who that guy was but he would find out, then have Boyle's replacement fire both him and Demarest; didn't need any Boyle loyalists hanging around. As he came closer, he could see Demarest was crying. That crying shit made women a real pain in the ass on the job; think she'd show a little more discretion.

The door from the outside hallway opened and two security guards stepped into the room. Good timing. "Here's something for you," he said to Boyle. He slid Samuels' letter across the boardroom table, careful to keep the wide table between himself and Boyle.

Boyle made no effort to pick the letter up, instead he kept focused on Demarest.

"Think you may want to read that, then join these gentlemen on the way out." Noren stood waiting.

Demarest waved Boyle away with her hand. "I'll be
okay."

"You sure?"

Demarest nodded yes. Boyle looked at Noren, glanced
at the letter, folded it and put in his pocket.

"What's her problem?" Noren asked Boyle, "Can't bear
to see you go?"

Boyle looked at Noren contemptuously. "Terry here,"
nodding at the young man sitting next to Fran, "just told
us they found Dom Mennotti's body in the garage behind
his home."

Noren took a step back, put one hand on the top of a
chair. "Who's Dom Mennotti?"

"Nobody you'd know of," Boyle stared at him coldly,
"for now." He stood and offered his hand to help
Demarest up.

She waved him off. "I'm okay," she said, "let's go."

The three of them turned to leave. Suddenly Boyle
whirled as if he were going to attack Noren again.

Noren jumped back.

Boyle grinned mirthlessly. "You and I are not finished
yet."

*   *   *

Dan Lipscomb knew he should have stayed longer over
at Lois's mother's place but he had to get away by himself,
have some time to think.

Lois had a big family—three sisters, two brothers,
they'd take care of the kids. Better they should be there

than here with him, just the three of them in this empty apartment.

They had some good times, he and Lois. All gone.

The TV was on. He focused on it when they said something about the crash, otherwise he just let his mind wander. To never see her again; that was a hard thought to bear. Another reporter was on now, saying something about the crash. Global fired the guy who ran the operations department. Boyle. Heard that name before, maybe Lois mentioned it. Firing has nothing necessarily to do with the crash. Sure. Planes don't fall out of the sky, cars don't drive themselves into lampposts, guns don't take it on themselves to kill someone; accidents happen cause somebody screws up real bad or doesn't care or plans it that way. Then they say, "Oh! Sorry, it was just an accident," like that makes it okay and everybody says, "Well, it was just an accident—why are you getting upset?"

They get away with it, just walk away as if nothing ever happened.

He stood up, went to the TV and looked at a photograph perched on top of it of Lois and himself. It's not fair; it's not right. And they get away with it, just walk away.

Lipscomb wandered into the kitchen, rummaged through note books and slips of paper in the drawer by the phone. He found the Global Air home directory for key employees and looked up the section starting with "B."

CHAPTER TEN

▼

PRE-DAWN

It was the first night in months they were together in their apartment again and finally the damned phone stopped ringing.

The early-evening calls were from Boyle loyalists in Europe who were trying one last time to make contact before calling it a night, mixed with close-of-the-business-day calls from U.S., Central and South American stations. About ten or so, Boyle could expect the early-morning calls from the Pacific stations. All the messages were variations on a theme: terrible news about the crash; say it's not true what we've heard about you; what are you going to do; can we be of help. The news media, in addition to calling about the accident were now demanding his reaction to being fired, particularly after Gene Olin's televised comments implying he was responsible for the crash.

Several government agencies called to remind him—rather officiously, in the case of the FAA rep—that regardless of his employment status, he would be expected to be available for their questions as the crash investigation proceeded.

"You getting hungry?", Kate asked after Boyle finished a lengthy conversation with the VP of Global's Western Division in Los Angeles about what was already being called the "Battle of the Board Room" on the company grapevine.

"Yeah, I could use something to eat. Want to go out?"

"Why don't I make something?"

Boyle was hoping she'd say that. Phone by his hand, he sat at the small kitchen table in their otherwise spacious apartment and watched Kate move from stove to refrigerator and back again. He was grateful for the sight.

"Were you really going to resign before this happened'?" she asked over her shoulder. She was busily engaged rinsing something in the sink. "All those years—the people, your friends?"

He had yet to explain his feelings, even to himself. Maybe now was the time. He stood and lumbered toward her. "It's changed so much, Kate. The people have changed. I thought maybe it was me, but...I mean, remember Charley Thurston?"

Boyle was at the sink now and saw her smile at the memory. Charley Thurston was a Korean War flying ace and long-time head of operations for Global Air. Pat Boyle was one of many young people he had hired and guided through their careers.

"There was a guy who was tough—tough, hell, courageous—and tight with a buck, God knows. But if he said something, you could believe it, you could trust him. He had...oh, I don't know..."

"Honor?"

"Yeah. Yeah, that was it...honor." Now it was the time: to tell her how much he missed her, how much he needed her to be with him, how much he loved her. Boyle swallowed, preparing to speak. "Ah...want me to help you with that?" He nodded at whatever it was she had in the sink.

Kate nodded no, head down and focused on the sink.

"I'm glad you're back." He sounded to himself as if had just made a boarding announcement on the airport PA system.

She looked up at him and smiled. "I needed the time away...I'm sorry if, well..."

He thought she might cry.

The intercom buzzed loudly—Boyle flinched at the sound.

"What can you do?" she mugged and wiped the back of her hand across her cheek.

The intercom buzzed again—he didn't recall it being so loud—as he moved toward it. "Yeah?" he said in the mouthpiece.

"Mr. Boyle?" came the brogue of Sean, the apartment's doorman.

"Uh-huh?"

"There's a police officer here..." a pause while he probably looked at a badge or something, "Sergeant Lipscomb. Says he's got to see you."

Boyle checked with Kate.

"This won't be ready for a while anyhow," she said.

"Okay Sean" Boyle said wearily into the mouthpiece, "send him up."

*   *   *

Noren thought more clearly when he was moving.

He had been in constant motion since returning to his apartment. He checked and double-checked the placement of the furniture, made sure he had a selection of wine, beer, liquor—even soda—anything she was likely to ask for, on hand. The balcony. The balcony was okay, on a night like this maybe a little chilly but tolerable and a great view—except for that damn railing! The railing was loose and shaky and the goddamn superintendent had done shit since he called him about it weeks ago!

But that wasn't important. Trish Peters was coming over. That was important...and about time. He nodded his head in confirmation of his success. Yeah! Spread those legs! Stopped by his office and said she had to see him tonight; privately...He checked again; the couch was okay, the bed was all made up if she wanted to make a night of it...Only two people were aware he had anything to do with the maintenance operation at Kennedy; one's gone—sure, it was a shame about Mennotti, not something to really rejoice over, but what the hell? Who knew what was bugging him? Noren stopped pacing and addressed himself sternly: whatever happened, you had nothing to do with it. If Mennotti did something stupid, it'll come out in the investigation. And whose name will come out? Patrick J. Boyle, Senior VP of Operations!

Now Trish Peters is a different story. She's probably a little concerned about the crash…that's understandable, time'll take care of that. She looked like hell in the office today. Hope she fixes herself up. He grinned. But then, who's going to be looking at her face?

       *   *   *

"You Pat Boyle?"

Boyle stood face-to-face with a large black man at the apartment door. The man was dressed in civvies—sport coat, shirt and tie, slacks; his shoes were highly polished.

"Yes."

The man halfheartedly held out a photo ID. Boyle squinted at it. "You know, Sergeant Lipscomb, if this is about the crash, I talked to one of your colleagues today before the press conference…"

Lipscomb was looking past Boyle into the apartment. "Isn't just about the crash."

Boyle sensed something wrong—the cop looked agitated. Would you hesitate if he were white, Boyle asked himself. He knew the obvious answer. "Come on in, Sergeant."

"Thanks." The tone seemed mocking.

Boyle followed Lipscomb into the large, comfortably furnished living room. The cop stopped and surveyed the room as if he were checking out a crime scene—he seemed to focus on a painting of a Boeing 707 hung between two handsome, built-in bookcases. The 707 was in Global Air colors and on final approach to Tokyo's old Haneda airport.

Boyle followed Lipscomb's gaze. "You an aviation fan, Sergeant?" Lipscomb continued to stare at the painting. "That was done by one of our captains, Johnnie Goodwin. Quite an artist, he studied...," Boyle's biography of the artist was cut short as Lipscomb turned an angry face to Boyle. "Make yourself comfortable, Sergeant." Boyle indicated the sofa.

Lipscomb walked over and sat in a Morris chair. Boyle's favorite chair.

"Hello, I'm Kate Boyle." She swept into the room and over to Lipscomb, her hand extended.

Lipscomb rose and shook her hand perfunctorily. "Mrs. Boyle."

"I'm doing some things in the kitchen and wonder if you'd like some coffee?"

"No thanks."

"Sure?"

"Sure."

He's never smiled, Boyle noted.

"Okay. But if you have any second thoughts, let me know." She smiled questioningly at Lipscomb, glanced at Boyle and headed back to the kitchen.

Boyle realized for some reason he was relieved she left the room. He walked to the sofa and sat down, facing Lipscomb in the Morris chair.

"How can I help you, Sergeant?"

"I want to know what happened."

"The crash?"

"Yeah."

"We don't know. Exactly."

He watched Lipscomb study him and had the feeling he was somehow on trial, standing before the judge. "I'm sure you're aware as anybody there's an investigation going on…"

"My wife was a flight attendant on that plane."

Boyle stared at him. "Lois?"

Lipscomb nodded, never taking his eyes off Boyle's.

"Oh, Jesus, Sergeant…I had no idea…I mean, if you had told me…I'm sorry…" Boyle knew he should do something but didn't know what. He stayed where he was. "She was one of our best…" It sounded like a performance appraisal. He shrugged. "I'm sorry."

Lipscomb continued to nod. "Watch a lot of TV, do ya?"

"TV?" What was this about? "Ah, no…"

"Don't watch local TV news?"

"Well, sometimes…"

"Man on the local news tonight said you'd been fired right after the crash. Sounded like maybe it had somethin' to do with crash."

"That's bullshit! Look Sergeant, if you think for a minute…"

Lipscomb waved off the objection. "Tell you what I think." Lipscomb sat back, his sport coat spreading open.

Boyle noticed the handle of a gun sticking out of a shoulder holster.

"I think someone fucked up real bad…"

Lipscomb's eyes were bloodshot—Boyle couldn't recall if they were that way when he entered the apartment.

"…and I think that someone might be you!"

"Coffee!"

Boyle leaped to his feet and whirled in the direction of Kate's voice—she was walking toward them, carrying a tray with a coffee pot, cups and saucers.

She looked at Boyle, obviously surprised by his reaction, but kept coming, heading for the table between the sofa and the Morris chair. "I know the officer said he didn't want coffee but there's no sense getting excited about it."

Lipscomb didn't move.

Boyle placed himself between Lipscomb and Kate as she bent over and set the tray on the table. "Sergeant Lipscomb is.... eh.... his wife was a flight attendant on 119." He tried to indicate with his head, his eyes—get the hell out of the room.

Before he could stop her, Kate brushed past him and went to Lipscomb's side. "I'm so sorry for your loss!"

Lipscomb jerked away, sat back in the chair, his hands gripping its arms.

Boyle calculated he could throw himself at Lipscomb if the cop went for his gun—certainly knock himself and the cop over, give Kate time to get out of the apartment.

Now Kate placed one of her hands over the cop's—he stiffened, looked away, but did not move. "There are no words I can give you..." she motioned with her head for Boyle to sit on the sofa—he stayed standing—"but we can listen."

"Listen?" He spat out the word in derision.

Boyle tensed for a leap.

Kate didn't move. "Listen," she affirmed softly.

Lipscomb shifted in the chair. Boyle noticed beads of sweat on his forehead. The cop lowered his gaze to the floor, then looked up and stared fiercely at Boyle. "Don't want no bullshit. Just wanna know why my Lois had to die."

Boyle turned his hands palms up and shook his head slightly. "We don't..."

Kate motioned again for Boyle to sit on the sofa—this time he did, but on its edge.

Lipscomb was rocking slightly in the chair. Then he stopped, as if he had made some decision. "Tell you something about me and Lois. You know Newark?" He was speaking toward Boyle but to Kate.

Boyle nodded.

"It's the asshole a Jersey. I was born there. Never saw my old man, he was long gone when I was a kid. Three of us, all boys, my mother. She was a good woman but then she died. We each went to live with kin. I went to Harlem, lived with my aunt."

"How old were you then?" Kate asked. She kept her hand on his but now was kneeling by the side of the chair, her legs tucked under her.

"'Leven, twelve, somethin' like that." Lipscomb still stared at Boyle.

"Finish grade school?" she prompted.

"Yeah, I graduated, got a piece a paper. Couldn't read it, though."

Kate sighed lightly.

"I hung around a lot, did a lotta things, some not so nice...Met Lois...didn't meet her actually. Just saw her once when my aunt took us to church one Sunday, started hangin' around. She'd say, 'Man, why don't you make somethin' a yourself?' and I'd say, 'Babe, only thing I wanna make around here is you!'...She'd laugh, oh she'd laugh...She'd say, 'Man, ain't no way you're gonna get those paws on this black beauty 'less you be some-body'…So I decided to be somebody. Started high school. Started to learn to read, liked it, read a lot. Read a whole lot, Lois kept after me. I stayed in school. We got mar-ried." Kate rose quietly and joined Boyle on the sofa.

Lipscomb rolled his head back and blinked his eyes, as if someone were putting drops in them. He looked back at Boyle. "After awhile, after I got on the force, we'd go out for an evenin' and I'd spot certain people and say, 'There's a whore and there's her pimp and there's a john all waitin' for the game to begin. And she'd say, 'Who you lookin' at? I see three people tired and lonely and maybe a little afraid. All they need is to take the hand of the Lord'."

Lipscomb gave in, grabbed the white pocket handker-chief from his sport coat and dabbed at his eyes. "She believed in all that shit, she really did."

"Sometimes belief is all we have," Kate suggested.

Lipscomb snapped out of his reverie. "Yeah, well I believe she died because someone…" he looked at Kate, then back at Boyle. "Because of someone. Not because of God or chance or fate…because of someone!"

Boyle flushed. "I know how you must feel…

"Ain't no way in hell you know how I feel!"

The two men stared at one another.

Kate started to say something, Lipscomb waved her silent.

"Let me put it this way: when was the last time some-body paid a personal price 'cause—'accidentally'— a plane crashed…or a bridge fell down or a boat sank?"

"So you're looking for vengeance," Boyle countered—it sounded different from what he meant.

"'Vengeance is mine; I will repay, saieth the Lord'." Lipscomb's voice resonated like that of a preacher, his head bobbed with conviction. "Lois believed that." He stood abruptly. "I don't." He turned toward the hallway.

"I'll see you out," Boyle said, as he and Kate rose from the couch.

Lipscomb suddenly turned back to Kate, took one of her hands and placed it between his, held it for a moment, then released it and walked rapidly from the room.

Boyle caught up to him at the apartment door and opened it.

Lipscomb fixed him with an intense stare. "Can't tell you what's gonna' happen…" He let the thought go, reached into his pocket and slowly pulled out his card. "If we ever need to talk."

Boyle reached out and took the card uncertainly.

"Man on TV tonight much as blamed you for the crash." Lipscomb looked at the card Boyle held. "You may need that."

Boyle had to clear his throat. He thought to extend his hand but realized it somehow would not be appropriate. "I only wish…"

"I know, I know." Solemnly, Lipscomb turned and left the apartment.

*   *   *

On the cab ride to Noren's apartment, Trish wondered again if she was doing the right thing.

Earlier in the day, when she heard the first rumors of the crash, she felt sick. When she got confirmation of the crash, she shut her office door, locked it, sat and stared at her desk. Her phone rang several times, various people came to her door, knocked and went away. At some point she must have cried, because there were several wads of Kleenex with mascara on them, balled up and scattered on her desk.

She stayed there for a while, thinking it couldn't be, endlessly re-playing her conversations with Noren, her meeting with Mennotti. It couldn't be. There was nothing she said or did that could in any way have caused the terrible thing that happened. These things always have an explanation, they happen, there is no possible way…it just couldn't be.

Then there was that awful meeting, poor Mr. Boyle. But Bill Noren was right, it was Boyle's department after all. You can delegate authority but you can't delegate responsibility; they taught you that at Wharton.

She was okay until she got the news about Mennotti. What made him do that? This was not the first plane to ever crash, it would not be the last. She kept seeing Mennotti in that greasy little diner, playing with the salt shaker, explaining…something. It was his idea, not hers. She had to talk to Noren about this but it shouldn't be in the office. Not the office, just in case…in case of what? Somebody gets the wrong idea. How could they get the wrong idea?

The cab pulled up to Noren's apartment. She could see the fare on the meter but couldn't figure out the tip, couldn't figure fifteen percent. Isn't that amusing, MBA and all. She gave the driver what had to be more than enough and got out of the cab. She was doing the right thing, going to talk to Noren without anyone knowing.

She stood on the sidewalk for a moment, looking at his apartment house and the nighttime sky. It couldn't be.

*   *   *

Tug Wallace looked in on Rick Wenthol in his cubicle. "You finished for the day?"

"They're finished with me but I haven't begun my 'day'." That was one of the real downsides of shift work for management; they'd call you in at all different times to accommodate the suits and their schedules, regardless what your work hours were. Wenthol had spent five hours of "his" time with various investigators. At least when they called the union in they got time-and-a-half. "You picked a helluva day to call in sick."

Wallace coughed, as if on cue. "Shouldn't be here now, got the flu." He coughed again.

"Then why don't y'quit coughing at me and go home? We're so backed up now, I'm gonna spend half the shift just figuring out what to do."

"Hear you turned in your resignation."

"Yeah." Great timing. He had been interviewed by the NTSB, FBI, NYPD and FAA, all of whom began with the same question: How come you're resigning? "I'm counting the days."

Tug went into a particularly elongated fit of coughing; must be getting ready to announce his departure. He wiped his eyes with the same gummy handkerchief he'd been blowing his nose into. "Well, I guess I better get going home."

"Go."

"That Mennotti was a shocker."

Wenthol shrugged. "Can't let this shit get to ya."

"Umm." Tug fired off one more good, hacking cough for effect and shuffled away.

Wenthol looked at the inventory list of aircraft for his shift. What a joke; couldn't fit another plane into the hangar and a dozen different investigator types are all saying, "My goodness! How could this have happened?" Just shoveling shit against the tide.

He opened his desk drawer, took out the pocket tape recorder, placed it against his ear and pushed the "play" button. He heard background noises, then Mennotti's voice, "Mr. Noren?", then the other voice, "Mennotti?". He clicked it off, rewound it and put it back in his desk drawer; re-thought that and put it in his coveralls pocket, zipping the pocket shut.

After they called him in early and finished questioning him, he had gone to his locker to get his coveralls for the shift. The recorder was in his locker, just sitting there. As far as he knew, only three keys to the locker were out: his own, Security's and his supervisor Mennotti's. No question who put it there, but why? Who knows, Mennotti was one strange fuck.

What now? The quick and easy thing to do is give it to one of the investigators. They'd love it, love him and he could spend the rest of his life answering their questions. Nooo thank you; thirteen days—actually nine working days left—a week to get there and a nice, clean, new job in an electronics plant in Renton, Washington, doing vendor work for Boeing.

The right thing to do is give it to Boyle. He's not a bad guy, God knows he could use it—someone said they did a

TV special saying he caused the crash—and then it becomes his problem, how to handle it.

But then there's Noren. Wenthol smiled, patted the recorder in his pocket. This little tape could hang Noren and he makes some real big bucks. Price of homes in Washington state supposed to be real low compared to New York, Noren might want to come up with a down payment. But that could be tricky, somebody might say it was blackmail. But it wouldn't be, really—all depends on how it was phrased.

"Hey Rick!" One of the lead mechanics was leaning in his cubicle, "Ya got our work sheets?"

"Gimme a minute, be right there."

Wenthol turned to his computer. Gotta give this some more thought. He punched up the priority order of aircraft awaiting maintenance, looked at it and sighed; it would be another night of pissing in the wind.

*   *   *

Trish didn't pay much attention to the apartment lobby or its decor, just walked up to the concierge who buzzed Noren's apartment and directed her to the elevator. This is the right thing to do, she knew, talk to him about what's happened. He'll understand, he'll know what to do.

Noren greeted her warmly and effusively at the door to his apartment; he looked very relaxed, considering everything that had happened. He seemed to take a long time removing her coat.

"Sit over here," he said. "It's the most comfortable seat in the house." She sat in the corner of the sofa. "How about a drink? I was just sipping a little white wine." He waved a half-full wine glass at her.

"No, no thanks, I'm fine."

He sat on the sofa, about halfway down, kind of close. "You look all stressed out." He looked concerned. "Now, what's up?"

"Oh Bill, the crash...and then Dom Mennotti!...I mean, I don't know what happened, what to do...I thought we should discuss this, make a plan or something."

He nodded his head gravely, put his glass of wine on the table in front of them and slid his hand along the back of the sofa, toward her.

"You're right Trish, we've got some serious matters to discuss." He smiled and moved closer to her. "I think you need my help."

"Your help? Well yes, but I thought we both..."

"You saw what happened to Boyle in the meeting today? Fired on the spot. They blame him for the crash." The word "crash" sent a shaft of ice through her stomach. "But we know better, don't we?" She went to speak, but he reached over and placed the index finger of his right hand on her lips. "Now, now," he said soothingly, "no one's aware of your meeting with Mennotti, and he's obviously not talking."

"But you told me..."

He dropped his hand to her knee. She squirmed back in the corner of the sofa. "Seems to me, you and I should have a little understanding." He slipped his hand beneath her skirt and moved closer. "After all, I'm prepared to do you a big favor."

She tried to say, "What favor?" but her throat was too dry. She said, "What..." very quietly.

He moved his hand up her thigh and placed it between her legs. He began to stroke her. She cried out softly and tried to remove his hand. He pressed harder.

"Trish, Trish...I can forget all about the plan you developed with Mennotti..."

"That...that wasn't my plan," she half-sobbed.

He smiled. "Trish...they fired Boyle today for denying his responsibility. He was a senior officer of the company. Who would believe you'?" He now twisted around on the sofa and ran his other hand up her thigh. He was tugging her pantyhose down.

"No...no," she began to plead.

"Trish...all those people dead..." she groaned and turned away her face. "And I'll never say anything...It will be our secret...I'll never tell."

He had her pantyhose down around her ankles, and now was pulling on the back of her legs, pulling her down on the sofa.

"Stop, please stop," she sobbed.

He put his left hand over her face. "Shh...it'll be all right." With his right hand, he pulled down the zipper on his fly.

She could feel him now, probing, thrusting, trying to force his way. Scream, scream! she thought...but what if he's right?...What if I killed those people?

She made an effort to sit up. He forced her down and with the effort of forcing her down, forced himself inside her. She froze and stopped struggling.

She kept her face away from him while it happened and tried to bury into the soft fabric of the sofa. Then she felt him remove himself and get up. She heard water running, somewhere in another part of the apartment.

He brought her a warm, wet hand towel and handed it to her. "You may want to freshen up a bit," he said.

*   *   *

It was after midnight. At last the phone calls from Global's Pacific stations had ceased, out of respect for the time in New York. Boyle sat across the kitchen table from Kate, the phone between them.

"Think that's it for the night?" she asked, looking at the phone.

"I hope so. Usually Australia's the last to check in and I've already heard from Derek."

"Did you get them all?" He flipped through a number of index cards and carefully sorted them out into several piles. "A few callbacks for the morning. I think I talked to everybody else."

"Those people love you, you know."

"No accounting for some people's taste," he mugged.

Kate stood, walked around the table—she was wearing her old terry cloth robe, the one he'd bought her years ago while on some trip and which she refused to give up, in spite of numerous robes of various materials and designs held purchased for her subsequently. Her favorite. She bent over to kiss his forehead. "Goodnight."

He moved to kiss her in return but she was already moving toward the door. It had been a while since they spent a night together.

She stopped at the door. "I have to get up early for work tomorrow."

"How early?"

"Not that early," she giggled.

"Damn right!" he said, jumping up from the table and knocking over the carefully-stacked notes in his haste.

CHAPTER ELEVEN

▼

New Day

Noren knew if Samuels was ever going to make him president of the airline, it had to be now.

Boyle had been Samuels' one-stop source of information for the temper of the airline and its people. Regardless
of how specialized or obscure the question—how the
pilots' union felt about feeder-airline contracts; what the
British Civil Aviation Authority might do about landing
rights in Manchester; why a widebody had to be placed on
the Miami/Dallas lane segment while a narrowbody would
suffice Miami/Seattle; all the infinite details it took to run
a worldwide airline operation—Boyle either had the

answer or knew where it could be found. To have removed him suddenly was like wiping out memory in a computer.

It would take Noren a little time to learn which buttons to push but what choice did Samuels have? If Samuels knew half a dozen Global Air people outside the Global Air building, that was a lot. Even at headquarters, aside from the ever-present Redmond, Dottie Allen—his cow of a secretary—the lawyer, the PR gal and Noren himself, Samuels hardly ever saw or spoke to any of the other employees. Boyle's departure left a gap; Noren would fill that gap, become the airline president de facto and Samuels would be forced to recognize him as such. At this particular moment, Noren was convinced Samuels needed him more than the other way round. Time to press that advantage.

His intercom buzzed. "Mr. Kreiger is here to see you, sir."

"Send him in." If you want a job, behave as though you had the job. The Kennedy situation was first on his list.

Arnold Kreiger, VP of Human Resources, had been very helpful when Noren axed three of Boyle's camp followers. Now he'd have another opportunity.

Kreiger entered the office tenuously, a child summoned to the principal's office. "Mr. Noren?"

"Yeah, Arnie. Sit down." Noren waved toward a chair in front of his desk. "What's the story on this woman at JFK?"

"Eh, Fran Demarest?" He sat down.

"She and Boyle...you know, friendly?"

Kreiger cleared his throat. "Well, she's reported to him for a number of years."

"Get rid of her."

"Get rid of her?"

"Yeah, like in fired, terminated, removed from the payroll."

Kreiger looked dumbfounded. "But she reports to Mr. Boyle."

"Reports to who?" This Kreiger is turning out to be one stupid guy.

"Ah well, she did..."

"**Did** is the operative word."

"I see." Kreiger shifted in his chair. "And you're..."

"I'm telling you to dump her."

Kreiger was carrying a vinyl portfolio; he now began to rub it with his fingertips as if he were trying to polish it. "Ah, as you probably know Mr. Noren, the only employees we can literally 'dump' these days are heterosexual white males under the age of forty who have no obvious disability, ethnic, racial or religious background..."

"So what'd we do with the other old woman?"

Kreiger looked like someone just goosed him with an ice-cold finger. "You mean Norma Jepson?"

"Whatever."

"Well, she resigned after..."

"Gary, right? She turned down the res job in Gary."

"Yes. . ."

"So offer this one something like that..."

"I think the station manager position in Omaha is open..."

"Do it." Noren turned away to look at his computer; Kreiger still sat there. Noren looked back at him. "I meant I want you to do that right now."

"We'll need to replace her."

"We'll as in **we**, Arnie?" Kreiger was looking dumbfounded again. "Isn't it your job to maintain an active file of replacement candidates?"

"Eh, yes…"

"So do your job, Arnie. Thanks for coming by."

Noren watched Kreiger stand and scuttle from the room. He knew a young woman in personnel at his last job who would fill Kreiger's position as head of Human Resources just fine and would be more than willing to express her gratitude for obtaining a VP slot with an airline. But first, he had to get the job he deserved—president of Global Air. The next step would be a little more tricky.

He picked up his phone and keyed in Redmond's extension.

"Mr. Redmond's office, Joannie speaking."

"Hi, Joannie."

"Oh hi, Bill."

"How'd you and your significant other like the show?"

"Oh, we loved it and the seats, I mean, we were like on the stage!"

"Anytime Joannie, anytime…Say, your boss around?"

"Sure is, want to speak to him?"

"Nah, just see if he's got a few minutes free now so I can pop down to chew the fat."

"Okay, hold on…he says sure, you bring the fat."

"Thanks, Joannie. Be right there." Had to play these cards carefully. If he did, it wouldn't be too long before Redmond was coming to his office.

*　　　　　　*　　　　　　*

The phone rang. Boyle looked at his wristwatch; seven twenty-eight. First time in a long time the phone didn't ring by six a.m. He walked from the living room to his new office—the kitchen table. All his notes were there from last night and this was probably one of those callbacks.

He picked up the phone. "Boyle." He would have to get over that habit of answering the phone with his last name; this was not work, after all.

"Mr. Boyle?"

"Yes."

"This is Sarah Litchfield from the NTSB, we met at the press conference yesterday."

"Oh yes, sure."

"Hope I'm not disturbing you…"

"I'm an early riser."

"…but they called me back to D.C. for a couple of days…"

"That explains the jet noise in the background. LaGuardia shuttle?"

"Uh-huh…and I just had a moment to call you and ask you about something that turned up when we interviewed the midnight crew last night."

"Sure."

"Why did you authorize a change in the engine/pylon procedure?"

Boyle looked at the phone—maybe the jet noise obscured what she said. "Excuse me?"

"Before you…eh, left, you authorized a change in engine/pylon procedures from separate handling to handling as a unit."

"No I didn't."

"We have a copy of your authorization."

"There's no way I would authorize a change in such a critical procedure without a full staff review—that would be totally irresponsible." He wondered if she knew what she was talking about. "Who did you talk to?"

"The shift supervisor, tall, kind of skinny fellow."

"Rick Wenthol?"

"Yes, along with a few of his people. He said his boss, the man who committed suicide…"

"Mennotti."

"Mr. Mennotti gave all his supervisors a copy of your authorization."

"I'd like to see a copy of that."

"I'll bring it when we meet."

"I'd like to see it now."

"Under the circumstances, that won't be possible."

"Now wait a minute…"

"They're calling my flight."

Boyle could hear the P.A. in the background.

"Mr. Boyle, you know we work backwards from the accident. We're concentrating on recovery operations now so my question may be a bit premature but I would like to sit down with you in the next week or so, go over this and a few other things."

"But there's a major discrepancy here!"

"And we can get into that when I return."

He could hear the final boarding call on the P.A. "Yes, but…"

"Mr. Boyle, I must get on my flight and I'll call you as soon as I get back."

"Who's running this while you're gone?"

"Mr. Boyle, please do not take this as me hanging up, but I have to go now!" The line went dead.

"Damn!" he said to the phone. Change the engine/pylon procedure? She said it casually, as if she were discussing a change in the in-flight menu. Has to be some sort of paperwork screw-up—wouldn't be the first time. But how could they have a copy of a change in procedure she said held signed? Wait till she gets back from Washington? Like hell—a few phone calls would straighten this out.

*   *   *

Samuels was waving a hard copy of Noren's e-mail in Redmond's face. "Have you gone totally nuts?"

"Gerry, I thought it was a good idea. I still do."

"Noren goes out to all the managers in the system with an E-mail that says not to talk to Boyle?"

"That is a good idea."

"I'm not saying it's not. Isolate Boyle from Global, no communication, fine. But who the hell gave Noren the idea he could give orders to the company? I mean, doesn't he just run marketing or did I miss something?"

"He's trying to help you, that's all. These are petty details, you don't have time for them."

"Bullshit. He's trying to leverage me to appoint him president. Lotsa luck."

"Might not be such a bad idea, take a lot a shit off your desk."

"You want to report to him?"

Redmond laughed louder than was necessary. "CFOs always report to the chairman Gerry, you know that."

Samuels glared at Redmond. "Stock opened down another point and a quarter, puts me negative two and an eighth. This keeps up, there'll be no airline to be CFO of." Samuels' eyes narrowed. "Why aren't you on the phone with the Germans?"

Redmond started for the door. "My next call." He stopped. "Oh, by the way, I will be on with Singapore tonight but I'll be out of the office."

"Where you gonna be?"

"Got some tickets for the Met, Madame Butterfly. I'll call from there."

Samuels scowled. "How'd you get tickets for that? I was told that thing's been sold out for months."

"Lucked into some, that's all."

*   *   *

Boyle thought it was strange that everybody he called at Global staff was "out" or "in a meeting" or "can't take your call right now".

Fran Demarest explained. "You've been deep-sixed. Anybody talks to you, lets you on Global property, it's their job." She had called him, the first and only call from anybody at Global today. "Noren sent out a systemwide E-mail, said it was 'imperative' for reasons of liability and corporate image that no one have any contact with you until the investigation is concluded, under 'pain of termination'. His exact words."

"So how come you're calling me?"

"I don't know, Pat. Guess my head is as thick as yours."

Boyle chuckled in appreciation; neither spoke for a moment.

"Besides, they're moving me out of harm's way. Arnie Kreiger called. I'm going to Omaha as station manager."

"Omaha? From Kennedy? From the hub to what, three, four flights a day?"

"Three. Two in the morning, one at night. All transits. Piece of cake."

"You'll go up a wall for things to do in a place like that."

"What's my choice?"

"Fran, you're still a young woman with a tremendous background..."

She laughed gently. "I think any youth I may have is in the eye of the beholder...I'm a thirty-something single parent with a high school education and one lovely son who I will see through college and beyond."

"Don't sell yourself short."

"Pat, if it hadn't been for you, I'd still be pounding on a typewriter and fetching coffee for eight dollars an hour. You know that."

"I only helped, you..."

"But you know something else? Call it intuition, whatever you want, you're not finished at Global yet."

It was Boyle's turn to laugh. "If I'm not finished at Global, I'm doing a pretty good imitation of it."

"Remember where I'll be, the land of the blue ice..."

They both laughed heartily; they shared a running gag that blue ice, the effluent that leaked from toilet holding tanks on aircraft and froze at cruising altitude, always seemed to break off and crash to the earth in the Great Plains states.

"I'll remember." He would miss her, her sense of humor; perhaps more?

"So this is not 'goodbye', it's 'till then'."

"Till then."

She hung up.

Boyle replaced the phone slowly. Fran had paid her penalty for being associated with him, just like the others—Clancy, Jepson, MacCready. He looked out the kitchen window at the East River, shimmering in the distance. What could he do about it, anything? He stood up and walked to the window. And what about that call from the NTSB; if no one at Global would see him, talk to him, how could he clear up this thing about a procedure change he never authorized? He returned to the phone. Dan Lipscomb's card was in the pile of notes—it would be awkward...yet it might be something he'd be interested in following up.

The phone rang as he rummaged through the scattered papers. Only the second call of the morning, quite a change from yesterday. He picked it up. "Boyle." There's that last-name habit again.

"Mr. Boyle? Hold for Mr. Trevnor, please." That was annoying. That sort of telephone one-upmanship at the office was bad enough; but at home it truly rankled.

"Mr. Boyle?"

"Yes?"

"This is Hal Trevnor of Trevnor and Associates."

"Uh-huh?"

"We've yet to meet, but perhaps you've heard of my firm?"

"It rings a bell, vaguely."

"We specialize in leveraged buyouts of large corporations. Renfrow Manufacturing was our latest endeavor."

"Yeah, well, as I say, vaguely..."

"I'd like to talk to you about an LBO…leveraged buy-out."

Boyle laughed. "I think you've got the wrong number. I've got nothing to sell, relatively little cash to buy anything with and, as you're probably aware, no longer with Global Air."

"Precisely. When can we meet?"

*   *   *

Leslie Foster—elegant, cool yet attentive—sat at the conference table in Noren's office and reminded herself again that advertising professionals do not allow themselves the emotional excesses their clients sometimes indulge in. She hoped her employees—art director on her left, account exec to her right—were equally determined and would maintain their equanimity.

Noren was furious, pacing the room, his arms and hands punctuating his words. "This is the fourth meeting in four days and I don't see shit!" He stopped pacing. "Don't you people understand?" he screamed the question, stared fiercely at each individual, then let out a theatrical sigh. He approached the conference table, leaned over and spread his hands out on it. "We've had a crash. People are concerned about flying on Global. And look at this!" He grabbed a stack of computer printouts on the table and flung them at the bug-eyed account exec. "We're losing market share!"

Noren resumed his pacing. "And you give me this drivel!" He waved at a mock-up of a print ad sitting on an easel next to the art director. Intended as a full-page newspaper insert, it had a banner headline across the top, "FLY

GLOBAL AIR…" and across the bottom, "…AND SAM-
PLE OUR SERVICE!" with four photos of a variety of
smiling couples eating and drinking on board various aircraft. "This is supposed to be ad for an airline, not a fucking restaurant!" he howled. He abruptly stopped pacing,
went to his desk, sat down and busied himself with some
paperwork.

There was an uncomfortable silence. The art director
and account executive glanced furtively at Leslie, awaiting
her lead. Finally, she spoke. "Just what is it you want?"

Noren shot back to his feet, pounded his fist on his
desk. "I want an ad that says it's safe to fly on Global Air!"

"That was the message in the first presentation we did
for you," she said, trying to remain as calm and non-con-
frontational as she could.

"Yeah, and that sucked!" He stalked over to where they
were sitting. "That said, 'Come fly Global Air and we
won't crash in the ocean anymore'!"

"That's obviously not how the copy read," she replied,
more a suggestion than a statement.

"That's the message it gave me!" he countered. He took
a deep breath; they waited for him to continue. "Look," he
sounded reasonable now, "what you've got to do is create
an ad that says it's safe to fly Global Air without actually
saying it in so many words." Leslie caught the eye of her
art director, who rubbed his jaw and looked away. The
account exec busied himself tiding up the market share
reports into a neat stack.

"Well, perhaps we're all just wasting each other's time."
Noren's voice was suddenly dampened and flat. He
returned to his desk and plopped down, as if he'd just been
told by the teacher to stay after class.

Foster bit her lip. "What does that mean?"

"Big town. Lotsa agencies," he shrugged.

She was furious; she hadn't humped this bastard all this time to take this shit. But then, she caught herself, business is business; never let your feelings show. If necessary, she would resign the account; but she would not be fired from it. She nodded to her two employees and they began to pack up their materials.

Leslie stood. "We'll be back tomorrow morning with a new presentation."

"If you like. Be here at eight," he said without looking up.

He knows that means we've got to work through the night, she thought. They straggled out of his office like remnants of a defeated army. Foster was last out and at the door as Noren called after her. "By the way Leslie, I'll be over tonight about nine. Don't worry about fixing me anything to eat."

"Not tonight."

"You don't have to stay in your office," he said petulantly. "You can have your staff put together the presentation."

"It's that time of the month," she lied sweetly, and left.

*   *   *

The lieutenant wanted Lipscomb to take some time off but Dan demurred, saying he needed to stay on the job to keep his mind occupied. He could use some personal time here and there as things came up, such as Boyle's call about Wenthol.

The way Boyle described it, this guy Wenthol should be able to fill in some of the details the investigator from the NTSB didn't have—like how did Boyle's signature show up on a document he claims he never signed? It sounded to Lipscomb like someone was playing fast and loose with Boyle's authority, for reasons not clear to Boyle or himself.

He pulled up outside an apartment in Forest Hills, best-known for once being the site of the tennis classic, now a woodsey home to many airline workers. Wenthol had said he preferred talking to Lipscomb at his apartment rather than come in early to the hangar and get involved in work problems before his shift began. Given all his years of shift work, Lipscomb could empathize.

The apartment was on the first floor. Lipscomb knocked on the door, which opened almost immediately. This guy must have been waiting for him.

"Dan Lipscomb, NYPD." He held his ID out.

"Yeah, hi. I'm Rick Wenthol. Come on in." His handshake was wet and clammy, he had a hard time looking Lipscomb in the eye. Maybe this guy was just nervous, having a cop—a big, black one at that—in his apartment. But maybe there was something else. "Have a seat, pardon the mess."

Wenthol had told him over the phone he was packing for a move to Washington. "Gettin' ready to pull up stakes, huh?"

"Yeah. Renton, Washington. Vendor work for Boeing."

Lipscomb remained standing. "Guess all the investigators you've talked to so far wonder about the coincidence, huh?"

"Coincidence?"

"Plane crashes, you resign."

"Hey, you got it backwards. I resign, plane crashes."
Wenthol looked like he knew that didn't sound good. "I
mean, one had nothin' to do with the other."

"Umm." Lipscomb wandered around the room; it was a
good-sized living room with a Pullman kitchen, bedroom
and bathroom down a short hallway. "So tell me about
this new procedure Mr. Boyle authorized."

"Not much to tell. My boss, Dom Mennotti…"

"He's the one committed suicide?"

"Uh-huh…he says we're gonna handle the engine and
pylon together instead of separate." Wenthol shrugged his
shoulders. "We did."

"What happened to Mennotti?"

"You mean why…?"

Lipscomb nodded.

"Damned if I know…I mean, he was the manager of
maintenance and all that but still…" Wenthol shook his
head.

"So how come Boyle said change procedures?" Wenthol
looked like an animal frozen in a car's headlights. "Uh…I
have no idea."

Lipscomb knew lying. "My wife was on that plane," he
said.

"Oh." Wenthol looked like he might faint.

"Senior flight attendant Lois Lipscomb."

"I…I…" Wenthol stared at the floor.

Lipscomb stood in front of him and placed his right
hand on Wenthol's shoulder; he could feel Wenthol shud-
der. "If you know something…look at me!"

Wenthol was sniveling now, trying to maintain control.
He raised his head but could not look at Lipscomb.

"If you know something you haven't told anybody you better tell me." Lipscomb still had his hand on Wenthol's shoulder; the shirt beneath his hand was wet with perspiration. He knew he could twist that shirt into a knot, twist it tight and squeeze the truth out. But that wouldn't hold up. "Big, bad black cop squeezes scum. Scum sues," would be the headline. He needed something voluntary. He snorted, slowly removed his hand from Wenthol's shoulder and reached inside his jacket pocket. Wenthol jumped back. It would have been funny if it were not so sad.

Lipscomb pulled a card out of his pocket and handed it to Wenthol. "Want you to think what we've talked about and gimme me a call." He lowered his head and bent it around to catch Wenthol's eyes. "You do that?"

Wenthol nodded quickly and affirmatively; he made a sound as if he were trying to say something but his voice wouldn't work.

Lipscomb backed up and stared at Wenthol. "Gonna be waitin' for that call." He turned toward the door. "Might wanna change your panties," he said over his shoulder.

A large, wet spot was beginning to form in the crotch area of Wenthol's pants.

*   *   *

Boyle thought the accommodations rather spartan for the office of a renowned deal-maker. He sat in a small, windowless, L-shaped waiting room painted institutional gray, furnished with vinyl chairs which looked as though they belonged in the Department of Motor Vehicles.

"Mr. Trevnor will see you now," said a dumpy-looking woman who peered around a corner of the room.

Trevnor's office, with one unwashed window looking out on an elevator shaft, was even less imposing. Small and narrow, with room for only one visitor's chair, it was piled from floor to halfway up the wall with files, books, reams of computer runs and financial publications. Trevnor, a slight, bespectacled and balding man of middle age, was surrounded by two computer terminals, a scanner, a telephone console which seemed to have all its buttons blinking, and a fax machine. The overall impression was that of a man engulfed in the flow of events, with no time to waste on frills or appearances.

"Mr. Boyle. Pleasure to meet you. Sit down please." They shook hands; Boyle sat.

"I guess my phone call was a bit perplexing," Trevnor began.

"You guess right."

"Let me tell you what we're up to."

Boyle nodded.

"Before we proceed, I'll need your word that anything we discuss today will be treated in complete confidence."

Boyle considered the request. "Quite frankly, Mr. Trevnor, I've always been reluctant to promise my confidence until I know just what it is we're talking about."

"Fair enough. Depending on how you react to some of the items I will discuss with you today, I plan to offer you the position of President and Chief Executive Officer of Global Air."

Boyle almost laughed out loud; instead, he smiled skeptically. "How do you plan to do that?"

"The answer to that question involves information about which I must have your pledge of confidence."

"You got it."

"Thank you."

Trevnor leaned back in his ergonomically designed chair, the only visible concession to office chic in the room and moved his eyeglasses on top of his head. "Trevnor and Associates consists of a few people like myself—lawyers or financial types or both…"

"You're?"

"I'm both. London School of Economics. Harvard Law. A few years at the Fed, then the SEC, then this." He smiled self-deprecatingly as he swung his arm around, indicating his office. "Low overhead, but we do get a nice return on our investment."

Boyle smiled and waited.

"We have a few investors who entrust us with their monies. Some corporate money managers. A few, rather wealthy private individuals. Some of our own money. We look for opportunities to invest that money."

"Sounds like my friend Samuels."

"Yes and no. Like Gerry Samuels, we seek out individual businesses and buy them. Unlike Gerry Samuels, we prefer to hold our assets and grow them and make our money that way. Samuels prefers to sell off assets, get his investment back real quick, then bleed what's left of a business for his profit."

"You sound noble by comparison."

"By comparison, perhaps. By intent, no. Both of us— Samuels, ourselves—want to make money. A lot of it. We believe—and, quite frankly, our experience has shown—that long-term investment in a basically solid but troubled company will bring greater returns. If that serves a noble purpose—maintaining jobs, community benefits, pensions—fine. But that's just a happy by-product, not the intent."

"Fair warning."

"Fair warning, indeed."

"How does this tie-in to Global Air?"

"Samuels bought an undervalued stock. Undervalued based on total asset value alone. His plan was to drive up the stock price, sell assets piecemeal, liquidate the airline, make another fortune."

"There were rumors…"

"Buyers lined up in Germany, Singapore, Las Vegas. Still pending, still haggling."

"So why doesn't he just sell out now?"

Trevnor's eyes widened, he was warming to his topic. "He's trapped by his own plan. Plan was, divvy up assets by three, sell them separately, maximize their potential. But he's dealing with some pretty sharp people who know exactly what he's trying to do. Then a plane crashes. The crash drives down the stock five, six points under what he paid for it. Let's say he's lost about twenty percent of his original investment, on paper. Now if he does get his price for one of the assets up for sale—say he sells the European routes to the Germans—Wall Street sees this as a liquidation move, everybody bails out of Global stock, the stock crashes and he's left trying to peddle non-liquid assets in a buyer's market, having just been wiped out in the stock market." Trevnor paused. "Gerry Samuels is on the edge of a financial meltdown."

Boyle smiled as he contemplated the thought. "And you want to buy the airline whole."

"We want to buy the airline whole and operate it at a fair profit; we believe it can be done."

The remark resonated with Boyle; in spite of years of erratic financial performance, he felt deeply Global Air could survive, even prosper. Maybe Trevnor had something.

"Our plan is to provide majority financing for a takeover, with subordinate financing through an ESOP."

"ESOP?"

"Employee Stock Ownership Program. It has tax benefits you can't imagine unless you've been involved in one. Have you?"

"I'm strictly an airline guy."

"Trust me."

"I guess I'll have to." Boyle could feel his skepticism being replaced by something that felt better.

"We've used ESOPs before in other deals and found they work very well. Gives the employees a piece of the pie. Takes the typical ten percent of any work force that're habitual troublemakers or complainers and turns them from lightning rods for problems into odd men out. Amazing how it works."

"Sounds like a way to put more hustle in the work force." He could see himself at the airport, walking the ramp, jacking up the troops—high-fives, shouts, smiles—Pat Boyle was back.

"That's it exactly. In a service business like the if airlines, where a sour face or curt reply…"

"…or lost piece of baggage…"

"…can lose a customer forever, an ESOP's better than sex!"

Boyle raised his eyebrows.

"I may have overstated my case," Trevnor smiled sheep-ishly. They both laughed.

"In any case," Trevnor continued, "to make an ESOP work, it needs a leader. Someone the other employees can respect and will work for. That's why we're coming to you."

"How about the crash and my being fired? And the news coverage I got?"

"You mean Olin's commentary on WPCT?" Boyle nodded.

"A plant."

"A plant?"

Trevnor looked away, as if weighing what he was about to say. "I really shouldn't be telling you this, but...you've given me your word..."

Boyle said nothing.

Trevnor stared at Boyle, then blinked; apparently he'd made some sort of decision. "One of our investors sits on the board of Innovative Communications. They own WPCT, among other media properties. Gene Olin, who's basically just a color man for their local TV outlet, was paid sixty-eight thousand dollars salary last year by Innovative. On that amount of money he's got an apart-ment in town, a condo in the Hamptons, two kids in pri-vate school, drives a new Lexus that costs fifty-plus and is completely paid for."

"Maybe he's invested well."

"They did some investigating. The car was purchased for him by Consolidated Industries."

"Noren's old company."

"William Noren's previous employer before he joined Global Air," Trevnor confirmed. He let the news sink in. "Olin doesn't know it yet, but his days at WPCT are numbered."

So are Noren's, the feeling grew in Boyle, so are Noren's.

CHAPTER TWELVE

▼

FIELD WORK

That they met at all was a great tribute to the respect the union leaders had for Pat Boyle; that they could agree to the proposition he placed before them was virtually unthinkable.

For Trevnor's strategy to work, Boyle had to get Global's unions to join the ESOP. Their combined membership in the airline—pilots, flight attendants and ground employees—was seventy-six percent of the airline's total employees. If they bought off on the plan, the deal was done.

Boyle and Hal Trevnor faced the three union leaders across a narrow conference table in a meeting room at the midtown Sheraton.

"Pat, this just isn't gonna fly," said Vito Simone, the diminutive but forceful Chairman of the U.S.E., the Union of Service Employees. Simone was known as the "Fucking Ferret" and took perverse pride in his nickname, often initialing in-house buckslips "FF." Some thought his pointed face, darting eyes and tic-prone mannerisms were the inspiration for the name, but those familiar with his leadership style knew better. His membership did most of the airline's ground service work and comprised the largest working group of the three unions. "The only thing my members want right now is job security. They take a look around the industry, see carriers going belly-up, and you want me to ask them to buy a piece of Global?…No way."

"As you know Pat, Mr. Simone and I seldom agree on anything," Captain Russell Miller—silver-haired, square-jawed and permanently tanned—was head of Global Air's Pilots' Association, "but my pilots would have to tap their pension funds to float this deal. To a pilot his pension fund is right up there with God, mother and country."

"Yeah, and from what I've seen of pilots, some of them would ditch their mothers for the pension," needled Simone. "I mean, we're talking serious cheap." He grinned at the Captain.

Captain Miller responded with an expression of pained forbearance toward the leader of the ground service employees. Some pilots considered themselves "employees" of airlines like superstar athletes were "employees" of the sports teams which paid their astronomical salaries; they had to tolerate distasteful others who did necessary labor.

"I wish I could be more optimistic, Pat." sighed Laurie Stephenson, President of the Airline Flight Professionals'

Union. Her slightly-frumpy-but-earnest appearance belied a shrewd negotiator and union leader. "My members are relatively young, have high turnover and live from pay-check to paycheck."

"Don't we all?" asked Boyle. The remark drew a sympathetic laugh from the group. They had been at it now for almost two hours. Trevnor had done his presentation on the numbers involved in the deal and painted a rosy picture of prospective gains for the participating employees: partial ownership of the company for which they worked; opportunity for upside appreciation of the stock; input to management policies and decisions; job security. The group appeared impressed but unmoved.

"Don't wanna rush you, Pat," said Simone, "but I gotta get outta here and crosstown for another meeting in about half an hour." He was simultaneously playing with the knot in his tie while pulling on an ear lobe. "Isn't it time to take a vote or somethin'?"

The three union leaders stared at Boyle. He turned to Trevnor, who shrugged and started putting his papers back in his attache case. No sale today.

"Yeah, I guess it is." Boyle paused. "When'd you start off with Global, Vito?" The question seemed innocuous, a graceful way to end a failed meeting.

"Me? Ah, sixty, sixty-one."

"At Kennedy?"

"Yeah. Actually, it was called Idlewild then...I remember my first winter on the ramp—cold as a bitch!"

"Global Air was a different airline back then, wasn't it?"

"Hell, yes. A good company. None better. The best."

"You know, looking around this table," said Boyle, "the four of us probably have what, over a hundred years total with Global?" The other three nodded in agreement.

"Maybe more like a hundred and twenty," suggested Captain Miller. Laurie Stephenson groaned.

"That's a lot of time," said Boyle, "and a lot's happened...What's happened to Global Air during that time?"

"It's the shits," answered Simone. "Last couple of years, we sat and watched other airlines grow up and steal our business, then Samuels and his crew came along and now we're just waitin' for the ax to fall."

"Laurie, do you recall how you felt when you first started flying for Global?"

"Proud. Very, very proud." She smiled at the reminiscence. "I was the first person from my high school in Falls Village, Connecticut, to get a job with an airline. They put it in the newspaper, the **Lakeville Journal.**"

"We were good then," Boyle suggested.

"Vito said it, we were the best." Her smile faded. "But that was a long time ago, Pat."

"Could we do it again, Laurie?" She considered the question but did not answer.

"It's possible," cut in Captain Miller. "Anything's possible. But where's the incentive? The motivation? Mr. Trevnor, your numbers look good."

Trevnor smiled with anticipation.

"But not good enough to take to my members. They're pretty well set financially, most of them. Another stock in their portfolios? Not that interesting."

"I'd like to think Global was more than just another stock in their portfolios." Boyle's tone carried a hint of sarcasm, almost anger. The Captain raised his eyebrows. "Think all your members are pleased with the way things are going at the airline now, Captain?"

The pilot considered Boyle frostily. His question appeared innocent enough but had distinct implications for Captain Miller, currently engaged in a quiet but fierce intra-union power struggle. "I don't think any of my members are pleased with the way this new management is handling things, if that's what you mean."

"Our plan brings Pat Boyle back to Global," Trevnor reminded him.

Miller looked uncomfortable. "There's no doubt professionals appreciate working with other professionals," he conceded.

Boyle allowed the response a moment to set in. "Vito. What would happen if you took this to your members?"

"Aw, Pat, you know how it works. I can bring anything I want before them. Problem is, there are always two or three guys who want my job. I back an issue, make it a major deal, put it up for a vote by the membership, it loses big, it could be my ass...and I don't think the members would go for this."

"Why?" pressed Boyle.

"Y'know Pat, you said earlier lots of things had changed over the years at Global. Well, some of the people have, too. I mean, I got a lot of members now could care less about Global. It's just another job. Global goes bust, they go someplace else. They don't care." Simone shrugged. "Why should they? That's the way it is."

Boyle pondered before replying. "You all know my background, how long I was with Global, how I got canned. Not a happy moment. But I guess no matter what, I always thought Global Air was something special. Like you said, Vito, the best. Proud to be there, like you Laurie. Playing with the pros, Captain. But all that pride and good feeling...no one just gave it to me. I got it because I worked hard with people who worked hard and we created it together."

Boyle concentrated on toying with the edge of a piece of paper in front of him, then looked directly at Simone. "People have changed, sure. And maybe it is harder to get some of them up and running these days. But it can be done! I believe that most people will respond well to good direction and fairness and in this case, a share in the company they're working for."

His voice was rising; he paused. "What happens if we do nothing? More of the same? A slow slide into mediocrity followed by a sell-out? To whom? Another bunch of financial bastards who'll cut Global up some more and spit out the rest?" He was almost shouting.

There was total silence in the room. He looked in the eyes of each of them before speaking again, his voice lower and calm. "Can we be proud again?"

No one said anything. Then Laurie Stephenson reached across the conference table to grasp Boyle's hand. "There'll be so many problems..." She smiled. "It's worth a try, Pat."

"We pilots may be frugal," Miller spoke judiciously, "but...I'm willing to go to the membership, let them make the call."

Vito Simone glanced at his watch. His membership could make or break the deal. "Yeah, well, I'm runnin' late for my next meeting and I gotta be goin'." He rose quickly and scurried to the door; hand on the doorknob, he turned. "Boyle, you're a sonafabitch, you know that? We've been sittin' on the opposite side of the table for all these years and you're still a sonafabitch!" He nodded at the wisdom of his words and made a decision. "Okay, I'll take it to the members. May be my last act as their chairman, but I'll take it to the members."

"Thanks, Vito."

"Up yours, pal. Up yours and twist hard to the right!"

*   *   *

Wenthol did one last walkaround of the apartment. He'd rented it furnished, so he didn't have to worry about moving or selling a whole load of furniture; just had to make sure all the drawers were empty.

They weren't particularly thrilled at Global Air when he told them he wasn't staying his full two-week notice but was taking off now. That was their problem; he had vacation time coming, he had comp time from last year he hadn't even taken yet and he was getting damned sick and tired of being called in early for his shift so he could sit around and bullshit with some clown from D.C. who was goin' to ask the same questions some other clown had, three days ago.

The big thing was the cop. No way he wanted to see that guy again, ever. There's plenty of much better things to see and do between here and Washington state than wait for another visit from him. That guy could be vicious, that was plain to see. Who knows? Next time maybe he'd bring a friend for corroboration—he could imagine the results.

"And you didn't see anything happen to this man, officer?"

"No sir. Sergeant Lipscomb and I were having this nice lit-tle visit with Mr. Wenthol when he ups and falls down the stairs in his apartment building."

"I thought he lived in a ground-floor apartment?"

"It was a nice night. We went up on the roof to look at the stars."

"Thank you, officer."

No thanks. He couldn't even buy into the "New York is a nice place to visit but I wouldn't want to live there" rou-tine. He wanted out now and would never come back.

The tour of the apartment was complete, everything was packed up and loaded. He went over to the table by the door and picked up the package. It was well wrapped with lots of heavy mailing tape and had enough postage to send it from here to hell and gone, instead of just down the road to the police station in Kew Gardens. He pur-posely overdid the postage; there was no return address on the package, so it had to get where it was going on the first try.

Lipscomb would probably guess who sent it but so what, he'd have a hard time proving it. The tape recorder and the cassette case were wiped as clean as they could be, the box they were in was made out of a cardboard stiffener for a shirt, the brown wrapping paper had been a bag with some Chinese takeout, tape was tape, the stamps came from a vending machine and he printed Lipscomb's name and address with his left hand, instead of his normal right hand. Besides, nobody was going to be interested in who sent the tape once they listened to it, the stuff on there was going to blow them away. To say nothing of Noren.

He smiled to himself. So much for his career as a black-mailer. Hey, it was a good idea but not worth the risk it entailed if something went wrong. Likely something would go wrong. He'd never forget the look on Lipscomb's face when he said, my wife was on that plane. That was one scary sight. Good luck to you, Mr. Noren.

*   *   *

The uninitiated view large organizations such as Global Air as a hierarchical model—orders issued from on high to compliant, waiting minions who carry them out faithfully, without second-guessing.

Pat Boyle knew better. Within the rigid framework of schedules, budget and equipment, Global Air was a seething, convoluted network of relationships and alliances fueled by rumor, innuendo and speculation. On his journey from ramp rat at Kennedy to Senior VP of Operations, Boyle had learned that reality as well as the phone numbers that went with it; though Noren had forbidden Global managers to communicate with Boyle, he never thought to preclude the workers.

The pilots' union was Boyle's first and most obvious target for the ESOP. The pilots had been working without a contract for the past year and a half. Their president, Captain Russ Miller, led the older faction of the union in their demands for increased pension payments while maintaining an inflexible seniority clause in their contract. The insurgents, led by Captain Larry Sundstrom, were far more concerned with job security and contract flexibility, which would allow pilots from Global's regional feeder services to join the master contract, increasing membership and diluting the power of current members.

Boyle's first call after meeting with the union leaders was to Larry Sundstrom.

The flight attendants were a different story. Though he felt sure Laurie Stephenson would push for the ESOP among her constituency and probably carry the vote domestically, the fact was that the overseas flight attendant bases in London, Tokyo and Sao Paulo together represented a majority of votes. As a flight attendant, Laurie had always chosen to fly domestic routes and was looked on with disdain and suspicion by some of her overseas membership. A totally negative international vote—while unlikely—was a risk he could not afford to take.

There was a simple solution; pick up the phone and call Penelope Warren in London, Sanko Kasamatsu in Tokyo and Gilberto Diaz in Sao Paulo. Each of those managers maintained excellent working relationships with the flight attendants—a discreet lobbying effort on their parts would bring in a positive international vote.

Except for Noren's e-mail.

Boyle knew if he called those people they would help out, no questions asked, Noren's threat notwithstanding. But he also knew word of their actions would inevitably filter back to Noren. No doubt what Noren would do. He couldn't ask these people to take that risk—he wouldn't ask them.

He flipped through his key employee's home phone directory, tapped in a number, listened while the phone rang and the recorder went through its greeting and beep. "Hi. I take it you haven't left town yet for the land of the blue ice. Give me a call soon as you can. 'Bye'." Boyle stood and stretched, walked around the kitchen. He smiled to himself; once it was just the kitchen in their apartment, now it had become Ops Control. A cordless phone with a single line replaced the telephone console, the hanging pots and pans did a passable imitation of the battery of clocks that tracked time in cities worldwide, and Pat Boyle was still running operations for Global Air.

He sighed, snapping out of the brief but pleasant reverie. It was time for the tough one—Vito Simone's United Service Employees.

The U.S.E. was Global's largest single group of employees, representing seventy-eight per cent of the unionized work force, sixty-one per cent of the total work force. Without the agreement of its mechanics, airport and ticket counter agents, baggage handlers, ramp workers, skycaps and food service workers, there would be no ESOP.

Vito Simone was a very impatient guy, hating wasted effort. He always introduced any contentious issue—such as the proposed ESOP—to the JFK local first, on the theory that as JFK went, so went the union. Experience and numbers backed his judgement. JFK was Global's hub, it had five times as many U.S.E. workers as any other station. U.S.E. workers elsewhere followed the lead of their brothers and sisters at JFK—if it works for them' at JFK, it's gonna work for us.

Without the U.S.E. Boyle would not get the ESOP; without their JFK local, he would not get the U.S.E. He strode quickly to the phone and punched in a number he knew through years of practice.

"Yeah?" Simone made it a point to answer his own phone. He was always on management's ass about Global having assistants to assistants and practiced what he preached.

"Pat Boyle, Vito."

"Yeah?" The nasal bark was non-committal, at least not hostile.

"Wondering if you've set a date with the JFK local about the ESOP."

"Yeah…" The reply drawn out to two syllables, suspicious in tone.

"I'd like to be there."

Silence for seconds. "You're shitting me."

*   *   *

Trish Peters had walked past the entrance of the battered women's shelter several times in the last few hours, but had yet to muster the courage to walk in, sit down at some stranger's desk and report her own rape. For what purpose? To become another statistic in some bureaucratic report? To file charges about something that had happened days ago? And the questions they'd ask. "Did you scream? Did you fight? No? Why not? Why did you wait so long to report it? Was this really a rape or did you do something yourself to encourage it?…Oh?…So what were you doing in his apartment in the first place?"…How could she prove anything?

Then there was the crash…The thought, the never-ending thought, the guilt…was she responsible for the crash? Wouldn't she have to tell them about the crash? If she didn't tell them, wouldn't they find out anyhow?

Trish Peters felt ill. Tired, cold and ill. She walked past the women's shelter again and continued on to the end of the block. There she would keep on walking. Walking was something to do. But maybe, maybe if she walked back to the shelter and looked in, maybe it was worth trying again. Or tomorrow. Yes, tomorrow would be better; she was too cold now. She would talk to somebody there tomorrow.

Kate Boyle's schedule was as full as any executive's; but the rewards for her efforts were mostly of the spirit. Beginning as a volunteer, now a paid worker—the pay barely covered her lunches and dry cleaning—she gave generously of her time to the clients of the Morningstar Clinic on East 67th Street. The clinic was something of an anomaly in this chic and upscale area, a definite nuisance to many of the neighborhood residents. After all, if one lacked the wits to avoid being "battered" (the word itself was so pedestrian) one was expected to deal with the situation discreetly, not slink into some clinic like a member of the working class.

Today Kate was doing double duty, holding down the front desk in the absence of the receptionist while reviewing the file of one of her clients, a woman badly beaten by her lover, prior to a court appearance. Through the double-glass doors of the shelter's entrance, she noticed the well-dressed but wan-looking young woman as she made what must have been her third pass in front of the shelter, stop, look in, and go on her way again. It was ironic, thought Kate, how many young women there were like that in the city: well educated, presumably independent, often employed at high-powered and well-paying jobs, yet also so obviously alone and frightened. Nowhere in their formidable education had anyone told them it was all right to ask for help.

The young woman approached the door and peered in; Kate thought she had seen that face before. She made a decision and got her coat.

Trish Roberts was walking away from the clinic. She had almost reached the end of the block when she felt someone lightly touch her arm.

"Excuse me," said Kate, "I hope I'm not intruding but I work at the shelter and I saw you looking in. Perhaps I could help?"

Trish looked at a face which was vaguely familiar. "Ah, no, no." She averted her eyes, afraid they would gave her away. "I was just looking for somebody."

"Are you sure? It's rather comfy in there; not as forbidding as it may appear from the outside. We could have some tea."

Trish studied the older woman's face and saw only kindness and concern. She felt so tired and alone. "Oh, okay. I guess a little tea would be nice on a day like this."

Kate showed Trish into the clinic and led her to a small consulting room off the main reception area. It was warmly and cheerfully decorated with handicrafts—needlepoint pillows, paintings, woven throw rugs and photographs—contributed by the many clients who had passed through the shelter and wanted to express their thanks for the help they received. She poured two cups of tea from the pot simmering on a hot plate and gave one to Trish. They sat side by side on a maple-framed sofa upholstered in colorful colonial prints.

"I hope you didn't mind my running after you like that," said Kate, "but I know from being here that oftentimes young people are very hesitant to take that first step through those doors."

"It was very kind of you. Actually, I've been walking past this place for hours."

"Would you like to talk to a counselor? I do talk to some of our clients, but I'm not part of the professional staff."

"No, please. I'd like to talk to you. You look so familiar."

"It's interesting you should say that; I thought the same about you. Do you work in the neighborhood?"

"No. I live close by but I work downtown at Global Air."

Kate's expression changed; she sat up straight. Trish was puzzled by her reaction. "Have I said something wrong?"

"No, no, not at all." She paused. "My husband used to work for Global Air."

The face and the identity clicked in Trish's memory. "You're Kate Boyle, Pat's wife. We met at a reception in the Wings Club this past summer. I'm Tricia Peters."

"Yes, yes—I recall. You'd recently graduated from Wharton." Kate put her teacup down on the table and took Trish's hands in hers. "What's happened?" she asked, as gently as she could.

Trish was shaking; she shut her eyes and tried to compose herself. Thoughts of the crash raged in her mind, forcing out all else. Her rape, how trivial. Punishment, fate; she deserved it.

"We're alone only if we choose to be," Kate said softly. Trish felt ice cold; the warmth of the woman's voice, her hands, drew her away from the crash.

"Oh, Mrs. Boyle...oh, Mrs. Boyle," cried Trish as she threw her arms around the older woman and began to sob uncontrollably. "The plane...all those people..."

Trish poured out her story. When she finished she was exhausted, but felt a relief, a lightness she had not known since the crash occurred.

Kate wanted her to talk to one of the staff counselors, but she demurred; all that was tearing her inside was released, exposed, vented. Whatever would happen to her now, at least she told someone else, someone she trusted, all she needed to say. She would not let Kate persuade her to stay at the Boyles' apartment till she felt better, nor even call for a cab to take her back to her own apartment. She would walk. She had the strength. She gave Kate her permission to repeat her story to Pat Boyle and Dan Lipscomb, and agreed to meet with them, if they so desired.

Kate escorted her through the glass doors of the entrance to the sidewalk.

"Oh, Kate, how can I thank you?"

"All I did was listen."

"It meant so much." Trish kissed Kate on the cheek.

Kate watched her disappear down the block, into a swirl of pedestrians, cars and traffic lights. She's so young, she thought.

*   *   *

Boyle was a slick one, no question about that. Simone offered to send his car into Manhattan, pick him up and bring him out to Queens for the meeting, but Boyle said no, how's about picking me up at the subway station on Queens Boulevard.

This guy was making big bucks and he's riding the fucking subway? He up for Proletarian of the Year or what?

Simone snickered with appreciation—smart move; some wiseguy at the meeting tonight says, "We all don't ride in limousines!" and Boyle shoots back, "I came out on the F train—how'd you get here?" Smart move.

Simone shot a glance at Boyle, sitting next to him in the back seat of the union's beat-up Plymouth Valiant. Boyle was just watching the lights flash by as they drove on the Van Wyck Expressway toward JFK. The guy didn't say much, never did, even when he was in the union. Big, strong, quiet kid then. Gotta have a lot on his mind. The crash, getting canned—word was he and the wife were splitsville.

Simone cleared his throat; he saw his driver check him out in the rear-view mirror. Had to be careful what you said. The driver was from the Chauffeur and Taxi Drivers Union and a lot of good union men thought Simone was nuts for allowing somebody from management—even if he was canned—into their meeting. Hell with 'em. Boyle had something important for them to listen to. Besides, he was a standup guy. "Ya know, Pat...you're not exactly gonna be talkin' to a group a Wall Street bankers tonight."

Boyle grinned. "I know, Vito, I know." He slapped Simone on the leg. "I appreciate you giving me this chance."

Damn—the slap stung. Boyle could take care of himself. Simone looked into the rear-view mirror; the driver flicked his eyes back toward the road.

A few hundred U.S.E. workers crammed into the well-worn Knights of Columbus hall on Conduit Avenue, close to Aqueduct Race Track, beneath the Canarsie flight approach to JFK. The JFK local was the most militant in the union. "They could go off anytime, like a torch that's been soaked in jet fuel," Simone typically warned management when a labor issue was in dispute. Management had learned through several bitter and lengthy disputes Simone knew what he was talking about.

Simone led Boyle to a seat on the makeshift stage as the members filed by. Even though the flyers announcing this special meeting advertised Boyle's appearance in bold headlines, some of the workers still reacted with surprise and anger to the presence in their meeting of one of the despised "they"—the suits, management, the pricks who schemed endlessly to make their lives unbearable. But Boyle was smiling and nodding, returning the occasional "hello", calling some members by their first names. Ballsey guy.

The program began with a scratchy recording of the Star-Spangled Banner—The Knights of Columbus had yet to get around to buying a tape deck or CD player—followed by the Pledge of Allegiance. As the members recited the Pledge, Simone eyed the shoe-box shaped hall. It was packed, lots of standees, maybe three hundred people in a room that could handle two hundred. He figured that like all smart businesses in New York City, the Knights made a monthly contribution to the Police and Fire Departments so bad things wouldn't happen to their establishments. He just hoped the Fire Department hadn't overlooked too many violations of the Building Code.

The shouting, hooting and laughing began as soon as the pledge ended; the membership was in high spirits tonight. Simone walked to the microphone. "Brothers," he began, "...and sisters...," he quickly added, paying homage to the changing demographics of his membership.

"Stand up, Vito!" shouted a voice.

"I can hear you, but I can't see yoooooo," crooned another to much laughter.

Simone nodded recognition of the tired jibes at his lack of height. He raised his arms wide and tried to wave the group quiet. "Okay, okay you guys. Settle down…settle down." They are in a good mood, he thought.

"There's an interestin' proposal for you to hear tonight." A few boos, some whistles and applause. "I want first of all for you to hear what Bill Denehey here has to say…" Someone in the audience imitated a very loud and long fart, which brought down the house. Simone waited for the reaction to subside. "After which we're gonna' hear from a guy I know a lot of you know or heard of, Pat Boyle."

Total silence. Simone was surprised; he expected some sort of reaction. Maybe that means they're really gonna listen. "So anyhow, here's our treasurer, Bill Denehey." The treasurer, a sprightly older man with a monk's tonsure of white hair set off by blazing pink skin, hopped up on the stage to a roar of approval.

Boyle and Simone had agreed for many reasons it was best to have the union's own treasurer explain an ESOP, how it worked, enumerate its pros and cons and the potential impact on the members. It was Boyle's job to sell it.

Simone was surprised when Denehey delivered anything but an unbiased presentation, harping constantly on the benefits to the members of owning stock—the more stock the better, from the union's viewpoint—in Global Air, while ignoring its downside risks. He concluded his presentation with a ringing, "We own enough stock, we got those guys by the balls—they'll never piss on us again!," which got a huge roar of approval from the membership.

"Hope I wasn't too hard on yer, Pat," whispered Denehey as he passed Boyle on his way off the stage.

"You've the makings of a poet, William," smiled Boyle.

"Yeah, okay, okay," Simone was back at the podium, waving at the group, "settle down, settle down." He looked in the general direction of Denehey. "Thanks, Bill, for givin' us the facts about this ESOP, which is real complicated, as you can see." He turned to Boyle. "Now I want to introduce a guy..." several boos were heard, "...hey, and I don' wanna' hear that. This man is our guest tonight, and I think we should treat him with respect, even if he was management." The boos ceased. "So here's Pat Boyle."

Boyle stood and covered the few steps to the microphone as a few members clapped perfunctorily.

"Hey! It's Captain Crash!," a voice sang out.

A brief silence, then a few coughs; even the rough-hewn humor of the members had its limits.

Boyle stared in the direction of the remark for what seemed a long time. "Ladies and gentlemen of the United Service Workers, thank you for allowing me to come here tonight."

They reacted like dead fish—nothing.

"Bill Denehey did a fine job outlining the benefits to you, your family and your union if you vote to participate in this Employee Stock Ownership Program." Boyle gave a little smile. "Almost too good."

Simone sat forward on his chair.

"There are a few negatives, and I want you to be aware of them."

Simone listened in disbelief as Boyle rattled off reasons why the members had to be wary of an ESOP—volatility of the stock market, a questionable outlook for Global Air (he even mentioned the word "bankruptcy"), a cut in take-home pay to fund the ESOP. Was this guy losing his marbles; why would he tell them this stuff?

"Now let me tell you why I think you should vote for this ESOP." Boyle had been holding a couple of 3"x5" index cards, consulting them occasionally. He made a big show of slipping them in the inside pocket of his suit jacket, placed both elbows on the rickety podium and leaned toward the audience. "I think what this is about is participation. A chance for you and your families to have a piece of the pie, a stake in the action. You know, I looked around the subway car as I was riding out here tonight on the F train…"

Simone's eyes darted around the audience—not a hoot, not a whistle of derision. Participation, ownership, pride, something tangible you could pass on to your kids; Boyle was reeling them in, slick as duck shit.

"What you do here tonight is very important. It's no secret the rest of the locals, the rest of the union, are watching—and waiting—to see what JFK is gonna do."

"Bullshit!" The high-pitched nasal whine came from the back of the hall. "This' just another way for you and the other fat cats to line your pockets at the workers' expense!"

Simone winced. It was the Punk from Bensonhurst, a spike-haired kid with rings in his ears, his fingers, his nose and, for all Simone knew, a ring pounded through his dick. "If this' such a good deal, why didn't we have it before?"

Several shouts of "Yeah!", "Right on, bro'!"

"We do all the work, take all the shit," the Punk was on his feet and waving now, "and you guys take all the money!"

Simone listened as murmurs of agreement swept the room. "Kid's right!" from somewhere in the middle of the audience. "Go back on the F train!", followed by a burst of laughter. Simone shrugged to himself. He'd warned Boyle—this wasn't a meeting of investment bankers.

"You ain't givin' us shit!", the Punk screamed in summation and flopped back in his seat to scattered applause.

"You're right kid!" Boyle shot back, "I ain't givin' you nothin'!" The anger and mockery in his voice stunned the members. "And you know something? There's nobody, nowhere, notime that's going to **qive** you a thing!" He was taking his wallet out of his pocket. "You're going to have to earn it!"

He had a card out of his wallet. "See this?" He held the card up to the crowd, then handed it to a startled man in the first row. "What is it?"

The man mumbled a reply.

"Into the mike, please."

The man got up and mumbled into the mike. "It's a U.S.E. card."

"Name?"

The man double-checked the card before speaking. "Patrick J. Boyle."

Boyle looked directly at the Punk. "You're not the only guy who ever sat out there and listened to some suit on a stage try to sell you something." His voice now was soft, understanding. "But you must understand not everything is a gimmick, not every proposal a lie. It would be very foolish if you simply allow your feelings to override a very unique chance to own part of the company you work for."

Simone realized he was holding his breath. Boyle waited at the podium.

A large, fiercely mustached, bald-headed man in the middle of the audience stood. Everybody knew Omar, the leader of the baggage handlers and ramp service workers. Nobody, including Simone, could recall his last name or even if he had one; he was just "Omar."

"Meester Boyle," shouted Omar in a booming voice that needed no amplification, "Meester Boyle, you know, sometimes I tell you I think management," he shrugged, "it talks through its asshole." The remark was met with cheers and laughter. "But tonight, tonight I think you tell a straight story." There was some applause. "I have been in this country ten, twelve years now and I thank God for every day! And I tell you this…" Omar's black, angry eyes swept the audience and came to rest on the Punk "…there is nowhere, nowhere when man like me can own company!" He spread his arms and turned his massive bulk to include all the members. "I want everybody in baggage handlers and ramp service to stand right now and say Yes!, we like this deal!"

Nobody moved.

Omar shot a fierce glance at the reedy little man sitting next to him. The man jumped to his feet as if held just been violated by a proctologist.

Slowly, then more rapidly, other members began to stand.

Wilma Kent, a large, black woman seated in the front row stood and faced the membership; she headed up the food service workers. "Well, seein's how I have to work with Omar here…" the crowd laughed loudly, none more so than Omar, "Food service workers, let us buy ourselves an airline!"

Simone knew that was it; the JFK local was going for the ESOP, the rest of the union was a done deal. Everybody—almost everybody—was standing, applauding, laughing. He looked at Boyle who was sweating, laughing, shaking hands. Then that sonofabitch Boyle looked over at him and winked.

*   *   *

"It's two out of three, Pat."

"Okay." Boyle appreciated the manner in which Fran Demarest gave her reports—summary first, followed by a few supporting details, ready for any questions. "Let me get some paper." He reached across the kitchen table and grabbed the pad he was using to record notes for his meeting with Trevnor later in the morning, then cradled the phone between his neck and ear. "Shoot."

"Spoke to Kasamatsu. Said he never received Noren's e-mail, thinks they may have had computer problems that day."

Boyle chuckled. He could see Kasamatsu sitting there, smiling, nodding politely; what e-mail?

"He said the Pacific flight attendants went for the ESOP eighty-one per cent yes, fourteen per cent no, five per cent no response. He apologizes for the fourteen per cent."

Perfect. "Okay."

"Penelope in London was a rip."

"Figures."

"She said she heard something about an e-mail from Noren and asked for a hard copy, but that was just the moment they ran out of toilet paper in the loo."

Boyle laughed.

"Said at least his message served some purpose. Also said not to worry about the vote. It was going to be unanimous for but she thought they should have a couple of no votes to make it look good."

"The British sense of fair play." Fran laughed at his jibe while he jotted down the numbers as ninety per cent for, ten per against, to be conservative in his estimate. "So two out of three'?" He waited for the bad news.

"Gilberto is nowhere to be found."

"Huh'?"

"Secretary says she doesn't know where he is, hasn't seen him for a couple of days, no answer at his apartment."

"Huh." That was disappointing; he hadn't counted on that. "She say he was on vacation or something?"

"Had no idea where he was." Fran's tone signalled her disbelief. She sighed. "Maybe…he just didn't want to give you bad news himself?"

"Yeah, that's always possible." Damn disappointing. Boyle did some calculations.

"What's that do to the vote?"

"Well, Laurie Stephenson says domestic division's going to be sixty/forty for, at best." He tapped a few numbers into a pocket-sized calculator, jotted down the results.

"She's got a lot of single mothers in the domestic division—and they don't get overseas allowance." Fran to the defense, rightly so.

"Yeah." He looked at the penciled figures. "But with all our domestic flight attendants, if they come in at fifty/fifty, even with an overwhelming yes from the Atlantic and Pacific, it's still going to be very close. We've got to at least split even in Caribbean/South America."

Fran was silent for a moment. "Remember my intuition."

"Umm." He remembered that and something else. "You given notice to your apartment manager yet?"

"I'm taking a few days off to tie things up. That's on my do-list."

"I'd hold off for a while."

"Something happening that soon?"

"Hopefully." The downstairs intercom buzzed. "Gotta go. Someone downstairs." He paused for a moment. "Thanks, Fran."

"I was only the messenger, Pat. It's you they're voting for." She hung up.

Boyle replaced the phone in its stand. Two out of three. You can't win 'em all, but still...The intercom buzzed again. He stood, turned to the wall and pressed the button. "Yeah?"

"Mr. Boyle, got a visitor here for you. A Mr...." a whispered prompt, "...Gilberto. Says he's got a sack of ballots..." another prompt, "and a few extra, in case you need them."

"Send him right up!" Boyle released the button. The surge of relief and joy he felt was tempered by his shame for doubting a friend.

    *   *   *

Sounds like it's show-and-tell time, Lipscomb thought as he ascended in the elevator to the Boyle's apartment. Strange how things sometimes happen together. Lois would've appreciated that. *We are all in the hands of the Lord.* She'd say that, somethin' like that…Wasn't the hand of the Lord brought that plane down.

He had received the package with Noren's tape, listened to it right before Boyle called him about Kate's meeting this Trish Peters. Hand of the Lord? No…No, anybody with half a brain could see how one man started a chain of events that ended in Lois' death, put a plane full a passengers on the bottom of the Atlantic. Not the Lord, not chance, not fate.

So what? When was the last time someone went to jail because of a plane crash?

Noren had connived and lied, that would earn him membership in the Businessmen's Hall of Fame or high political office. With the right lawyer, this guy doesn't have a problem in the world—might even come up with a defamation of character suit of his own if there was an admissibility problem with the tape. And there would be, always is. The rape? The alleged rape, he reminded himself officially. Gonna be his version against hers if she brings charges, which she probably won't and would be smart not to, 'less she's into public humiliation. That Noren's gonna walk away from this with no more personal pain than if he stepped in some dog shit. Life in the big city.

The elevator stopped and Lipscomb got off. He knew he needed to get to the gym; hit, hit, hit the heavy bag, hit it hard as he could and try to break it, watch its guts spill out on the floor. Instead he walked down the hall to the Boyles' apartment.

"Dan. Thanks for coming over." The two men shook hands as Lipscomb entered the apartment. Kate came up and kissed him on his cheek. "Dan, so good to see you. I've got some coffee set down by the sofa." Lipscomb nodded silently; Kate led him toward the living room.

Boyle followed them, a little disappointed that Lipscomb did not seem buoyed by the developing evidence—the tape, Trish Peters' testimony; things were looking up.

Lipscomb sat in the Morris chair, waved off the coffee Kate offered.

"Are the children alright?" she asked.

Lipscomb looked momentarily stunned, as if he'd forgotten about his children. "Oh, yeah, fine...they're with Lois' mother." He looked blankly at Kate for a moment, then his expression hardened as he removed a black microcassette recorder from his jacket pocket. "This' it." He pushed the playback button and placed it on the table in front of the sofa. Boyle and Kate sat on the sofa and watched as the tape hissed to life.

The tape ended. Lipscomb reached out, picked up the recorder and flicked on rewind. The three watched as it rewound, the only sound the occasional squeal of the tape.

Boyle knew he should be elated; the forging of his signature, the surreptitious change in procedure which
would explain the crash—Noren's scheme was exposed.
Instead, he felt sad, disgusted, but most of all, tired, very
tired. "We'll need to get that to the NTSB."

"Soon as I make some copies." The tape had rewound,
Lipscomb slipped the recorder back into his pocket.

No copies? Boyle assumed making copies would be the
first thing anybody would do with a tape like that, let
alone a cop. But that was a minor point. "Okay, then do
you want to send them directly to the NTSB yourself?"

"Maybe the FBI."

The FBI? A criminal investigation? "Well, usually the
FBI gets involved only after the NTSB has developed evidence, unless the crash was caused by obvious criminal
activity—a bomb or something like that."

"Don't think this was criminal?"

"Ah…well, yes…criminal in the sense that it happened,
and there'd be forgery, I guess…" Boyle was uncomfortable with himself for equivocating, but Lipscomb's tack
surprised him.

"Mennotti did the forgery."

"Yes, but…"

"Mennotti's dead. If I'm Noren's lawyer, all I hear is a
man trying to save his company some money. Dead man's
the one who…" he looked at Kate, "screwed up."

"Dan, what are you trying to say?"

Lipscomb ignored the question and kept his focus on
Kate.

"Now 'bout Ms. Peters."

Kate sat on the sofa's edge.

"Noren and her...seen one case like that, ya seen 'em all, right?"

She glanced at the floor. "Unfortunately, her situation is...not untypical."

"Ever been in court on one a these cases?"

Kate nodded.

"What kinda shape she gonna be in when his scumbag lawyer gets through with her?"

She made no response.

"Lawyer's gonna make her look like a two-bit hooker, right?"

"The system's brutal Sergeant. You should know that." Kate shot back her reply with a depth of anger that seemed to take Lipscomb by surprise. "But if you're asking me..." The ringing phone interrupted her. It rang again.

"I don't think the recorder's on," Boyle said.

"I'll get it." She seemed reluctant to leave, but stood and walked rapidly toward the kitchen.

Boyle welcomed the break—where was Lipscomb going with this? "You know, Dan..."

"You're home free."

"Excuse me?"

"Game's over, you won. Just a question who gets to break the news to Noren." He shrugged. "For what that'll be worth."

"I don't look at it quite like that."

Lipscomb mugged skepticism.

"It's Hal Trevnor on the line." Kate was at the kitchen door. "He says he has to speak to you right now—the pilots vote is in."

The pilots; this could be it for the ESOP. "Ah, Dan..."

Lipscomb was already standing.

"Sounds important." The mocking tone again.

"Well yeah, but…"

He was in the departure lounge in Hong Kong; it was hot and steamy and they were holding the flight to Jakarta, waiting for him to get off the phone.

He could barely hear Kate's voice with the poor connection. "His fever's very high, but…"

"Do you want me to come back?" he shouted into the phone. "I can go to Tokyo, get the non-stop…"

"No, no, stay there. It'll be alright." He was relieved to hear her say that; he had business to do.

Lipscomb was headed toward the hallway.

"Dan, can you wait a minute? I've got to take this call."

"Later." The reply was terse, over-the-shoulder.

Boyle looked questioningly at Kate.

"He's lost the most precious thing in his life," she said as she started after Lipscomb, "you expect logic?"

CHAPTER THIRTEEN

▼

CONVERGENCE

Boyle sat across the desk from Trevnor. Somehow the man had crammed yet another stack of paper into his office. This one was about three feet high, perched on top of another stack. It was covered by a roll of computer printout, "Global Air" written on one side.

Trevnor handed Boyle a sheet of paper. "This is the investment advice the pilots got."

The paper was heavy bond, the letterhead that of the investment firm Inverness, Walpole & Straggle. "**It is the opinion of the undersigned that, while this Employee Stock Ownership Program (ESOP)_carries the risks inherent in any such plan, its timing in relation to**

Global Air's present and likely future financial condition, assuming its acceptance by the other employee groups affected, is a viable endeavor. While there is a good deal of upside potential, the downside exposure should not be discounted. [see attached]"

Boyle noted the three scrawled signatures of Messrs. Inverness, Walpole & Straggle took up more space than the text and handed the letter back to Trevnor. "Do I translate this correctly as a recommendation for a yes vote?"

"That plus this," Trevnor hefted the attachment, a document the size of a phone directory for a mid-sized city, "equals a highly-qualified yes."

"Think any of the pilots read that?" Boyle nodded at the attachment.

"Investors never read this stuff. Investment houses throw it in just in case they ever get sued—shows they did their due diligence." Trevnor tossed the attachment to one side of his desk. "From what I hear, the real reason for the pilots' yes vote was that somebody leaked news of the ESOP to the leader of an insurgent movement in their union and this guy used it to show how out of touch with things the old guard was."

Boyle stared at Trevnor. "Huh."

Trevnor smiled. "Got some very interesting news from another source."

"Oh?"

"Damon Redmond is sniffing around Western States Engineering. There's a saying on the Street, 'Where Redmond sniffs, Samuels trods.'"

"Western States Engineering?"

"Makes a lot of sense for Samuels. They've got extensive mining, real-estate interests in the western U. S. and Chile, a significantly undervalued company. We were looking at it ourselves, but…" Trevnor paused. "Funny. We've got a couple of investors won't touch anything south of the Rio Grande—unstable governments-pho-bia—but they'll still pour their money into Asia." He shrugged. "Anyhow, that's what Samuels is up to."

"How can he afford another company?"

"He can't!" Trevnor smiled triumphantly. "He needs cash and he needs it now and the crash has all three of his would-be buyers doing the same thing—leverage down his asking price, wait for the distress sale." He flicked through his Rolodex. "Timing. Timing is everything." He nodded at the telephone console as he keyed in a number. Similar to phones in many offices in Europe, it was fitted with an earpiece for listening.

Boyle picked up the earpiece and held it to his ear. His hand was dry and steady.

"Mr. Samuels' office," answered Dottie Allen.

"Can I speak to him, please? It's Hal Trevnor calling."

"May I tell him what company you're with?"

"He'll recognize the name," Trevnor assured her.

"Hold on please, Mr. Trevnor." She buzzed Samuels on his intercom.

"Yes?"

"There's a Mr. Trevnor on your private line, Mr. Samuels.."

Samuels was reading a financial report; he placed it on his desk.

"…he'd like to speak to you."

Samuels didn't hesitate. "I'll take the call."

"Thank you, Mr. Samuels."

Hal Trevnor. Samuels recalled the name. Sharp mind, knowledgeable investor, access to some heavy money. They'd done several deals together in the past but on the same side of the table. Samuels assumed they would be on opposite sides now; the sharks were circling. He picked up the phone.

"Hal, how are you?"

"Just fine, Gerry. Yourself?" Along with Damon Redmond and few others, Trevnor had the standing in the investment community to address Samuels by his first name.

"I've been better."

"I guess owning an airline isn't everything it's cracked up to be."

Samuels remained silent.

"Gerry, let me get right to the point. Trevnor and Associates are planning a tender offer for your stock in Global Air. I wanted you to know as a matter of courtesy, before the media pick it up."

Samuels smiled ironically at the last sentence; how often did he begin a takeover with the same words? "What are you offering, Hal?"

"Nineteen dollars a share."

"That's outrageous. I bought at twenty-two."

"Nineteen's a fair offer. It's at sixteen and an eighth right now. Been as low as fifteen and a quarter. Don't think it'll see the twenties anytime soon."

"Book value's higher than nineteen."

"I don't think my people would buy that as book value, Gerry. You've got some very old aircraft."

Neither man spoke for a moment.

"Gerry, I should also let you know minority financing for the deal is being furnished by an ESOP."

"What?" The emotion in Samuels' voice was real.

"All your unions have bought off on it."

"That can't be!" shouted Samuels. "No one told me anything about that!" Samuels did not allow his emotions to move him; he was immediately aware he had said the wrong thing. An ESOP. Samuels knew Trevnor would not dare fabricate the existence of an ESOP; it was too easy a lie to expose and its exposure would stigmatize the liar to his peers as an amateur in a thoroughly professional sport. An ESOP. Samuels had only contempt for an owner caught unaware of his own employees' plans to buy him out: either he was totally out of touch with the vital details of his business or criminally uninformed by his staff.

Trevnor broke the silence. "I'd like to put this together in a friendly manner if we could, Gerry."

Revelation of the ESOP had taken some of the fight out of Samuels. "Nineteen's too low but have your people get together with mine. We'll see." He replaced the phone in its cradle and stared past the balcony and its view of lower Manhattan.

Trevnor jumped to his feet, his right hand stretched out to Boyle. "We got Global!"

Boyle replaced the earpiece and shook hands tentatively. "Don't think this is a little early to celebrate?"

"You hear the steam go out of his voice about the ESOP? He's gone, done for!" Trevnor was back on the phone, punching a button. "Pat, go home, get some rest, we're calling a press conference as soon as we settle on a price." Someone answered his call. "Johnny, get everybody in the war room right away! We need to get talking to

Samuels' people, now!" Trevnor looked back at Boyle as if he forgot he was still there. "I'll call you as soon as we settle—stay loose."

Boyle smiled and headed for the door; while he couldn't quite share Trevnor's conviction, he felt better than he had in a long time.

"Pat?", Trevnor's voice stopped him at the door. "You did a great job! Thanks, Mr. President."

Trevnor was back on the phone. As he left the office, Boyle realized how much he liked the sound of his new title.

*   *   *

Samuels sat back in his tufted red-leather chair and gazed idly at the rich surroundings of his office. Suddenly they had lost some of their colors, some of their life.

Gerald S. Samuels was a businessman, a very good one, one of the best. He had made a fortune that other men could only dream of; he did that by working through his head, not his heart. Though the buyout offer was insulting and the ESOP reprehensible, he began to look for the opportunities presented in the situation. "Cut your losses, maximize your opportunities," was advice he offered others; time to practice what he preached.

A buyout at twenty at the most...say, nineteen and a half at the worst...he'd take a loss, yes, but that would finance his run at Western States Engineering. An undervalued gem, if ever he saw one. He could then turn around and use some of his Global Air losses to offset profits in one of his other companies. That would be a substantial amount, might even put him dollars ahead, net after taxes;

have to run the numbers on that. Best of all, he would be finished with the airline and its problems. The problems simply weren't worth the effort. Dismember the airline with a sale of assets? Cold day in hell that would happen; each buyers' group was waiting for the other to make the first move. So much for Redmond and his advice.

Samuels stood and began to pace the room. What really stung, a slap in the face, was the employee buyout...and being totally unaware such an attempt was even going on!

He thought of his father, his small dry-goods store on Manhattan's lower Eastside. When the old man died, hundreds of people came to his funeral to pay their respects: relatives, neighbors, customers, vendors—even competitors. The man was beloved in the community.

Samuels held out no such illusions about himself; no one would consider him a beloved figure; no one. But he had not sought such sentiment. He had sought—and found—overwhelming financial success in business.

Just as his father had provided good value in his business and looked after his employees, so did he. As far as he was concerned, he took very good care of his employees. Who did they think provided their jobs? Did they believe they were entitled to a job by birthright? Had they any idea what it was like to meet a payroll? And now those back-stabbers were trying to buy him out and no one had even warned him about it!

The more Samuels churned these thoughts the more coldly furious he became. He paid too many people too much money not to be advised that his own employees were trying to buy him out. Were they simply stupid or not attending to the job for which they were paid so well? He stabbed the intercom for Dottie Allen.

"Yes, Mr. Samuels?"

"Have Noren come here immediately."

"Yes, sir."

Noren. Obviously made quite a mistake in hiring this man who wants to be president of the airline but doesn't even know of the employees' buyout plan...Maybe he knew but was afraid to tell...Maybe he's part of the plan! He pounded the intercom again. "Where is Noren?!"

"Oh, I'm sorry Mr. Samuels," Dottie Allen replied, "Mr. Noren's secretary says he's already left for lunch at the Cloud Club. He's meeting a delegation of English businessmen there. Shall I have him paged?"

"No, godammit!" Samuels was furious; facing a buyout—an employee buyout!—and Noren's taking someone to lunch? "Call Lucello at the club, tell him to have Noren call me as soon as..." Samuels had a sudden and icy-clear insight; this man is making a fool of me. No one made a fool of Gerald S. Samuels. "Get Lucello on the line. I want to speak to him myself."

*   *   *

Noren had suggested meeting the distinguished British delegation at the Cloud Club. They were on a tight schedule and he knew how upperclass Brits lap up the club scene.

Besides, he was relieved to get out of the office. Ever since that asshole Boyle got canned, it had been remarkably quiet. The crash investigation had a life of its own, no one bothered him about it. Trish Peters was taking some vacation time—probably looking for another job, which might be a good idea for both of them. Redmond at first seemed all fired up about pushing him to Samuels as the airline's president, but his enthusiasm flagged once he got the opera tickets. About the only people talking to him regularly were a handful of sycophants in the marketing department and they seemed to be completely out of touch with what was going on with the rest of the airline. Even Samuels seemed sort of lethargic. He entered the private elevator to the Cloud Club.

Ah, well. A good and productive meeting today would put things back on track. The president of Global Air must have the wit, style and panache to deal effectively with individuals of high standing on the world scene; make them grateful they're customers.

The elevator eased to a smooth stop at the sixty-fourth floor. Alighting, Noren saw a group of three distinguished-looking gentlemen in the Club's waiting area and recognized them immediately. Sir Francis Buckmaster, honorary head of the British Tourist Authority, vaguely related to the Queen. Alistair Holmes, president of the biggest travel agency in the U.K., Global Air's largest offshore account. Dunston Smathers, Deputy Head of the British mission to the U.N. Quite a group!

Noren greeted each one effusively, immensely buoyed to be hosting such a singular collection of high-ranking individuals. He led the way into the dining room, where he stopped in anger and disgust—another party was seated at the table he had specified. "Lucello," Noren said loudly as the maitre d' approached the group, "my table is occupied. I want you to correct the situation immediately!"

His voice carried. Several diners looked up—it was unusual to hear a loud voice in the Cloud Club. His British guests exchanged glances among themselves.

"Didn't you hear me, Lucello? I want my table now!" Noren snapped his fingers.

The maitre d' dipped his head deferentially. Lucello was a hard worker, raising a family of four in Staten Island, going daily from his midday job at the Cloud Club to his evening job as second chef at a midtown French restaurant. He needed his position at the Club and the money it provided. But he was also a proud man. You only snap your fingers at a dog.

"Mr. Noren," Lucello said, in a loud, clear voice, "you are no longer a member of this Club."

"What?" Noren exclaimed. The subdued conversations of the other diners grew even quieter or halted altogether.

Lucello continued, "Perhaps Mr. Samuels has neglected to tell you but your membership has been canceled."

Noren looked around, stricken. His British guests turned away, embarrassed.

"And Mr. Noren," added Lucello in the same loud, clear voice, "Mr. Samuels asked me to tell you it will not be necessary to return to your office at Global Air."

Dunston Smathers leaned toward his two compatriots. "I believe he's just been fired by the maitre d'...how extraordinary."

Noren turned; without looking back at his guests or the other members, he walked directly to the waiting elevator and pressed the down button. To hell with them, he thought, to hell with them all.

CHAPTER FOURTEEN

▼

"...SAITH THE LORD"

"I'm real glad to hear that, Hal...You don't know how good it'll be to be back in harness...Okay, first thing in the morning, I'll be there...Right. Thanks for calling." Boyle slammed the phone back in its cradle as if he were spiking a football after intercepting a pass and taking it in for a touchdown. "We got it!" he shouted.

Kate came running into the kitchen. "It's done?"

"Done! Samuels agreed to the terms, the new owners take over..."

"With a new president!"

"With a new president, press conference at nine-thirty tomorrow morning!" He picked her up by the waist and twirled her around the floor. "Thank God it's over!" Even though he was carrying her, he felt fifty pounds lighter. "That calls for a celebration!"

Kate laughed delightedly. "If you put me down and give me a little time to finish a report, you can buy me dinner."

*   *   *

The apartment—once so neat, clean and cozy—showed the effects of Lois's absence. Paper plates were scattered about, a TV tray held a half-empty can of Diet Coke, dirty laundry was piled on the bedroom floor.

Dan Lipscomb sat on the sofa, spinning the empty chamber of his Police Special Smith & Wesson .38. He sighted an imaginary target and pulled the trigger. To his left, on the end-table by the sofa, was an eight-by-eleven color photograph of Lois, taken of her in her flight attendant's uniform. The light in the lamp above the photo was on even during the day. Lipscomb fired off a few more imaginary rounds, then flipped open the empty chamber. He took several bullets from the box on the coffee table and loaded the pistol, flicking back the loaded chamber with a jerk of his hand. He put the safety in the "on" position and slipped the pistol into the shoulder holster on his left-hand side.

He rose from the sofa and walked across the room to pick up his blue suit jacket from the chair on which he'd placed it earlier. He put it on, checked himself in the mirror above the chair: good blue suit, white dress shirt, dark maroon tie and white handkerchief just poking out of the corner of his breast pocket. Lois always insisted he wear a handkerchief in his breast pocket; she said it was the mark of a gentleman. Lois would be proud.

He went back to the end-table by the sofa and bent over to put out the lamp behind Lois' picture. She had always been very careful about not wasting electricity.

Lipscomb turned and headed to the door. Neglecting to put on a topcoat against the evening chill, he left the darkened apartment.

*   *   *

Noren paced. He was spending too much time holed up in this dumpy apartment. He needed to go to his athletic club—play racquetball, work out with the weights, do something—but some asshole might say something, make a joke. Fuck. He needed a plan. Get even.

Shit-canned. No one had ever fired William Noren. No one had ever even **thought** of firing William Noren.

Except that prick Samuels.

Samuels...He would get him back. It would be difficult, but somehow he would do it. Somehow he would get him back for his firing, that shit at the Cloud Club. He did not permit himself to dwell on it, or even think of what happened. All his focus was revenge, payback, getting even.

Including that bitch Foster at the ad agency. She wouldn't even return his phone calls. He found her when she was a copywriter in some little scumbag ad agency, brought her along job by job and now she wouldn't even return his phone calls.

Well, there'd be plenty of opportunity to get back at her. Guaranteed. William Noren was a marketing genius and he'd have ad agencies kissing his ass and sucking his dick again to get his business, and she'd lead the parade. Of that he was sure; just a question of time.

He walked to the glass door to his balcony and looked out. Even that depressed him. For many people, an apartment with a balcony on the Eastside of Manhattan would be a life's dream come true. But not to William Noren.

The building was in the unfashionable 40's. Its construction was ugly grey brick, hurriedly thrown up by a developer during the last real-estate boom to cash in on a wildly escalating market. The ceilings were eight feet high, not ten, and had no moldings, no character. The balcony was a joke: it would accommodate three people, maybe. Already it was beginning to fall apart. They had put up cheap little metal handrails and siderails on the balcony when they built the place and now part of the railing, where it joined the outside wall by the balcony door, had fallen off. That part of the balcony had a sheet of plywood where the handrail and siderail should be. Everything about the place was cheap, except the monthly rent.

Noren had planned on making enough money at Global Air to acquire the kind of apartment he deserved, but now that would have to wait awhile; he'd have to put up with this shit-box a little longer.

The doorbell rang. That was strange. Normally, the receptionist downstairs in the lobby would announce visitors on the intercom. Had they fired the receptionist to save a buck and not told the tenants? Wouldn't surprise him.

He went to the door and looked through the security viewer. Big black cop holding up a police badge standing there. What the hell now?

He opened the door but kept the security chain in place. "Yes?"

"Mr. Noren? I'm Sergeant Dan Lipscomb of the New York Police Department. I need to talk to you."

*   *   *

It's changed quite a bit and not for the best, but to be in New York City as the lights of night come on is to be somewhere special. Boyle charged along Third Avenue, headed downtown. Daylight was departing the late afternoon, replaced by a purplish glow serrated by lights twinkling in windows of stores and apartments, on cars, buses and cabs. The air smelled wet; were it a little colder, it might mean snow. Looks like we'll be catching a little rain, he guessed.

Kate said she needed about an hour and a half to finish a report, then they'd go out to dinner and celebrate. Meantime, he needed the walk. At the pace he maintained, it was almost a trot.

Boyle had another purpose in mind and stopped in front of St. Al's. It had been awhile since last he paid his respects. The church was dimly lit and virtually deserted. One grey-haired woman knelt at the altar rail. The smell of incense hung in the still air. Boyle knelt in a pew at the back of the church and took in the scene, the wooden kneeler creaking under his weight.

He let his thoughts drift over the events in the jumble of the past, wandering like a tourist among scenes painted and hung in some gallery.

Thy will be done. The phrase insinuated itself into the wanderings of his mind. *Thy will be done.* Then it was gone, like some distant music heard, then vanished, on a long-ago summer's night.

Boyle looked at the altar without focusing on it. Some phrase, some similar phrase taunted his memory but he couldn't quite grasp it. Recently. A similar phrase. He had spoken it; somebody had spoken it.

Vengeance is mine...

Dan. It was Dan Lipscomb.

I will repay...

Boyle felt a chill, a twinge of apprehension. He thought about a brief conversation he'd had with Lipscomb earlier that afternoon, right before Hal Trevnor called with news of the sale. Kate said he should call Lipscomb, check in on him. "I'm worried about Dan," she said. "You really ought to keep in touch."

He got him on the phone but Lipscomb hadn't said much, talked about finishing it tonight, something like that; Boyle's mind was on the pending sale, he didn't listen that closely.

Vengeance is mine...

It wouldn't go away.

Mechanically he reached inside his jacket pocket for his monthly calendar, carried out of long years of habit. At the back of its leather case were the names, home addresses and telephone numbers of all Global Air executives, in case he needed to reach them outside normal working hours.

I will repay...

He found Noren's address. East 48th Street, minutes away. He replaced the calendar in his pocket and remained on his knees, eyes now focused on the altar. This doesn't make any sense, no sense at all.

...*saith the Lord.*

*   *   *

Should have known better, thought Noren; should've known better. Badge or no badge, blacks mean trouble; should never have let him in.

The man had introduced himself as Sergeant Lipscomb. "Maybe you heard the name?"

"Doesn't register, Sergeant." The man walked past Noren and into the apartment. Noren left the front door slightly open, in case he wanted to leave quickly. Never lock yourself in a room with a black man, thought Noren. At least I did that right. He followed Lipscomb into the apartment.

"Nice place you got here." Lipscomb was looking at various lithographs on the wall.

"It's adequate." Noren hoped the cop wouldn't touch anything with what he assumed were dirty hands.

Lipscomb walked to the sliding glass door to the balcony. "Looks like we're gettin' some rain." The first drops had begun to splatter on the glass.

"Yes. Would you mind telling me what I can do for you?"

Lipscomb turned slowly to face Noren and considered the question as he walked past him to the sofa and sat down.

Noren followed his movement and remained standing. "I asked you a question, Sergeant...and I don't recall asking you to sit down."

"Uh-huh." Lipscomb reached out and began toying with a Chinese lacquered box on the coffee table. Noren visibly flinched. Lipscomb noted the reaction. "Guess you don't entertain a whole lotta the brothers up here, huh?" Lipscomb smiled sardonically. "I came to talk about the crash."

"The Global Air crash?"

"Yeah."

"You're talking to the wrong man, Sergeant. I'm no longer with Global Air."

"You were there when it happened."

"So were a lot of other people. Look," he walked over to an easy chair opposite Lipscomb and sat down, "maybe you don't understand my position there. I was in charge of marketing, not operations. The only time I went near an airport was to get on a plane. I had absolutely nothing to do with those people."

Lipscomb nodded as if in agreement. He reached into his inside breast pocket, pulled out a small wire-bound notepad and consulted it.

"You know Trish Peters?"

Trish. This could be a little tricky, Noren realized. "She worked for me briefly. Hysteric."

"Hysteric?"

"Yeah, a real hysteric. Couldn't trust anything she said. Very unstable." Maybe she'd filed a complaint or something after that session up here. Better get the paper trail straight. "You know how it is, Sergeant." Noren grimaced a smile and tried to sound as man-to-man as he could. "You have a position with a lot of visibility in a large airline, big expense account, lots of free travel to exotic spots. You take a young woman who's very ambitious and wants to get ahead real bad…why…they can claim all sorts of things." He winked.

"You dick'er a lot?"

Jesus, thought Noren. You give them an inch and they take a mile. "What I'm trying to tell you is that Trish Peters is a very unstable young woman who, quite frankly, tried to make herself available to me on several occasions to advance her career. I, of course, would have nothing to do with that."

Lipscomb nodded his head as if in sympathy. "Must be difficult, tryin' to keep your cherry."

"I think you're more than a little out of line there, Sergeant."

"Uh-huh." Lipscomb consulted his notepad again. "How 'bout Dom Mennotti?"

Noren responded quite abruptly. "Some operations flunky, had nothing to do with him." He stood up. "Now look, Sergeant. I'm a very busy person, I'm sure you are, too. All I know about the Global Air crash is what I read in the papers. If you want anything more than that, you'd better talk to my attorney." He started to move toward the door.

"Siddown, Noren." Lipscomb's voice was quiet, but the tone was angry, almost fierce; it was an order you would ignore only at risk. Noren retreated the few steps he'd taken and sat down.

"Lemme tell you a little story 'bout one a the people on that plane, Mister Noren." He ground the "mister" with his voice.

*   *   *

Boyle entered the lobby of Noren's apartment house. It was full of all the glitz Boyle associated with the man—a gurgling fountain splashing on pastel-colored plastic flowers, gold-flecked black marble floors framed by red flocked-velvet walls and a doorman dressed up to look like a character out of India under the Raj; a little touch of Miami Beach decor in New York City. He went to the reception desk.

"Good evening," he said to the young woman behind the desk. "What apartment is Mr. Noren in?"

The young woman glanced at the tenant board in front of her. Her green-streaked brown hair seemed to be as tall as her face was long. She was working on a big wad of gum. "24 C. You another cop?"

"Another cop?"

She looked around, then leaned over the counter to whisper confidentially. "Big, black cop." Her eyes widened. "Looked mean." Her eyes returned to their half-mast position, she straightened up and pushed an old-fashioned dial phone toward him. "Just dial 243."

Boyle dialed and waited through four rings. "No answer. They must be busy talking." He replaced the phone. "I might as well go up."

The girl was involved in an intense study of her long, talon-shaped nails from which various metal items dangled. "Whatever."

Boyle went to the elevator, entered it and pushed the button for the twenty-fourth floor. He was unsure of what he would find or what he would do, or even what he wanted to do. Certainly he wanted to prevent Dan Lipscomb from doing anything foolish if in fact, it was Dan who was up there now. He'd just have to see.

The elevator stopped at twenty-four. He stepped through the opened doors. Apartments A, B and C were to his left. He walked down the corridor to Apartment C. Surprisingly, the door was partially open. He could recognize voices in the apartment; Noren's, sounding unnaturally strained and forced, Lipscomb's, low and rumbling. He pushed open the door quietly, slipped into the apartment and closed the door behind him.

Lipscomb, his pistol drawn, had backed Noren up to the open glass door leading to the balcony. The rain was falling more heavily now and both men were getting wet from the blowing rain.

Noren saw Boyle over Lipscomb's right shoulder. "Boyle!" he half-shouted, half-cried. "Boyle, he's trying to kill me!"

Lipscomb had too much training and experience to allow the cry to distract his attention from Noren; it could be a ruse. He inclined his head slightly up and to his right and spoke over his shoulder. "That you, Boyle?"

"It is, Dan."

"You shouldn't be here, man. Move over to where I can see you."

"Don't do it, Dan. Don't do anything you'll regret." Boyle moved to Lipscomb's right side, far enough away so he wouldn't appear threatening.

"Boyle, this asshole's going to kill me!" cried Noren, framed in the open doorway.

"Don't do it, Dan. He's not worth it." Lipscomb flicked his eyes toward Boyle, then immediately returned to focus on Noren. He inclined his head toward Boyle. "He killed her, man. He killed my Lois just like all those people on that plane and he ain't gonna get away with it!"

"That's bullshit!" cried Noren. "Bullshit. All I did was try to save some money…the girl and Mennotti cooked the whole thing up, not me!"

Lipscomb stared at Noren. "One man made the difference. You're that man…if you're not there, Lois'd be here now."

"There's nothing, no evidence…no judge or jury would convict me of anything!"

"Noren, I am your judge and jury."

I will repay. "Dan, Dan—think of your kids! What will happen to them?"

The kids. Momentarily caught off-guard, Lipscomb turned to respond.

Noren saw the movement, sensed Lipscomb's distraction and lunged for the gun in his right hand.

Lipscomb whirled toward the sound, blocked Noren's lunge with his left arm and, with a mighty and furious effort, flung the man backwards.

Noren, off-balance and falling, staggered backwards onto the balcony and crashed against the plywood barrier. For one slight moment it appeared to support him, then snapped loudly and give way.

Falling into space, Noren grasped at the remaining metal handrail, slipped and grabbed a metal side rail as he fell. He could feel the metal strain in its concrete base as he held on with his left hand, his body swinging in open space twenty-four stories over the street below.

As Noren crashed through the plywood barrier, Lipscomb's training took over. He shoved his gun in his shoulder holster as he simultaneously lunged after the falling man. Lying fully stretched out on the floor of the balcony, he grasped Noren by the wrist of his hand holding on to the siderail. "Boyle," he shouted, "get ahold a my legs!"

Boyle threw himself on Lipscomb's legs as they lay half-in, half-out of the doorway.

For a moment, all seemed suspended in time: Noren, his left hand locked around the metal siderail, his wrist in Lipscomb's vise-like grip; Lipscomb, flat-out on the balcony floor, his left hand wrapped around Noren's wrist, his right hand struggling to gain a grasp on the wet and slippery floor; Boyle, arms now wrapped around Lipscomb's legs, his body thrust perpendicular to the doorway and wedged against the open door as support against the weight he was trying to hold.

Then Noren could feel the slow slide begin. Greased by the falling rain, he could feel his fingers slowly, inexorably loosen their grip on the metal siderail. He could feel his wrist oozing out of Lipscomb's grasp.

His body swaying in the wind, left arm aching, he tried to swing his right hand up to grasp Lipscomb's extended arm. He clammed on with his right hand momentarily, then felt it slipping too. The sweat, the rain, the effort; he felt the slipping continue.

Lipscomb tried to move his right hand over to aid in the effort as he felt Norton slipping, but lying at an angle rather than head-on to the struggling man, he couldn't reach. He felt the slow movement of flesh on flesh and knew the inevitable. Was this how Lois felt when the plane nosed over and fell to the ocean?

Then a convulsion, then no more weight on his arm, then the scream disappearing down, muffled by the rain.

Boyle felt the sudden twinge and relaxation in the weight he was straining to hold, like hanging onto a fishing pole when a hooked fish had just broken the line. He tugged and pulled the legs backwards from the edge of the doorway until Lipscomb could recover his balance and stand.

The back of Lipscomb's left hand was covered with blood from the scratches Norton made as he dug in his nails before his fall.

"I'd better call the local precinct," said Lipscomb. Boyle nodded agreement. In the distance, the wail of sirens on their way to the scene could already be heard. He sat on the sofa and watched Lipscomb place the call.

The phone conversation was brief. Lipscomb returned and sat in the easy chair opposite Boyle.

"What'd you say?" asked Boyle.

"Man slipped off the balcony. Crashed through some makeshift thing, piece a plywood or somethin'. I tried to save him."

"Umm."

"What you gonna say?"

"I don't know…I'm not sure." *Vengeance is mine…*

Lipscomb looked at him with a calm, level stare. "It ain't for me. It's for my kids…and Lois."

Boyle returned the stare.

Two cops arrived swiftly; that one of their own was involved may have had something to do with their reaction time.

Boyle listened as Lipscomb gave his statement. He said he'd been talking to Noren about the crash—his friends on the force knew he had been trying to piece together on his own the details of the crash for some obscure, quixotic reason. Noren was on the balcony. Needed some fresh air or something. Balcony was wet, he slipped and crashed through the plywood. I couldn't hold him. I tried.

"No previous physical contact with the deceased?"

"None."

The cop nodded solemnly as he made his notes, then turned to Boyle. "Mr. Boyle?"

"Yes, officer?"

"We'd like your statement, please."

Lipscomb turned away, as if to avoid influencing Boyle's decision.

One wrong does not, cannot, make a right...However painful or unfair, Boyle knew what he had to do.

"Mr. Boyle?"

Boyle stared at the cop.

"What you saw, sir?"

Boyle looked toward the balcony, then beyond.

The cop waited, cleared his throat.

"It's as Sergeant Lipscomb described it. Mr. Noren lost his balance, fell through that flimsy barrier. Sergeant Lipscomb tried to save him."

Thy will be done.

Lipscomb nodded his head, affirming something known only to himself. His eyes appeared to glisten.

"We're gonna need you at the station, Sarge," the older cop reminded Lipscomb. "Wally, you handle the write-up?"

The younger cop was already writing a description of the apartment. "Gotcha."

Lipscomb turned away and followed the older cop out.

Boyle looked around the apartment. The younger cop was taking detailed notes, obviously impressed with the apartment and its contents. "This' some place, huh?"

Boyle didn't reply.

"What d'ya think it costs to live in a place like this?"

Boyle thought about that. "Too much," he said.

*   *   *

The rain had stopped falling, the night became clear and cold. Boyle returned the thirty-some blocks to his apartment at a much slower pace.

When you make a decision, you move on. A decision can always be modified, adjusted, shaded, but you don't second-guess yourself on major decisions—that's weak and vacillating management. Boyle could not shake the feeling he had made the wrong decision in what he told the police about Noren's death and Lipscomb's involvement.

When he entered their apartment, Kate was on the sofa, reading a book. A mood music radio station was on, insinuating its homogenized but relaxing tones. She closed the book and put it aside as he entered the living room.

"That must have been some walk," she said. She rose from the sofa and went to him.

"I'm sorry, should've called…

She stood on her toes and kissed him on the cheek. "I made you some tea."

Tea? He seldom drank tea and needed a drink—she knew that.

"It won't be that bad," she smiled, reading his thoughts. "Come on." She took his hand and led him into the kitchen, to the kitchen table where two cups awaited filling. The phone and pile of notes had been pushed off to one side.

He sat down and watched her fussing with a tea pot on the stove.

"The news on the radio said Noren is dead." She didn't turn around, still occupied with the tea pot.

He had debated how to tell her that. "How'd they announce it?"

She turned and walked toward the table, steaming tea pot in hand. "Just on the news. Said the police were called to where some man fell from his apartment balcony, then they gave his name." She poured the tea for both of them, placed the tea pot on a trivet and sat down opposite him. "Appeared to be an accident."

"Umm." He blew on the tea and sipped it. "I was there."

She did not appear to be surprised.

"Dan Lipscomb." He took another sip of the tea—it didn't taste that bad. "They had a struggle..."

"It was an accident?" She spoke softly, slowly—more like a statement than a question.

He stared into the cup of tea, sloshed it around.

"Every day I see people who've been hurt so badly by other people," she put her cup down, "and some of them ask me—no harm in asking—how can I get back at the person who beat me, who lied to me, the person who...stole my youth?"

"There is the law."

"There's also economics."

The quickness and intensity of her reply surprised him.

"How is a Dan Lipscomb ever going to 'get back' at a William Noren?" She waited for his answer as if she had not posed a rhetorical question. "The law? Lawyers and courtrooms? He can't afford it." She picked up her cup and sipped some tea, watching him over the rim.

"I'm not saying Dan did the wrong thing, but I was there, I saw what happened, I told the police..."

She had replaced the cup and now wrapped both her hands around his. "I tell some of my cases—it's cold comfort, I know—they should never confuse the law with justice."

Boyle thought about that and knew he had made the right decision.

CHAPTER FIFTEEN

▼

DEALS

The President's office occupied the northeast corner of the fifty-first floor of the Global Air Building. Its views extended north, beyond the wooded rectangle of Central Park to the spires of the George Washington Bridge, standing abrupt sentinels above the Hudson River. To the east, the cannon-like smokestacks of power plants in Norwalk, Connecticut, and Port Jefferson, Long Island, pointed their slim barrels toward the sky.

"Nice scenery you've got here." Hal Trevnor gazed through the floor-to-ceiling windows, enjoying the warmth of the mid-morning sun which flooded the office.

"When I'm not on the phone, I try to keep my eyes fixed on the top of my shoes," cracked Pat Boyle. "How about you? Are you going to move into Samuels' old office?" The former chairman's office was located on the building's southeast corner and included a view of Wall Street among its vistas.

"Not me. All that glass and the height make me nervous. I'm far better off and more productive in my little rat's nest, playing with my computers."

"Have you heard from Samuels since he left?"

"Nope—don't expect to. Not his style."

Boyle stroked his face. "How did he do it?"

"Huh?"

"How was he able to walk out of here with a multi-million dollar loss, turn around, buy another company and all of a sudden be on his way to a huge profit?" The morning's **Journal** gushed over Samuels' purchase of Western States Engineering, "one of Wall Street's best-kept secrets" and the likelihood it could turn into a money machine for Gerald S. Samuels.

"The **Journal** story?"

Boyle nodded.

"Well, first of all, you can't believe everything you read. But…" Trevnor smiled and rubbed his hands together, "…this was a beauty."

As many a top-drawer executive or entrepreneur thoroughly caught up with his life's work, Trevnor was also an enthusiastic teacher, eager to explain a highly sophisticated and arcane maneuver by a master of the trade. He explained how part of Samuels' loss on his sale of Global Air stock would be absorbed as a tax loss by his holding company, Samuels Investments, offsetting extraordinary profits generated by another of his subsidiaries, a biotech firm headquartered in San Diego.

"But that's the easy part, anybody can do that," commented Trevnor. "The interesting part is he set up another subsidiary, Aurora Fund, which issued a huge amount of debt, mainly high-yield securities—we used to call them junk bonds—to buy control of Western States Engineering." He described a series of complex maneuvers, exchange of the Western States' stock between Samuels' own holding companies for more debt paper, leading to the eventual control of the Western States stock by Samuels himself, rather than one of his holding companies. "So, if the stock goes up or if he can sell the company at a higher price, he stands to make another personal fortune. If it dives, he can fold up his investment subsidiary, walk away from it, his investors are left holding the bag. In other words, he can't lose: it's genius!"

"Is all of that legal?"

Trevnor looked suddenly deflated, like a comedian who just had someone step on his punch line. "Legal?" He sounded disappointed with the question. "Legal is not the point. The point is, he pulled off one helluva deal!" Trevnor sighed. "Sometimes I think we're like artists and our work is hard to appreciate." His messianic juices were flowing; maybe there was another way to explain this. "Pat, look out the window. What do you see?"

Boyle appraised the man and the question. "I suspect I see something quite different from what you see."

"You see buildings, right?"

Boyle nodded.

"I see deals," said Trevnor. "Lots and lots of deals. None of those buildings—not one—got put up because of truth, justice or beauty; they got put up because somebody made a buck off the deal." Trevnor stared at Boyle like a professor about to spell out the point of his lecture for a rather obtuse class. "And that's all there is, the deal!"

Boyle was back on familiar ground; the name and the player had changed but not the game. He took a deep breath. "I see what you mean."

"Course you do." Trevnor clapped Boyle on his arm, as if congratulating him for some achievement, then studied him, obviously trying to decide what to say next. "You know, Pat," he tried to slip his arm over the taller man's shoulders but couldn't quite reach, "at some point you and I need to sit down and go over your..new realities."

"New realities?"

"Yeah, I mean Christ, you're the best operations guy in the business, we all know that. But, as president of Global, you got to maybe take a little broader look at things, know what I mean?"

"I think I do."

"Sure, I mean I know we got to be very sensitive to all these safety issues and whatnot, but I was looking over this year's budget last night..."

Boyle grabbed Trevnor by his arm. Trevnor shut up, looking surprised and not a little alarmed.

"Let me show you something." Boyle walked Trevnor toward the window; the shorter man had to stand on tiptoe to keep up.

"Let me tell you what I see out this window. I see buildings...and I see the people who built those buildings and dug those trenches and paved those streets...and I see the families they raised all the time they were out killing themselves on the job so guys like you could come along and make a buck off the deal!" He relaxed his grip on Trevnor's arm; Trevnor rocked floorward from his tiptoe position.

Boyle leaned close to Trevnor's face. "If you don't like what you just heard, then you better fire my ass right now."

*   *   *

It was the morning rush at JFK; the noise was ear-numbing with jet engines whining, roaring into life as aircraft were pushed back or powered away from their gates.

Omar and the Punk from Bensonhurst were furiously loading passenger luggage into the belly of an MD-80. Omar wrenched bags out of a covered baggage cart and slapped them on the conveyor belt while the Punk, scrunched in the pit of the aircraft, tossed the bags behind him as they rolled off the belt.

A large suitcase, held together with a thick piece of rope, toppled from the belt and landed on the tarmac. Neither ramper paid it any attention, continuing the rapid pace of their work.

As Omar leaned into the baggage cart to wrestle out a bag lodged in the back, he caught a glance of a man wearing a business suit stop by the belt and bend over to the ground. He heard a grunt of exertion, the slap of a bag on the belt and a familiar voice.

"Make a note, Fran. We need younger and better-looking rampers out here. The old ones are frightening all the customers away."

Omar uncoiled from the baggage cart and saw a beaming Pat Boyle, accompanied by Fran Demarest. "Ah, Meester Boyle," he said, his massive arms held wide in greeting. "You are back, Meester Boyle!" He went over to Boyle and gave him a bear hug, actually lifting him off the ground.

"Whoa," said Boyle, as Omar plunked him back on the ground.

Omar checked out Boyle's suit by rubbing his palms up and down the back of its lapels. "Nice suit, Meester Boyle, but Omar can get you better ones wholesale."

Boyle laughed and patted him on the cheek. "Omar, before I buy suits from you, let me check and see if we've got any claims pending at the cargo terminal."

Everybody laughed heartily except Omar, who roared.

When he finished laughing, Omar went back to loading bags on the belt. "Better get these bags on plane so plane gets out on time so Ms. Fran does not blame Omar."

"Good idea!" laughed Fran, as she and Boyle started to walk away.

Omar ran after Boyle and grabbed his hand. "You keep us flying, eh?"

"I'll do that Omar, I will," Boyle said.

Solemnly, the two men shook hands. Omar nodded at Boyle, turned and walked back to the baggage cart.

Fran noticed Boyle fumble with a handkerchief and dab his eyes as they walked toward the next aircraft loading. "You okay?" she asked.

"Oh yeah, yeah, just some particles from the jet exhaust."

Boyle turned, squinting into the distance where planes of differing size, manufacture and colors were lining up on the taxiways. One by one these graceful machines would move into position at the head of the runway, hold, then start their takeoff roll, roaring skyward, into the new day.

ABOUT THE AUTHOR

───────────────▼───────────────

Walter Carlin is a veteran of the airline industry. Originally selected by Pan Am for its operations management program, he was subsequently recruited by Eastern, TWA, PSA and American as a problem-solver in their marketing departments.